# The Renegades' Reward

Maddie Taylor

Maddie Taylor

---

Copyright © 2017 by Maddie Taylor
All rights reserved.

This book is a work of fiction. The characters, incidents and dialogue are products of the author's imagination and as such, any similarity to existing persons, places, or events must be considered purely coincidental.

This book contains content for adult audiences and is not suitable for readers aged 17 and under.

**For mature readers, only.**

Published in the United States of America

First Electronic Edition: July 2017
First Paperback Edition: August 2017

Cover Art by No Sweat Graphics
Editing by Wizards of Publishing

# The Renegades' Reward

# Maddie Taylor

# Chapter One

At the top of the grand marble staircase, in front of the main entrance to the Elzorian royal family's residence, Daniella Alltryp paused and closed her eyes.

*Breathe,* she urged herself silently.

Following her own sage advice, Dani inhaled deeply and filled her lungs to capacity. She did so for two very sound reasons. First, to soak up as much of the cool, fresh morning air as possible before embarking on the seventy-two-hour space flight home—not the most pleasant experience for a moderate claustrophobic and dedicated landlubber. And second, to calm her jagged nerves so she could walk, rather than fall, down the fifty narrow steps in front of the massive gathering of onlookers below.

Feeling a bit better after breathing in and blowing out slowly several times, she opened her eyes and looked down. Big mistake!

She swayed on weak knees, a sudden head rush making her world tilt on end. Reaching out with a trembling hand, she grabbed hold of the carved balustrade. Time to add fear of heights to her phobia list. When she swept her gaze over the crowd of thousands, each face angled up to where she stood, all eyes fixed on her, her pulse jumped, and she tacked on agoraphobia to her growing list. She averted her eyes, picking a focal point straight ahead, and tried to steady herself.

Dani had always wanted to travel, to visit all thirty-seven Intergalactic Alliance planets. So far, she'd only made it to two, including Earth. She used to blame her father and all his rules as the reason. After this trip to Elzor, she realized being a space tourist wasn't all the travel brochures and getaway infomercials made it seem.

Granted, if she had stayed home, she would have missed the beautiful landscapes and stunning vistas which made up the Dominion of Elzor. Appropriately named the Blue Planet, the color dominated every setting, from the spectacular cyan mountains in the distance, to the nearby bay with its deep-sapphire waters glistening in the morning sun, and, above it all, the azure sky laced with fingers of ice-blue feathery clouds as far as the eye could see. This majesty exemplified the reason she wanted to spread her wings and move beyond her narrow existence in her father's Long Island suburban home.

Considering the disaster this past week had been, she had grave reservations of ever doing so again.

Things had gone awry soon after liftoff when the ship's course took them through a meteor stream. For almost three hours, she sat strapped in her flight chair while millions of jagged boulders came hurtling at them.

Okay, perhaps millions was a slight exaggeration, but there had to have been hundreds, at least, maybe thousands.

Dani thought for sure they would die as the space rocks banged and bounced off the shields. While she held on with a white-knuckled grip, graphic images of her imminent demise flashed in her head. Mostly, of a giant boulder colliding with one of the external fuel cells and turning them into a celestial fireball. At least it would be a quick ending. Not true for what she feared more should the safety shields fail and a meteorite knock a gaping hole in the hull. She pictured herself being sucked out into the vacuum of space, gasping for breath without oxygen, and suffering a horrible, painful death when her lungs expanded and burst, or all the blood in her body vaporized.

Even now, she couldn't keep from shuddering at the horrifying prospect.

To her relief, she didn't meet with an untimely demise and the ship didn't go up in flames, although it sustained external damage. Nothing life-threatening, but important navigation and communication components had to be repaired before they could safely continue their journey. This resulted in a two-day layover at a nearby spaceport.

When it came time to leave, the captain himself escorted her on board. His reassurances had done little to calm her twisting, churning stomach. The three-day flight turned into five, and it had taken her another six — until yesterday — to settle her nerves, and the resulting queasiness, enough to eat.

Now, with it time to head home, she dreaded going through anything close to the same ordeal again.

As bad as the incoming flight had been, it didn't end up being the worst part of the trip, believe it or not. In fact, the entire visit had been rather strange, and nothing had gone as planned. From the moment she arrived, she noticed wherever she went, crowds gathered, and she drew curious stares. At first, she thought her appearance turned heads because at five feet eight, she towered over the petite Elzorian women. Where they were pixyish and reed slender, Dani had curves and meat on her bones. Not overweight, but she liked to eat and would never achieve a concave belly or a six-pack.

Her auburn hair stood out amidst a sea of silver and champagne blondes, as did her rosy-hued complexion because the people of Elzor had blue skin to match their planet. Not a dark shade, but a light grayish-blue, almost ashen, which Dani found eerie and corpse-like. She'd spotted other humans amid the onlookers and knew many of her kind worked and lived on Elzor. They had for decades, ever since Earth joined the Alliance in 2273. She'd also read there'd been a few interspecies marriages and some of those couples had children. They must be accustomed to seeing human women, so she couldn't figure out why they seemed so fascinated with her.

What was going on didn't become clear until midweek. Then, the news knocked her for a loop, although it became less shocking when she learned her father had a hand in it.

Initially, she'd been surprised when she found out he had arranged for her to stay with the royal family, and a little uncomfortable, though they were gracious and welcoming. By itself, this wouldn't have been all bad, but he had also neglected to inform her of the sole purpose of the holiday. Prince Ivar needed a wife, and she'd been sent specifically to meet him and be considered as a potential bride. And dear ole dad hadn't mentioned a word about it.

*Holy freaking crap!*

The prince didn't have the final say, however. If Ivar approved, it fell to his parents, the king and queen of Elzor, to decide if she was good enough for their son, suitable to bear the title of royal princess, and worthy of being the mother to the next heir to the throne.

It bore repeating... *Ho-ly fah-reaking crap!*

When the prince explained this, she had burst into laughter. A rude reaction, yet what he'd told her had to have been one of the most outlandish stories she'd ever heard. But he hadn't chuckled, cracked a smile, or given the least little twitch of his blue lips. Once she realized he was serious, she'd embarrassed herself further by getting weak in the knees, which had required his help to a chair or risk falling flat on her face.

The rest of the stay had been a blur of social events with her trotted out and put through her paces—the prize mare analogy both spot-on and insulting.

"Broodmare is more like it," she muttered to herself.

Remembering how her potential in-laws had scrutinized her all week, she wouldn't be at all surprised if they were off somewhere now comparing notes and tallying up her score card.

Dani's anger, which had been simmering under the surface the past few days, reignited. So much so, her jaw clenched while her heart thudded in her ears.

The nerve of her underhanded, dictatorial parent father as though it was the dark ages, although she shouldn't be shocked. He'd always been highhanded and taken charge of her life, making decisions without caring what she wanted. Telling her how to dress, where she could go, what school to attend, who her friends could and couldn't be.

Correction! He never told her, at least not to her face. It came in a directive through one of his assistants, or barked as an order over his shoulder while he walked out the door—not once expecting her to do anything other than obey.

"Two more weeks," she whispered under her breath. "A short time to endure before you are free for good."

The pounding in her ears became louder all at once. It took her a moment to realize it wasn't her thudding pulse, but rhythmic clapping from the crowd below. The next instant, it grew in volume, and raucous cheering erupted. At the same time, a hand came to rest on her back.

"Daniella, surely you weren't going to leave without saying good-bye."

Her head snapped around, and she found Ivar, her husband wannabe, standing beside her. Chin tilted up—yes, up. The men of Elzor may not be pixie-sized like their women, but they were close. Only of average height, Dani had a good two inches on the prince, five if she counted her heels.

While he waited for her answer, his blond brows inched higher.

"I, um…thought we said our farewells after supper last night. I know I expressed my thanks to your parents for welcoming me into their home." Afterward, she had avoided him like he had a plague, figuring if they weren't alone, he couldn't ask the dreaded question, something she hoped and prayed he wouldn't do here on the steps.

"Yes, but I planned to have a private word with you after breakfast." His tone held unmistakable censure when he added, "A meal you skipped."

"I wasn't feeling well. My stomach is nervous about the upcoming flight. You understand, after the very unpleasant trip here."

"Perhaps you should postpone your return if you're ill."

"No!" she blurted out, regretting her lack of finesse when a dark-blue shadow crossed his face.

*Shit!* It wouldn't do to anger the man or insult the Elzorian royalty.

She rushed to cover her faux pas. "I'm sorry and appreciate your concern for my health, your highness, but I can't stay. I have other engagements I've committed to and must keep to the schedule."

His stiff expression relaxed somewhat, and she mentally sighed in relief.

"I understand obligations, Daniella. As a royal princess, I dare say your calendar would be more demanding. It pleases me to hear you take your obligations seriously."

She swallowed, not liking where this was heading at all. She'd been polite to him, but not overly approachable since she had no intention of marrying the man. And, although beautiful, Elzor wasn't a place she wanted to live, princess or not.

"Oh, look," she exclaimed, determined to stop any other mention of weddings, princesses, or royal engagements. *Yikes!* "My ride to the landing pad has arrived."

Taking a hasty step forward, which put her up against the edge of the first stair leading down, she teetered then staggered, catching herself on the railing. Ivar hurried to assist, his arms encircling her waist to steady her.

Excited cheers and the chant of "Daniella" erupted from the avid spectators, reading much more into her stumble and Ivar's rescue than she wanted. She pulled away, covering her obvious reluctance to be close to him by tugging down her lightweight fitted jacket and smoothing the front of her skirt. Once set to rights, she thanked him and carefully turned back to the stairs.

"I have business in New York City. I'll be making a trip there soon. While I'm there, we'll have more time together, and more privacy. If you don't break your neck on the descent, that is. Let me assist you."

When he took her arm, she had no choice other than to accept. It wouldn't do for her to make a scene by pulling away and refusing his help. With thousands watching, including a good number of photographers, anything perceived to be a snub would hit the news links and become fodder for the tabloids. It could turn into an interplanetary incident. Her father, who had business ties to Elzor, would be livid. With so much at stake, she plastered on a fake smile for Ivar and any cameras aimed her way.

Taking the stairs at a slow pace, the prince didn't speak further. Dani was grateful because she needed to focus on putting one foot in front of the other and not being her usual klutzy self by tumbling head over heels down the hard, unforgiving marble, landing in a broken heap at the bottom, and taking Ivar with her.

Wouldn't that be a sight?

They crossed the landing midway without misstep, no thanks to the butterflies dancing furiously in her stomach. Another twenty-five narrow treads and she'd be almost home free. Not for the first time this week, Dani wondered why they couldn't have a lift, or a moving staircase at the very least, like everyone else in the modernized universe.

With her heart racing, she forced her chin up, facing the thousands who had turned out to see her off today. Seeing their excitement, she felt like a fraud, though she had done nothing to concoct this farce. She would let her father break the news to Ivar, and subsequently to the people of Elzor. No way would she say yes to becoming their future princess, no matter how much Daniel Alltryp ranted and railed at her.

Still, he could make the next fourteen days until her birthday difficult. She needed to come up with a way to delay a proposal and, heaven forbid, any rush to the altar, which she wouldn't put past her father. Once she turned twenty-five, the age of majority on Earth, she'd come into her inheritance from her grandmother, held in trust for her since birth, something he couldn't touch.

She felt the need to pinch herself to make sure she wasn't in the middle of a crazy dream. Like most little girls, she'd fantasized about marrying a handsome prince and being whisked away to a fairy-tale castle to live happily ever after. In her dream, however, he hadn't been blue or short, and her prince charming had fallen in love with her. And he didn't have the entire thing arranged by a third party. Something seemed fishy, but she had yet to figure out what.

Arriving at the bottom, she took a breath and stepped off the last stair onto the thick plush red carpet. Yes, they had rolled out an actual red carpet for her, a nobody from Earth, not royalty, merely the daughter of a businessman. A very wealthy businessman—some even called him a mogul—and the one most often in the spotlight. This wasn't for her, someone quiet and reserved, not a media whore interested in fame, fortune, and being sucked up to by the little people, like her father.

Dani didn't have time to dwell on anything to do with him right now, or anything else other than moving the thirty feet between the stairs and the waiting vehicle. To do so, she had to run the gauntlet made up by the cheering, clamoring crowd lining the walkway.

"I will be in touch with your father, Daniella." Ivar raised her hand to his mouth. When he pressed a lingering kiss to her knuckles, his warmth surprised her, expecting icy cold.

Imagining his blue lips on hers, or his ghoulish fingers touching her body intimately, made her cringe inside. She barely managed to tamp down a shiver. Eager to get away from him, she nodded and stepped forward, her eyes on the uniformed driver who stood beside the hovering glider, hand on the latch, ready to open the door for her.

She counted down the diminishing distance, from twenty-five, to twenty, to fifteen. Just a few more feet…

"Princess Dani," a young girl called out. She ducked under the velvet perimeter rope, her youthful agility and the crowd's excitement making it easy to scoot away from her mother. Arriving in front of Daniella, she dropped to her knees, her skirt pooling around her as she looked up in awe.

"Not a princess yet, sweetheart," Dani told her, cupping her upturned face.

"But you will be soon," she replied with childlike giddiness. "You said yes to Prince Ivar, didn't you? He is getting quite old, and we worry if he waits much longer, he might not be able to—"

"Find a bride," a woman finished for her as she rushed up. "We're thrilled for you and the prince, miss." She began hauling the little girl away.

"But, Mother, she didn't answer my question," the child protested. "I wanted to know if she said yes."

The people had quieted, trying to hear the exchange. Now, they looked at her with anticipation, the ones toward the back, leaning in to catch her answer, which she judiciously withheld.

"There will be a formal announcement very soon. Thank you for coming to see me off."

Feeling more awkward and knowing her imminent decision would disappoint the child and so many others who had turned out today, she patted her on the head and moved past her, eager to get in the waiting car and be on her way.

After taking no more than a few steps, from the corner of her eye, she spied a young man drop to one knee, his head bowed in a show of respect. Still unused to this reaction, Daniella inclined her head and continued past him, trying not to hurry, and seem obvious, when she really wanted to sprint as fast as her feet would take her.

Another man followed suit, so did another. Soon, the sea of people formed a rippling wave as they knelt, the girls and women who were able, dipping into a floor-sweeping curtsy.

*Oh my!*

Never had she received such an outpouring of attention, and, considering the circumstances, she found it very off-putting. She decided some sort of public gift to show her gratitude for their gracious welcome would be appropriate before the news broke she'd declined Ivar's offer. They might not want it afterward.

At the vehicle, when she turned in the open door to give them a farewell smile and a wave, another young girl came forward with an armful of fresh-cut flowers tied with a pink bow. A sense of regret gripped her insides—she could get used to this part of being a princess.

After accepting the bouquet, and with one final wave, her gaze collided with Ivar's, where he stood on the second step watching her. She ducked inside, heaving a sigh of relief when the door slammed shut.

As the glider moved forward, Dani trembled with anger. All of it directed at her father. Why had he made her come here only to go through the motions of considering the prince when he had to know she'd never wed the man? What twisted game had he come up with now? And why, when Ivar could have his choice of brides among Elzor's women, did he want her?

So many unanswered questions. In frustration, she hit her fist against the empty seat beside her.

"You've had a rough week."

The very American-sounding voice made her bolt upright, her eyes meeting those of her driver when he glanced her way. He surprised her further by twisting in his seat and hooking his arm over the back as if settling in for a chat.

She glanced at the road ahead, the one he wasn't watching. "Uh, don't you need to drive or something?"

"I switched on the auto-navigation. It's a straight shot from here to the landing port. When we're close, I'll take back control. Until then, I've got twenty minutes to listen, and you sure look like you could use a good ear." He smiled at her, his straight white teeth gleaming against his tanned face. Something about him put her instantly at ease. Handsome, with silver at his temples, he had little crinkles fanning out beside his eyes, and around his mouth, as though he laughed often. By her guess, he was in his mid-fifties, about her father's age, though he looked nothing like him.

Best of all, she took comfort in his voice because he spoke English, with a distinct drawl. "Do I detect a hint of a southern accent?"

His lips tipped into a grin, increasing the crinkles. "Yes, ma'am. You've got an excellent ear. I'm Blake Askins. Born and raised in Nashville, Tennessee."

"I'm Dani, from New York City."

"Yeah? I might have heard a little buzz around town about you."

"Of course," she said, flushing hot. Unless he'd been living under a rock for the past week, he would have known of her visit. "Do you work for the royal family?"

"No, I'm employed by Alltryp Universal."

"You're kidding!"

"No. My wife works for the company, too, as a geologist. We moved here ten years ago when they began exploring the north region. While she digs in the dirt, I pilot shuttles and, on occasion, get assigned to chauffeur dignitaries around, or a pretty girl with sadness in her eyes."

She glanced out the window, sorry she hadn't done a better job at hiding her emotions. A skill that had never been her strong suit.

"So, you're not keen on becoming an Elzorian princess?"

"It shows, huh?"

"Yeah, darlin'. Did the visit not go well?"

"It was a disaster from the start, but with good reason. I have no plans of becoming Prince Ivar's bride, and that's what this week turned out to be all about."

"Then why did you come?"

"Silly me. I thought my father was being nice. I've been bugging him about traveling and thought he'd finally caved." What a fool she had been. When had her father done anything nice, let alone without an underlying, self-indulgent purpose?

"Daniel Alltryp is a putz."

She blinked, her lips parting.

"No offense, but he is."

A small humorless laugh slipped out. "You aren't telling me something I don't know, Mr. Askins."

"Please, I'm Blake. And I figured as much if he sent you here for a marriage setup and didn't clue you in."

"He knew I'd refuse to come."

"Smart girl. Overall, the Elzorians are nice people, a bit staid and boring, and most of them are well intended. Things can get political here, like back home. Until recently, they have been adamant about keeping to their own kind. That Ivar is considering an off-worlder for a royal bride, and the mother of the future king has rocked some of the old conservative types to their core. Though they don't have much choice, now."

"What do you mean?"

He shifted, appearing uncomfortable, his jaw clenching.

"I reckon if your daddy didn't inform you of a potential engagement, he wouldn't have told you the rest of the story, about why Ivar intends to take an Earth bride." He paused, his blue eyes coming back to her. "As I said, folks here are nice, in general, and almost painfully polite people — aside from the nobility who put those niceties aside whenever it suits them — but they aren't the most robust species. They're small, have a weak immune system, and they're getting more fragile with each generation. The scientists have recommended introducing a stouter set of genes into the pool."

"By crossbreeding."

"Yes. And they've decided humans are ideal to meet their needs. There have already been a few interspecies marriages which have produced offspring."

"I heard, though I'm shocked by the dispassionate, clinical intent behind them."

"Arranged unions for gains not involving love and romance have existed for centuries, including on our world. Here, the first few were purely experimental. They jumped on board with the plan after the twentieth mixed-species child reached the age of ten. If commoners could successfully breed with human females, why not the royal family?"

"But why Ivar? He is the fourth son. Why not the heir to the throne, or the other two older brothers?"

"They're shooting blanks, apparently."

She blinked. "Excuse me?"

Blake chuckled softly. "Sorry to be blunt, but it's true. For a decade, neither the crown prince nor his brothers have been able to produce an heir. When the attempts to conceive the old-fashioned way failed, they turned to science. This produced a few pregnancies, yet they all ended in miscarriages when the royal princesses couldn't carry to term for one reason or another. It goes back to the weaknesses they want to breed out. Now, the millennium old royal family line is in jeopardy, and they are desperate."

"But I was told they are all single. What happened to their wives?"

"Dead, under suspicious circumstances."

"Dear heaven. They had them killed? Why not simply divorce them?"

"Divorce doesn't exist; Elzorians wed for life. And it's a pride thing for the princes. Can't have ex-wives talking about their prowess, or lack thereof, in the bedroom, now can we?"

"They killed three innocent women," she whispered in horror.

"More like ten."

"What?"

"There have been ten royal princesses by marriage. Four each for the two oldest sons. The third tried and failed twice, and has now fallen ill. The king is impatient and won't wait to see if he will recover. It has come down to the youngest son, and his biological clock is ticking. Evidently, at the age of forty, their sperm count diminishes, and the odds of fathering a child become nonexistent."

"Ivar told me he was thirty-eight."

"Yeah, tick-tock, tick-tock."

Aghast, the next piece of the puzzle fell into place for her. "If we married, and he ends up shooting blanks, too, it would make me dead princess number eleven."

Compassion filled his kind eyes as Blake's gaze met hers. "I'm sorry you had to hear it this way, from a stranger, but this would be the risk you'd take by marrying the man. I'm surprised you haven't heard the rumors. They've been floating around for over a year. The story goes, Ivar's sperm is viable, and they found a compatible recipient, a young woman not of this world."

"Enter me," she stated in a dismal tone.

"Yes. You, dear Dani, are their greatest hope, though it must be a bitter pill for the royal family, snobs that they are, thinking their race is far superior to any other, especially humans. I'm sure they think your father is a representative of every man on Earth. They must be plagued with nightmares, of you and Ivar successfully producing an heir, but ending up with a future king just like him."

"It's what they deserve, only not at my expense," she replied, adding silently that one Daniel Alltryp in the vast universe was enough. "But if they're so snobby, why are the people so accepting of me? And of the other mixed marriages?"

"It seems the birth rate overall is on the decline."

"The infertility affliction is spreading beyond the heirs," she surmised.

"Yes, so now it's either lower their lofty standards and breed with humans, or risk not only the family line dying out, but their species too. Ironic, isn't it? Though not everyone is in favor of crossbreeding. Ustis, a first cousin with a mounting following, is firmly against it. He also wants to close access to outsiders and cease the constant exploration in the north region. They think the environmental changes are part of the problem. He's been vocal about shutting your father's research down."

"What research?"

"You aren't aware of his business with Elzor?"

"He doesn't speak to me about his work." She didn't mention he rarely spoke to her at all.

"It's very secretive, but my wife, she shares. From what I know, there is buzz about a new energy source. It isn't her area, still, she hears the talk. The north region is ripe with radioactivity, evidently. This concerns the opposition, who believe all the digging is damaging the planet and affecting the people. They want it stopped."

"This all boils down to greed, then. If the current family is out, and this Ustis takes over, my father loses his contract and billions in a potential new energy source."

"That's my thinking."

"He is sacrificing me, my womb, and perhaps my very life for money." She frowned. "Why are you telling me this? You don't know me, and if my father finds out you said something, it will be your job, and your wife's, no doubt."

"The one thing not widely known is what they discovered in the north region. Most everything else is common knowledge."

"Not to me."

"You must be very isolated, darlin'."

A knot formed in the pit of her stomach. He had described her life in a single word. She'd gotten a small taste of freedom during college. Since graduation two years ago, she'd lived like a hermit. Her father said there were threats and she could be targeted. About that time her security detail had doubled and contact with her friends had been curtailed. *He'd been planning this, for that long. Oh my God!*

"You asked why I took this risk. I have a daughter," Blake told her quietly. "Rebecca is your age. She's attending college at home in Tennessee, studying to be a doctor. Like you, she's a beauty, with the same auburn hair. I couldn't sit back and not share. I'd never be able to look my girl in the eyes again."

"You love her."

"Of course. She's my baby, my only child. I love her with all my heart."

"I wouldn't know about that," Dani whispered.

"Knowing the kind of man your father is, I arranged to be your driver today. I thought someone's daddy needed to look out for you."

Her eyes pooled with tears until, one after another, they overflowed. He reached into his jacket pocket and pulled out a wad of tissues. The man obviously knew women and came prepared. As he passed them to her, an alarm on the control console beeped.

"We're almost there. Dry your tears. We can't let on you know or that I told you."

"Never. I owe you, Mr. Askins."

"It's Blake. And if ever you need anything…anything at all, you call on me. Do you hear?"

Unable to speak, Dani nodded, while wiping her wet cheeks. It was all they had time for because they had arrived at the landing port, and yet another crowd awaited her. All the cheering, knowing smiles, curious gazes, and the little girl who bowed at Daniella's knees made sense. It hadn't been evident then, her mother quickly covering for her, but the words came flooding back.

*If he waits much longer, he might not be able to…*

All the blanks had been filled in, the many questions answered. In another year or two, it might be too late for him. Even the girl knew who and what Dani meant to their people.

It had been a wise decision to skip breakfast. With the way her stomach rebelled at the plotting against her by so many, she would have lost everything in it.

When Blake drew the glider to a halt and came around to open her door, she slid out, her movements sluggish as she stared at the ship which would bring her home. Though crowded with a staff of many, she'd be alone, the crew and security personnel all employed by Daniel Alltryp. How could she trust any of them?

"Be strong, darlin'," her well-meaning informant murmured as she passed. "And watch your back."

With a slight nod, she left him behind, wondering why fate hadn't gifted her with a man like Blake Askins for a father. But wishing things had been different would get her nowhere. She had her own harsh reality to face. Somehow, she had to get through the next two weeks unscathed by her father's manipulations and his unreasonable hatred.

\*\*\*

For most of the long two days that followed, Dani stayed in her quarters, often sitting motionless, staring out the window into space. Her mind whirled with tormented thoughts of how she had come to this low point in her life. And, like she had done many times before, brooded over what could she have possibly done to earn her father's ill will?

Ever since she could remember, he'd barely tolerated her presence and made great strides to avoid her company. Aside from him, she had no one. Her mother had died when Dani was two. She had no memories of her, no pictures, and her father never spoke of her. If she had relatives, she didn't know them. No one ever called or tried to contact her. It made for a lonely existence, raised by nannies, tutors, and household staff.

The only time she experienced a semblance of normalcy had been in college where she formed a few lasting friendships. Otherwise, she never had a chance to get close to anyone, including her father who preferred it that way. They had a cold, distant relationship, not from a lack of effort on her part to change things, but she had given up trying years ago.

Lost in thought and indulging in a good deal of well-deserved self-pity, Dani started when an alarm screeched and the overhead warning lights began to flash. Rising from her chair, she hurried to the door. The moment it opened, an acrid odor filled her nostrils.

Looking both ways, she saw a cloud of smoke filling the corridor and rolling her way. When it engulfed a crewman running in her direction, he crumpled to the floor and laid motionless without so much as coughing.

"That's not smoke," she uttered in horror. Dani whirled. Before she could reenter her quarters, the cloud surrounded her. Her head swam, and the bitter gas coated her tongue. She fell to her knees with a thud. An instant later, the floor rose toward her face, but she didn't feel the impact, blackness enveloping her instead.

# Chapter Two

The magnets inlaid in the heels of Jaylin's boots echoed off the tile floor with each step he took across the enormous room. Like a king receiving one of his lowly subjects, Daniel Alltryp sat on a gilded, red-velvet throne-like chair. Disgust for the odious man consumed him. If the filthy rich human didn't hold the title to his ship, he would have enjoyed putting his fist through his contemptuous face.

"Captain Sin-Naysir." When Alltryp said his name, his upper lip curled, and his nostrils flared as if he had found something foul on the sole of his shoe. "You're late," the older man snapped.

"I had important things to do today," Jaylin replied. "Visiting a rich fuck with a galaxy-sized ego wasn't one of them."

"You're one to talk," he shot back. "Your reputation for arrogance precedes you."

"You confuse self-confidence with arrogance. On me, it's swagger, and it works. On you, it's exaggerated self-importance, which is repulsive."

The man's already-ruddy face turned crimson, and Jaylin was sure he'd stroke out right there in front of him—not that he cared. The universe would be better off without the prick. It was widely known they despised one another, if the old guy keeled over with him in the room, there might be questions. After several past run-ins with Earth's global security force, he'd rather not have another.

"Let's cut the chitchat, Alltryp. Why don't you explain why you summoned me here?"

"I have a job for you."

Jaylin had listened long enough to this total waste of time. Without hesitation, he turned to leave.

"Wait! You haven't heard the details," came the man's sputtering protest.

His steps didn't slow. "I'm well versed on how you do business. You'll excuse me, but when I want to get fucked, I'll find a woman."

"What if I return your ship? Free and clear?"

This got his attention.

Trilorian by birth, he hadn't called Trilor home in years. Instead, he lived, worked, and played—which hadn't been often of late—on the Renegade, his somewhat dated, though well-maintained, heavily armed space cruiser. Once confiscated by the court based on a bogus breach of contract claim from Alltryp, he'd been stuck on Earth. A nice place to visit and all, except the lack of work had tapped into his income stream. An interstellar mercenary for hire was of little use without a ship, after all.

Turning back, he crossed his arms over his chest, eyeing the worm. "I'm listening," he murmured, prepared to take in Alltryp's proposal with a healthy dose of skepticism.

"My personal spacecraft has been taken."

"What a shame."

"My daughter was on board," he snapped. "Pirates overtook it on the return trip from the Dominion of Elzor where Daniella was meeting her soon-to-be in-laws." He pulled a folded sheet of white paper out of his inner breast pocket, and held it up. "I received this ransom demand three days ago."

"On paper, how quaint." Jaylin glanced at it, making no move to take it. "Why did you wait until now to contact me for assistance?"

"My other options didn't pan out."

Jaylin smirked. He wasn't the only one Alltryp had screwed over. Nobody wanted to work for the jackweed. Moving forward, he snatched the paper from between his fat fingers, being careful not to touch his skin.

*Alltryp,*

*We have your daughter. Deposit five million credits into our universal account, or we put her up for auction. You have one Earth week to comply.*

"Four days from now," he observed, his tone sharp. "You didn't leave me much time."

"I went through proper channels—a mistake. I should have called you in first. I regret the wasted time. I need Daniella returned, and I have to admit I'm at my wits' end."

Jaylin glanced up in surprise. He'd always assumed Alltryp's concerns lay solely with himself and his money, nothing more. "You must care for your daughter very much."

"Fuck no. She's the product of a youthful indiscretion, an influential man's daughter I knocked up and had to marry. But Daniella's bitch of a mother is long gone, so is her daddy. The only thing I care about is the billion credits she's bringing as a bride price, and the future billions I'll earn in joint ventures with her in-laws, the ruling king and queen of Elzor."

Watching the man salivating with avarice made Jaylin's stomach turn. Heartily sorry for the daughter of the unfeeling sperm donor sitting on his pretentious throne, he backed away for fear he'd be tainted by his callousness. "I knew you were a heartless bastard, but this shit is fucked up."

"Coming from a mercenary for sale to the highest bidder, just breaks my heart." From a side table, he picked up a data stick. "My investigators have done half the work for you. Pictures, bio, the ship's specs, and its tracking key; they're all here. And before you ask, they sold the Titan within hours to a resale dealer for a fraction of its worth. Which means I'm out the cost of a damn expensive spacecraft on top of everything else."

Being in the same room with the asshole made Jaylin's skin crawl. This said a lot considering the lowlifes he interacted with daily in his line of work. He wanted the deal done and to be out of here. He would take the job, but it would cost.

"Return of the Renegade with clear title, now. And, when I return the girl, I want one hundred thousand credits for all the shit I've had to put up with from you this past year."

"The ship alone is worth ten times as much!" he whined. "Forget it, I'll find someone else."

He snorted. Alltryp's bluff wasn't close to convincing. "I wouldn't be standing here if you could find anyone else willing to deal with you. And, considering the ship you're returning doesn't belong to you, one hundred thousand for an extraction-and-rescue mission is dirt cheap. For someone with my skill, who can do the impossible and get her back inside of a week, it's insulting. But go right ahead, find another merc. I'll enjoy watching you sweat while you try."

He started toward the door again, Alltryp muttering angrily behind him, "Filthy lowlife pirate scum."

"Insults aren't getting your daughter back, Danny-boy. The clock is ticking, and you're wasting valuable time. If I reach the door before you change your mind, I won't be back."

"Fine. One hundred thousand and the return of your damn ship."

He stopped, turning back, not done with his demands. He had safeguards in mind to keep Alltryp from screwing him over, again. "I want the deed and the Renegade in space dock within the hour, and a receipt of the credits deposited in a trust at the 1st Global Bank. The manager there is Alaan St. Justice. A fitting name for an impartial trustee who will oversee the money and complete the transfer when the girl is returned."

"I'm good for it. There's no need—"

"There's every need, you corrupt fuck. This is the deal, or there is no deal."

The older man's double chin wobbled as he shook with outrage, unused to being on the short end of the negotiations. Jaylin enjoyed every moment the bastard squirmed. He'd make the right decision because no other remained.

"Deal," Alltryp snapped after a prolonged pause.

"I'm leaving now to prepare. In the meantime, get your shit together, Dan." He took several strides forward, stopping close enough to meet the other man's shifty-eyed stare. "Don't fuck around and make me wait, or you put your daughter at risk. Strike that. You put the billion credits and your future joint ventures at risk. The thought of all the money you stand to lose should be enough to spark a fire in your cold heart to get you motivated." He paused. "I'll need the data."

On reflex, Jaylin caught the small computer storage stick Alltryp threw at him. He stared at it a moment, his conscience battling over doing business with such a man. His livelihood depended on getting the Renegade back and staying out of prison. With no other option to get out of his own predicament, he slipped it in his pocket and headed for the door.

"There is one other thing," Alltryp announced.

He froze. *Shit. What now?*

"She's a virgin."

His head came around, looking over his shoulder in amazement. "Considering your age, I didn't think we were talking about a child. How old is she?"

"Twenty-four, at least for a few more weeks."

"You're not serious." Earth women had a universally renowned reputation for being free sexually. For this girl to have reached her mid-twenties and remained untouched was unheard of.

"I'm quite serious. With a slut for a mother, I've spent considerable time and expense preventing Daniella from turning out the same way. And, believe me, her college years tested my purse strings. I'm about to get restitution, however. Return her as she left here, or the deal is off."

"What if the current kidnappers have already removed the barrier?"

"This would be unfortunate for both of us. We won't know until you recover her, but it's the chance you'll have to take for your ship and your freedom."

He scowled, his fists clenched at his sides to keep from surrendering to the temptation of kicking a fifty-year-old fat man's ass. The energy it took to do so was better served finding the girl. Turning, he left the room and Alltryp's loathsome presence without looking back.

\*\*\*

"I don't like this, not one bit. You know how I feel about having a woman aboard ship. They're trouble."

*You don't have to like it, but I gave you an order, which you do have to follow.*

"Always pulling rank when it's something I object to."

*That's the privilege of rank, brother. You get to pull it whenever you want.*

When silence greeted him, Jaylin paused, glancing up from where he entered search parameters into the Renegade's computer. He took in Malik's mulish expression. They didn't have time to debate this. With each minute, the clock ticked closer to the deadline, and the pirates' ship moved farther from their grasp, along with the solution to their current financial dilemma. He rose to his feet, staring unblinking at his younger brother.

"Need I remind you who is the captain?" he asked aloud. Most often, they communicated with mind-speak, a benefit of their twin link. But, after being alone on a ship for so long just the two of them, they needed sound, especially when they became frustrated or angry, like he was now. "More to the point, do you need help recalling who is the first twin?"

Jaw clenched tight like his fists, his brother's golden eyes, so different from his own silver ones, darkened. He knew what it meant, so he waited.

It had been this way for thirty-two years. Jaylin, as the eldest, the first twin, meant he was the dominant one of the pair—the same for all Trilorian males, always born as twins. The more powerful of the two, the first was the leader, the protector, the decision maker, and the one who sought out the woman the brothers would share as their life mate. It had been the natural order of things on Trilor since the beginning.

Malik, as the second was steadfast, protective of his first, but more passive in general—though not a pushover. Often, the younger twin grew bigger. His brother topped him by an inch, at least. His size made him self-confident, assertive, and when necessary, forceful. The difference? Malik had less need for control, which made him a good follower. He took orders well, had been an excellent soldier in the past, and now, served as first mate for the Renegade. In fact, since there were only the two of them, he also comprised the entire crew.

Jaylin didn't take his brother's loyalty for granted and never ran roughshod over his second, nor did he bark orders solely because he could. Malik was intelligent, a skilled medic, and had trained in the military for warfare. As captain, Jaylin relied on and respected his opinion. As twins, they were close. Inseparable when children, they'd remained fast friends into adulthood. This didn't mean they always saw eye to eye.

Like brothers did, they argued, and their disagreements had, at times, become physical, although they hadn't had a fist fight since their youth. Still, when vying factions conflicted, chaos could result unless a leader emerged to restore order, make decisions, or to mediate and compromise when necessary. Malik knew his role, remained unwavering in his support—most often—offered counsel when needed, and followed orders, like any crewman did with his captain. Sometimes, though, it took a moment for him to yield and accept his authority—especially when a situation stirred up emotions he'd rather suppress. Jaylin gave him time, knowing he would inevitably do what must be done.

When the tension left his brother's jaw and his fists unclenched, Jaylin also stood at ease.

"You don't need to remind me. You are the captain, of course," Malik conceded, "and always the first."

He clamped his hand on his shoulder and squeezed. "I listen, brother, but in this case, we are out of options."

Multitasking due to the ticking clock, Jaylin set the program to run and moved to the interactive map on the far wall. He keyed in the coordinates of the pirates' last transmission. Once the computer assimilated all the information, it would produce a narrowed-down list of probable sites where they would likely hide out while waiting for the ransom deadline.

One by one, locator flags popped up on the map—too many for Jaylin's liking. Malik moved to his side, watching the results along with him. Several minutes later, the program ended. With his hands on his hips, Jaylin stared at the thirty computer projections spanning ten sectors.

"It would take ten teams working round the clock to search all these sites by the deadline," his brother stated, and he was right.

"We don't have ten teams, and since there is little time to do the impossible, this is the only recourse available to pay back these ridiculous fines. Despite Alltryp returning the Renegade, the Interstellar Council could take it away again and imprison us if we don't make full payment in thirty days."

"Damn trumped-up charges. A decent attorney would have had this dismissed without court fees and exorbitant fines," Malik grumbled.

"Our funds were limited. A second-rate shyster is all we could afford."

"This mess is Alltryp's fault to begin with. He's corrupt, and here we are crawling back in bed with him."

An image of the red-faced, balding man with his considerable paunch made him grimace. "Please, I'd like to keep thoughts of the bastard anywhere near my bed out of my head."

"You realize he's nothing but a crook?"

"I'm not an idiot, Mal. I know exactly what kind of man he is."

"Then why are we doing this?"

He glanced over his shoulder at his twin's disgruntled face. This job was too big to do solo. When they located the pirates, he'd need Malik at the helm while he boarded the pirates' vessel and recovered the girl. Not that he expected other than his full compliance, it would make the mission much easier — not to mention more peaceful — if he had his support.

"Do you have a better idea?" Jaylin asked.

"Not at this time," he admitted.

"Time is something we don't have, thanks to our subpar attorney-at-law. I made him regret his incompetence, although doing so doesn't eliminate our fifty thousand credit debt."

A wry smile twisted Malik's lips. "I would have enjoyed seeing you crush him, at least I'd have gleaned some satisfaction out of this shit show."

Fed up with his malcontent of a first officer and having his orders questioned, he snapped. "This contract pays out twice what we owe and gives us the Renegade free and clear. Stop your bitchin'."

"Who are we rescuing, royalty?"

"No, but once Daniella Alltryp weds the Elzorian prince, she will be."

"Elzor! I heard the heir to the throne and his brothers are all sterile, and because they are too arrogant to believe their regal gonads are at fault, despite medical science that proves it, they blame their wives, getting rid of them when they don't produce an heir — naturally, or otherwise — within a year. Returning the girl to them could be the same as signing her death warrant."

Jaylin had struggled with his decision, and how the girl's ultimate fate and being party to it would weigh on their consciences. But mercenaries rarely worked for clients with morals. And scruples didn't play a part in their business, nor would they keep them fed or get their ship back. "It isn't our concern.

Our mission is to rescue the girl and return her to her father. What happens afterward is between them. Besides, is leaving her to the mercy of pirates any better?"

"Sacrificing his own daughter." Malik shook his head in disgust. "He's a bigger prick than I thought."

"Agreed, but he's a wealthy prick and we need the reward. And, Alltryp being reprehensible may be our ace in the hole."

"What do you mean?"

Jaylin dug into his shirt pocket, removed the data stick, and laid it on the computer console between them.

"What is that?"

"Daniella's file. I reviewed some of it. There are a few surprises, specifically a tracking code. We'll be able to pick up her signal if we get within range."

"I thought Alltryp told you they sold his ship."

"They did."

Malik arched a brow, waiting.

"It doesn't track Alltryp's ship."

"What then?"

"Not what, who. The file says it's embedded on the back of Daniella's right thigh, just below her ass cheek."

"He chipped her? Like a pet?" He paled, taking on a greenish tint as if he might get sick. "You know he stands to gain from this. But Elzor isn't known for its fortune. The question remains, why is he so keen on this marriage? I smell something foul in this deal, Jay."

"I didn't ask, nor do I care. We'll rescue this Earth mogul's spoiled daughter, collect our fee, pay off our debt, and be on our way."

"You don't care she might be an innocent pawn in all of this?"

"Yes, except I can't afford to be swayed by it, and you shouldn't be either. We don't need your altruism resurfacing at a time like this, Malik. And that is a direct order!"

"You play your first twin card easily when it suits you."

"We've already determined it is a privilege of birth order, deal with it."

"Fine. But she stays in her quarters, and far away from you. If she's the least bit attractive, I don't want you getting ideas."

"I haven't seen the girl, not that it matters. She's Daniel Alltryp's daughter. Odds are she's a bitch, cold and calculating like her daddy. You've heard the Earth expression about the apple not falling far from the tree? His kind of greed tends to run in families. Trust me, brother, she could be a raving beauty, and I wouldn't be tempted."

"Bullshit, you're always up for a quick fuck, which is precisely what I'm afraid of." He grabbed the data stick off the desk and inserted it into one of the access ports. Seconds later, the files appeared. With a few swipes, Malik brought up an image on-screen.

Jaylin froze at the sight of the auburn-haired, green-eyed beauty, her fair skin and delicate features taking his breath away. "Fuck me!" he murmured, his body stirring.

"No! Absolutely not! You may be the captain, but as part owner of the Renegade, I have a say in what affects this ship. And I say that"—he jabbed his index finger at the screen—"is trouble. We need to find another way to pay off this debt."

"Too late. I agreed. The credits have been deposited and the title to the ship signed over to us."

"Dammit, Jaylin! No way can you bring her on board and not be tempted."

"I'm not a boy who can't control his libido."

A few more swipes and Malik pulled up a full-length image of Daniella Alltryp. She had curves—plentiful enough to make his teeth ache and his dick hard. She had the body type he preferred on a woman, and it had always been his brother's preference, too. He was right. She would be pure temptation; however, if she had inherited a hint of her father's black soul—greedy and heartless, trampling on anything and anyone to get ahead—he wanted no part of her.

Jaylin shrugged. "So, she's beautiful. I don't want a cold as ice, spoiled rich girl in my bed. She'd probably freeze my prick off. Besides, we have to return her with her virginity still intact or we're back to square one."

"A fact you forgot to mention, brother. What if the pirates have taken the prize?"

"We'll deal with it if, or when, the time comes."

"This is a futile mission."

"Have faith, Malik. In two weeks, all of this will be a bad memory and we can return to living our lives, which means finding a woman to complete our triad. If she looks like our target, redheaded, creamy skin, curves to overflow our hands, and has the power to bring your dormant dick back to life, all the better."

Malik growled. "How many times do I have to tell you there won't be another triad?"

This time, Jaylin pointed at the screen. "Do you mean to tell me you wouldn't fuck a woman who looks like that?" He goaded him on purpose. He'd felt like he did once, but time had passed, and although he would never forget, he had moved on. His brother had gotten stuck, and it fell to him, as the first twin, to get him moving again. "Someone will come along who will stir your blood, Malik. I'm sure of it. I know you disagree, but there is more than one perfect match for us out there. And when we find her, when the benevolence of the Creators brings another treasure into our lives, we will accept the gift and rejoice in being favored, twice."

"Favored! Bah. Mahlia was supposed to be our gift of a lifetime, yet after less than two years with her, they took her away. The Creators play a cruel game, with us as the pawns." Bitterness pervaded Malik's words. "I don't like the odds, or the rules, and decided long ago never to play again. A beautiful redheaded human is not going to make me change my mind."

His brother's face, usually a flat, emotionless mask of indifference, had darkened with anger and what Jaylin recognized as deep-rooted fear. The loss of their beloved wife had been heartbreaking, their grief unremitting. Jaylin thought the anguish would last an eternity. He had struggled to move forward, too, but, after a year had passed, although it still hurt, he realized a long, solitary life stretched out ahead of him if he didn't break free of the pall of sorrow. And he missed the softness a woman brought to his hard life, the affection, the laughter, and, yes, regular sex.

Not true for Malik, who, as a second twin, had an intense sense of loyalty and devotion, one stronger than his own, it seemed. Five years later, he remained frozen and embittered. It had been as long since they had shared a female, something instinctive, like breathing among their kind. One-on-one sex was possible, physically gratifying, although not more than that. It scratched an itch, but didn't satisfy the intuitive bonding necessary for a Trilorian male to be fulfilled. Somehow, he had to break through the glacial barrier his twin had erected around his heart and end this self-imposed celibacy, so they could both move on, together, how they were meant to.

He eyed the fiery-haired beauty on the screen. Perhaps someone like Daniella Alltryp could revive his brother's hibernating sexuality and, once awakened, remind him how much loving—and living—he had ahead of him. After this mission concluded, he'd make getting Malik laid a top priority.

"I know what you are thinking. You can forget it. I won't go there again."

Jaylin looked up, certain he'd concealed his thoughts, but after thirty-two years, his twin knew him well.

"I loved her," he went on to say in a harsh whisper. "I know you did, too. The difference is you're stronger than me. I can't endure another loss like that, Jay. It almost killed me. If it happens again, I'm not sure I can survive."

He didn't know what to say, stunned his twin's ever-present shields had vanished. Gone was the mask of cool indifference, and before him stood the man he once knew, one who felt deeply, too much so, because he appeared shaken, raw, and afraid.

Still, it gave Jaylin hope. He hadn't seen the real man in so long he'd begun to think him lost forever. "Mal—"

"No, please. We'll find the girl and return her to Alltryp. But I'm keeping my distance, and so should you. Afterward, we reinstitute our no-females-on-board policy." He spun on his heel and moved to the door. Facing away from him, he added, "I ask little of you, brother. My entire life I've followed your lead, watched your back, and have done what you've asked. In this, however, I will have my way."

He glanced over his shoulder at him, and, in a blink, the damned mask slipped into place again. Jaylin wanted to roar in anger, demanding he return. Instead, he stared in helpless frustration at the brother he loved.

"I'll go set the course."

For a long time, Jaylin gazed at the empty doorway, at a loss for what to do. But he was stubborn like his twin, maybe more so because the determination to bring his shattered brother out of this perpetual limbo, surged within him. The only question that remained…how.

# Chapter Three

Curled into a ball in the corner of the unheated cargo hold, Dani could focus on nothing except combatting the bone-chilling cold. Exhausted by overwhelming fear which had kept her awake these past three days, it didn't seem relief would be coming anytime soon as she lay on the hard, unyielding floor without a blanket, much less a pillow for comfort.

Bound with her hands behind her back and to the wall by an ankle shackle, she had been this way ever since she awoke groggy from the gas they'd deployed. She hadn't seen anyone else from her ship. She'd asked about the crew, but her questions had been met by silence from her captors.

Two more attempts to communicate had received the same response with the addition of a filthy rag stuffed in her mouth. It had remained in place, choking her for hours, until she thought for sure she'd die by suffocation. She hadn't been so lucky, thinking death a better fate than whatever they had in mind for her. Finally, one of them came in with a tray of disgusting food, removed the gag, and untied her. With her throat parched, dry lips sore and cracked, and her stomach in knots, she hadn't attempted to force a single bite down though she needed to keep her strength up to fight.

They removed the constricting shackle every so often to drag her to the toilet. Everyone gave her a few moments of privacy except Nestor, a disgusting, bug-eyed pervert who leered at her, making lewd comments. She tried to ignore him, but he made it impossible by insisting she beg to be untied. When she refused, he threatened to leave her bound and take down her pants and panties himself, something far worse since it meant he'd be touching her.

Hopelessness assailed her, and she closed her eyes, tired of fighting sleep. Except, in the dark, the sounds in the room grew louder, from the click of her chattering teeth, to the chug of the engines which had to be situated against the wall behind her because it vibrated with a metallic ring. All of it combined to keep her frazzled nerves on edge.

A boot jabbing into her ribs told her she was no longer alone. She flinched, guarding her tender side since this tended to be their typical greeting. Any movement wracked her body with pain. To prevent another kick, she forced her stiff body from its cramped position, a tug on her tender ankle reminding her of the heavy chain and shackle she wore.

When she didn't move fast enough, an angry curse accompanied another sharp blow. Whimpering in agony, she rolled onto her back, her body weight pinching her hands against the hard floor. At the sight of the ugly, hooked nosed, sneering face leaning over her, she shrank back, although it wasn't far enough to escape his breath which reeked from his rotten teeth.

If she'd had anything in her stomach, it would have come up all over him, earning her yet another hard boot tip between the ribs.

"Daddy's time is up, princess," he informed her, a cold edge to his nasty tone. "He didn't pay, so you get to."

She snorted in derision. "My father cares about two things, himself and lining his pockets. I told you he wouldn't part with any of his precious credits, you fool—"

Another vicious jolt rammed home, this one aimed at her belly. It knocked the wind out of her, making her wheeze and cough until her eyes watered.

Spittle spattered her face when the captain shouted at her. "I told you to stop calling me stupid, bitch." Hard fingers dug into her arms as he hauled her to her feet, and shoved her at one of his men.

Other rough hands caught her, and the man turned her to face him. With his pockmarked sallow skin, sunken eyes, and one brown snaggletooth hanging down in front, this pirate terrified Dani the most. Because, as cruel as Captain Rondo Cobb ever thought to be, this man, who they called Nestor, was worse. And he had one thing on his mind—getting in her pants.

"Strip the slut," Rondo ordered. "And get pictures of all her fuckable parts. We'll upload her profile to the intergalactic slave auction. Her pretty white skin, big tits, and fresh pussy should earn us enough to make this fiasco of a kidnapping worth our while."

"No, please," she cried.

The third man, who didn't say much, grabbed her ankle and released the shackle. He got her feet while Nestor took hold of her under the arms, and, together, they lifted and started carrying her. Sobbing and struggling, she kicked, twisted, and clawed, not caring if she fell and broke her neck. They dropped her on a hard, flat surface, pinning her down with harsh hands. Nestor's malicious grin filled her vision. He leered at her, licking his lips obscenely which sent a chill racing down her spine. Her reaction didn't go unnoticed, and he laughed.

Wasting no time, he ripped her already-torn dress down the front, tugged down her bra, putting on a show like he was following orders and stripping her, but, really, he groped what he had lusted after for days.

"Can I have me some before we sell her, Cobb?"

"I don't give a fuck, and neither will her buyers." The captain's orders for her to remain unharmed and the expected ransom from her father had been all that stood between her and certain rape. She had to endure Nestor's lewd looks and sly touches whenever Rondo wasn't around, but nothing more, except their rough handling. With her protection eliminated, he was free to molest and rape at will, which he clearly intended to do straightaway.

He tore apart the front clasp of her bra, baring her breasts then began pinching and twisting her nipples. Her cries of pain and pleas for mercy only entertained him. Dani tried to get away. With her hands still bound and his buddy holding her ankles — waiting to be next in line, no doubt — her weak efforts were futile.

They were bigger, stronger, and had probably eaten in the past few days, where she had not. Desperate, she used the one weapon available, her teeth. When he rolled her toward him, to strip off the rest of her clothes, she bit the fleshy part of his arm and clamped down hard.

His sudden shriek of pain startled his partner who loosened his grip. Free, Dani came off the table.

Without a plan, other than getting away, she lurched forward. She didn't get far before a hand caught her hair and spun her back around, at which point, Nestor repaid her by landing a vicious backhand slap across her cheek and sent her reeling.

"Idiot!" Cobb roared. "Her price will suffer if she's marked. Fuck her all you want, just be careful with the merchandise."

"The bitch made me bleed," he spluttered. "She deserves to suffer."

"Go easy or you'll get no pussy at all, hear me?"

"Won't you get more money for a virgin?" she cried out, frantic to stop Nestor, who bore down on her.

"She's lying," he accused.

"I'm not. I swear. If my father won't pay, contact Prince Ivar."

"Quit spewing stories, cunt," her would-be rapist ordered. His fingers curled into the waistband of her panties and twisted. They gave way like tissue paper in his grip, leaving her bare except for her shoes.

"Please, I'm telling the truth!" Sobbing and screaming at the same time, she made a desperate plea to the captain. "Do you think the Elzorian prince would consider me for his bride and the mother of the heir to the throne, if I wasn't pure? He'll pay. I know he will."

"Hold," Rondo called. "She's right. If Daddy won't meet our price, maybe her pathetic excuse for a groom will."

"Aw, fuck, Cobb," Nestor whined. "I need it bad."

"And I don't give a shit. Haul her back to the table. I'll examine her and see for myself if she's telling the truth or just lying to keep from taking your disease-riddled cock."

"You know I took the medicine to clear that up," he grumbled, though still followed orders, hauling her up by her hair. "Damn. You won't ever shut up about it. I make one mistake with a whore and I'm tainted forever."

At the thought of him passing something nasty onto her, she gagged, tasting the bitter gall rise in her throat. Back at the table, he twisted the fistful of hair, pulling her across the top, when a deafening bang and violent shudder rocked the ship. Everything not nailed down went flying, including Dani. When she landed, her shoulder took the brunt of the impact and exploded in agony.

The next instant, the ship shook again, this time listing sharply sideways. Again, she slammed into something hard, this time a shipping crate. Before she could get her bearings, the breath left her body with a whoosh when a heavy weight fell on her back, trapping her beneath it and the floor.

"What the hell?" Cobb growled close to her ear, which explained what had landed on top of her. Another bang and the ship shuddered again.

"We're under attack," someone yelled.

The old spacecraft creaked and groaned, then tilted the other way. She and Cobb began sliding. Still bound, Dani only had her feet to try to save herself. She kicked out wildly, hoping, as her world shifted, she could catch herself before she slammed into something for a third time. Clawing with her fingers, she tried to grab hold of anything. Once, she caught a seam in the floor, but couldn't stop her momentum and she lost her tiny grip, ripping out a nail or two in the process.

Another thunderous boom rocked the ship. She shifted direction, colliding with something soft and warm for a change. It ended up being the pirate captain tossed about as if he weighed nothing, too.

"Someone find out what the fuck is going on," he roared, making her ears ring more than the nonstop shriek of the alarm.

"We're taking heavy fire from an unidentified craft," a voice shouted over the speakers. It was Rylon, the fourth man who had apparently been left in control of the bridge.

"What's the damage?" Cobb barked while scrambling to his feet, uncaring that he stepped on her.

"Stabilizers are out, and we've had a hull breach— Brace for impact!" he screamed right before a bone-jarring thud shook the ship.

"Evasive maneuvers or return fire, dammit. We can't sustain much more of this." His words hadn't faded when a flash of brilliant light filled the room.

When it dissipated, the form of a large man became visible for a split second before the lights went out and blackness engulfed them. After that, all she could see were flashes of weapons firing, red from a photon torch, beams of blue from where she'd last seen the stranger. One of the men cried out in pain.

Terrified, Dani curled into a ball on the floor, longing for her quiet, solitary existence back home. With certain death a heartbeat away, she closed her eyes, covered her head with her arms, and prayed for it to be swift and painless.

"The last hit took out environmental controls and life support, and there's a fire in the engine room," Rylon announced, his voice shaky with undisguised panic. "I got smoke on the bridge and nothing is responding. Hellfire, Cobb, we're sitting ducks."

"Open communication. Tell them we are willing to negotiate. Find out what they want."

"I want the girl," a deadly cold voice stated. "A demand which is non-negotiable."

"No!" Nestor roared.

The captain shouted, "Take her, but leave us in one piece."

"The hell with that!" her primary tormentor called out. "He can't have her. She's worth a fortune and I haven't gotten to fuck her yet."

"Get your mind off your prick, asshole," Rylon grumbled through the speaker. "It's give up the girl, or get blasted out of the sky."

"If we give her up, what's to keep them from doing it anyway?" Nestor demanded.

"Nothing. It's a chance we gotta take, like it or not, when he's the one with the fucking gun and his ship is pummeling us with vortex cannon fire," the captain snapped. To the stranger, he growled, "You can have her."

"Smart," came his low, rumbling reply, barely audible over her would-be rapist who angrily cursed a blue streak.

"Shut up, you idiot," Cobb raged. "You can't get any pussy when you're dead."

"Enough squabbling!" the newcomer warned. "I'm taking her now. The first one that moves I blast into bits."

Heavy footsteps approached at the same time the auxiliary lights came on.

"At least something works on this tin can," the captain grumbled.

Temporarily blinded by the sudden flood of light after total blackness, Dani squinched her eyes shut. She thought she heard someone running and some scuffling. Next, came a ghastly choking sound. Squinting against the brightness, she could make out the outline of two men.

One was huge and made Nestor look petite while holding him with one hand by the throat, his feet dangling above the floor by a foot. Then, with what to her seemed like an effortless flick of his wrist—like the two-hundred-pound man weighed no more than a pesky fly—he launched him into a stack of shipping crates. The nasty pirate fell hard, landing with a sickening crunch of bones, lying in a motionless heap, his head at an awkward angle. Although it seemed wrong, Dani reveled in his death and would have cheered if she hadn't been paralyzed with fear.

Done with Nestor, the big man turned, his gaze sweeping over the two remaining pirates. "Any other heroes who want to meet their Creator today?" he drawled coolly.

A pulse beat later, Rylon's voice filled the room.

"Cobb, the ship identifies as the Renegade, and the captain is—"

"Mother fucking Jaylin Sin-Naysir," he finished for him. "I know. I'm lookin' at him. He's the same bastard who's been a thorn in my side for five goddamn years."

Dani looked at him, too, which required craning her neck, considering there was a lot of him. Several inches over six feet tall, with thick blond hair reaching past his shoulders, and he had golden-hued skin, indicating he wasn't human. Although battered and banged up, she could still appreciate all that he was—the most handsome man she'd ever laid eyes on.

In the next instant, he smiled, revealing gleaming white teeth, and her heart fluttered.

"Rondo Cobb." He chuckled, the huskiness of his laugh washing over her, creating goose bumps across her skin. "You're the oily pirate whose ass I've been kicking all over the galaxy. Even though I have thoroughly enjoyed doing it all this time, I can't say I'm pleased to meet you." His eyes flicked to Dani for a split second before sliding back to Cobb, all amusement wiped from his face. He raised his weapon, aiming it dead center at the captain's chest. "You put the mark on her cheek?"

"No. The backhand came courtesy of Nestor." Cobb jerked his chin toward where her abuser lay.

His gun hand didn't waver, only his chin moved, and no more than a fraction. He stared at the lifeless form among the splintered wood for a moment, then he grunted—sounding satisfied. His free hand extended her way. "Come to me, Daniella."

Startled by his deep baritone saying her name, she didn't move, unable to. Did she take her chances here, with the devils she knew, or go with him, the devil she didn't? Trembling with fear, she could only gaze back at him while a cold knot of uncertainty formed in her stomach.

He took the decision from her by moving in and pulling her up with an arm around her waist.

"Please, no…" she whimpered, wishing this nightmare would end.

"Shh, sweetness," he murmured, and she thought he added, "trust me."

But she couldn't be sure because Rylon announced through the speakers, "He's locked onto all life-forms in the cargo hold. He says to get out or he'll transport everyone, and vaporize any uninvited guests upon arrival."

The two remaining pirates scrambled for the doors. A moment later, the prickly tingling sensation of transporting took hold, her molecules disassembling, scattering across time and space, only to come together again in a flash of light moments later. She'd done it twice in her life, and never forgot it, hating the process which always left her dazed and weak-kneed. It also freaked her out, each time expecting to wind up with an arm sticking out of her forehead or her feet facing backward.

Nothing horrible happened this time, except her legs gave way. She didn't puddle on the floor, however, thanks to the hold the large alien had on her waist. He went a step further and caught her behind the knees, scooping her naked body—save for her shoes—up in his arms.

"I can walk," she protested.

"You can barely stand." He stepped out of the semi-circular glass booth.

She peeked up at him. This close, she noticed he had a blond scruff of beard, light next to his tawny skin. She wanted to reach up and touch it, to feel the texture on her fingertips, but that would be insane. No matter his handsomeness, he was a stranger and an alien. She stiffened instinctively, pushing against his chest. "What do you want with me?"

His face angled down to her. When their eyes met, she sucked in a startled breath. His were a stunning silver shade, and, up close, better looking, something she wouldn't have believed possible. And strong enough to lift her off the floor one-handed, and capable of saving her from the cruel pirates who'd outnumbered him three- to-one. He'd also ended Nestor without batting an eye.

The last fact sobered her. The pirates had called him a mercenary. She didn't know if it was true, but she had no guarantee she was any better off now than ten minutes ago. Panicking, she struggled to get free, twisting in his arms. "Put me down."

Her resistance had the opposite effect. Like steel bands, his inflexible hold tightened.

"Easy, Daniella. I'm one of the good guys. You're safe."

"I don't know that." Struggling, she found she was helpless against his strength. "And you didn't answer my question. What do you want? Who sent you?"

"Daniel Alltryp."

His answer stabbed into her heart. Her father meant to sell her to Ivar, like the pirates had to a slave auction, so she'd be no better off. "You work for him?"

"On contract only." He strode forward. "I'll explain everything later. Right now, I need to get you secured. Cobb's rattletrap is going to blow at any moment, and I don't want you injured from any subsequent shock waves."

"Brace, Jaylin," a deep voice called over the com. "Blast wave in five, four, three…"

Her rescuer moved into action. Dropping her on her feet, he pinned her to the wall.

"Not again," she whimpered.

By the count of one, the floor beneath her feet and everything around her jerked violently. This time, she felt no pain, just the pressure of his big body constraining hers while he grasped the vertical beams on either side of them.

Having been through this one too many times of late, she freaked. Unable to suppress the frightened sob rising from her throat, she clutched at the closest thing within reach. Unfortunately, the only solid thing around was him.

"Easy, Daniella, I've got you," he murmured.

Unlike the pirates' ship, this one seemed sound. Though it shook, it didn't creak and

groan, or give the impression it would break into bits at any second. Still, the awful experience brought her phobia about being sucked into space front and center.

Big and solid, even though he was a stranger, she wanted to wrap her arms around his waist and cling to him, like her life depended on it because, as far as she knew, it did. Except she couldn't, not with her arms bound behind her back. Instead, she leaned into him and buried her face in his chest, hoping he wouldn't let her fall.

Before long, the shaking stopped, and the same deep voice called the all clear.

"Does that mean…?" Her question came out muffled by his shirt, but he answered.

"Yep. Cobb and the rest of his vile crew won't bother you ever again."

She wilted, only noticing a few minutes later, he'd released the beams and curled his arms around her. It felt nice, and reassuring. Tipping her head back, she looked up at him.

"Are you all right?" he asked, his low voice warm with concern.

Sudden tears made his image waver; she didn't think she'd ever be all right again.

"Sweetness…" He used his thumbs to wipe the wetness from her cheeks, his touch gentle.

Standing naked in his arms, she became self-conscious, well aware she hadn't washed in days. "I'm fine," she whispered, hiding her face in his shirt when she really wanted to find a corner to curl up in and lick her wounds. Second on her list, a hot shower. Except she couldn't do any of those things, not with her wrists tied. Nor did she pull away, or else she'd expose herself.

He leaned away, nudged up her chin, his silver eyes searching. "I doubt you're fine, Daniella. You've been through quite an ordeal."

With his chin tucked to look down at her, she became aware of how very big he was. Tall, and thickly muscled, his chest at least triple the breadth of Ivar's, it tested the constraints of his white shirt. With his hair swirling around his shoulders, he reminded her of a pirate of old, the swashbuckling kind from romantic tales, lacking only a sword and a scabbard. And he smelled wonderful, the opposite of the stale fetid breath of Nestor and his ilk.

She breathed him in, having no choice since he surrounded her. When he tilted his head, peering down at her in concern, it came to her she'd been gaping at him like a smitten fool. She racked her brain to recall his last comment.

"Uh, well…yes," she stammered, before coming up with a response. "It has been a harrowing few days."

"I bet." He gave her a squeeze. He also slid his hands down her arms and, with a snap, released her bindings.

Moving her hands in front, she stayed close to him, concealing her nudity while also flexing her fingers, trying to restore the blood. "Thank you," she murmured. "Much longer, and my shoulders would have been forever frozen in that position." Her stomach growled, which mortified her on top of everything else.

His full, sensual lips curved upward, teeth flashing dazzling white against his golden skin, and those eyes, they gleamed as he smiled transforming his face from handsome to gorgeous. And it didn't help her schoolgirl giddiness when he brushed back strands of hair from her cheeks and forehead, tucking the long tendrils behind her ears.

"Things are looking up for you because I see a hot shower and food in your future."

"Yes, please."

"After, I'll have Malik check your injuries. He's at the helm, right now."

"Is he your captain?"

"No, I command the Renegade. Malik is my crew."

"Your crew consists of one man?"

"Yes, he's my copilot, cooks because I've tried and am hopeless, and he's also our medic. We're lean on numbers but make up for it in skill and determination." He slid his long finger down her cheek, and then tapped her nose. "Now, how about a shower."

Her face flooded with heat at the reminder. After three days, she must really stink. "I'm sorry. This close, you must not be able to stand me."

"You misunderstood, Daniella. You're warm and soft against me, and your skin is very silky smooth. I'm trying to be a gentleman and not kiss your tears away, so I need to put some space between us. Your father might frown upon you standing naked in my arms since it's not exactly part of the first-class rescue and protection service he hired me to deliver."

"As if my father would care," she retorted, unable to hide her hurt.

"He's paying a lot of credits to get you back."

"Only to hand me over to the Elzorians and certain death."

A shadow crossed his face. "Let's take care of your immediate needs. After you're settled you can tell me all about it."

When he began to step back, her arms tightened. "Wait! I'm naked."

"I'm aware, sweetness, believe me. But you have nothing to fear from me, and nothing to be ashamed of. You have a beautiful body, which we, Malik and I, intend to protect to the death to keep that way." With his back to her, he held his hand bent up behind him. "Grab hold and I'll take you to your quarters while on the Renegade."

Reassured by his consideration of her modesty, she set her palm in his, amazed at how its bigness engulfed hers. As he led her out of the transporter room and into a large circular deck, she marveled at what she saw. State-of-the-art, immaculate, and in excellent condition, a far cry from the dirty, dilapidated ship where she'd spent the past few days.

Small rooms surrounded the large center space, some stood open, others had clear double doors which allowed her to see inside. They passed a roomy galley kitchen, an exercise area with all sorts of equipment, and a smaller, darkened room with a thickly padded reclining chair, floor-to-ceiling screens on the walls, and nothing else. Beyond stood a control console in an alcove with a mini observation screen, and on it a multitude of stars twinkled in the black heavens.

He veered right down a short hall with several frosted glass doors.

"These are the crew quarters. Although modestly sized and nothing fancy, I think you'll find them comfortable. Yours is at the end of the hall. I'll give you a tour of the rest of the ship later, after you've rested." He stopped in front of the last door. "Here we are."

He pressed his palm over a sensor near the ceiling, far above her head.

"Will I be locked in?"

"No, why would you think that?"

"I won't be able to reach the control."

He raised his hand again and made an adjustment.

"Now it's set on automatic."

"I can't lock it?"

"I'd prefer you didn't for your safety, but I'll get you something to stand on so you can if it makes you more comfortable."

"Thank you." She peeked around him, taking in the tempting bed with its plush navy comforter, and thick blue-and-white striped pillows. So easily, she could crawl into it, curl under the covers, and sleep for a week. On the wall to her left stood a recessed door which she hoped led to a bathroom.

"You'll find the shower through there." He nodded at the door, like he'd read her mind.

When she glanced up, she decided it was because he watched her so closely.

"I don't have any clothes," she whispered, crossing her arms over her bare breasts while her gaze swept the room, searching for a robe or a towel, a doily would do, anything to cover herself. Not seeing any of those things, she dashed to the bed and grabbed one of the pillows, holding it longways against her front.

When she turned back, his eyes had become gleaming pools of silver, locked on her.

"We have a facsimulator," he said after a pause. "It can create whatever you'd like to wear. A dress? Trousers and a shirt? Or, I could order up a tunic and leggings. What shall it be?"

"A tunic and leggings sounds comfortable."

"What's your favorite color?"

"It used to be blue." After Elzor, she hated it. "How about purple?"

"Done." His gaze moved over her hair. "Mine has recently become red."

Flushing, she hurried toward the bathroom, not an easy task while walking backward and hiding behind a pillow. She didn't miss his lips twitching with amusement.

"How about a hairbrush?"

"There is a cabinet inside. You should find everything you need. If not, call me."

When she reached the door, instead of scurrying through when it slid open as she'd planned, Dani paused. Hearing all was in readiness for her, she asked something that had occurred to her, bothered her actually, though it shouldn't. "Do you do this often? Rescue women, I mean?"

"We aren't in the business of recovering kidnap victims, no. This is an all-male enterprise, all two of us. We didn't have provisions for a woman and wanted to ensure your comfort during your trip home."

A heaviness centered in her chest at the word home. An hour ago, she'd have given anything to be there. Now, with what her father had done, she couldn't imagine it. "Thank you for considering my needs and for caring. I don't get a lot of that."

"You should." The sudden sharpness of his tone drew her eyes to his face. He frowned briefly, then his features smoothed out. What had he been thinking? "I'll leave you to your shower. Should I plan for supper in say, thirty minutes? Or will you require longer?"

"Any longer and I might fall asleep. I've hardly closed my eyes since the day I was taken."

"And I'm sure you haven't eaten. We'll get you fed, have those bruises checked out, and, afterward, you can sleep clear on through to morning."

"Thank you, Captain, that sounds wonderful."
"I'm Jaylin, please."
"And most people call me Dani."
"Thirty minutes, Dani. Or I'm coming in to check on you." He said it softly, with a kind smile, though she didn't doubt for a minute he'd meant it as an order.

"Yes, sir," she replied, snapping off a salute as if one of his crew, and totally forgetting her state of undress. Her pillow slipped. She caught it before she revealed everything, but a blush flooded her face, spreading down her neck to the tops of her breasts which peeked above the blue-and-white makeshift shield. His attention dipped to where she clutched it to her chest, only making things worse.

He didn't comment or tease her in any way. Instead, with one last intense glance, he strode out the door.

# Chapter Four

Busy in the galley making a meal for their guest, Malik turned when he heard footsteps. His brother's hair was damp from a shower, and though he should be relaxed after accomplishing their mission so efficiently, he read tension and anger on his face.

"How is she?"

"Rattled, as any young woman would be after being subjected to Cobb and Nestor's company for three long days. I tried to set her at ease. She'll need your attention after she gets cleaned up. I saw bruises on her hips, wrists, and several ugly ones over her ribs. The bastards were damn rough. I would have had you see to her first thing, except she seemed more desperate for a shower, than in pain. And she hasn't eaten or slept."

"I figured she'd be hungry. It's almost ready. After she eats, if she can't sleep, restless with bad memories, I can give her something to help."

"That might be a good idea, regardless."

Malik asked the yet-unspoken question. "Was she harmed more than outwardly, do you think? Nestor is a devout rapist, or he used to be until I scattered his atoms across the galaxy."

"She's skittish, so I didn't press her on that yet." A muscle ticked in Jaylin's cheek. "They had her stripped bare when I found her, with her hands bound behind her back."

"Creators damn them to hell," he growled.

"If there is justice, they are burning there now. I'll regret their end came so hastily if they violated her. Inquire when you examine her, Mal, but go easy."

He nodded, another dismal thought occurring to him. "If the deed is done, what becomes of her?"

"I don't know. Alltryp seemed concerned only about her bride price and the credits he'd earn in his alliance with Elzor." Jaylin's troubled gaze bored into him when he stated, "I can't fathom how a father can be so cold. She's beautiful, Malik. More so than her pictures. Young, wide-eyed, and so helpless when I found her. What could she have done to earn his hatred?"

"Be careful, brother, your protective nature and kind heart are showing."

Jaylin snorted. "Both have been buried so long, I'd forgotten I had either one."

"This is what I was afraid of. Remember what we discussed. We can't. I can't. Not again."

"Am I interrupting?" Husky as though strained, her soft voice cut through his increasing anxiety. When he glanced at her, he understood why his brother had been taken with her so quickly. He'd seen her picture, but it in no way did her justice.

"Dani, you look—" Jaylin paused. "I had thought to say better. That isn't true, you just look different."

"I have clothes on and my hair isn't going in a million directions."

He noticed his brother's eyes run over her long, dark-red hair. And they didn't stop there, moving on to the clingy tunic and form-fitting tights accentuating her ample curves. Fully covered from her neck to the ankle-high boots on her small feet, a lace nightgown wouldn't have been more alluring. This didn't escape Jaylin's notice, either.

"The new clothes," he murmured. "They fit very well."

The girl flushed, already falling under the spell of his dominant brother's allure. And, he, in turn, was far from immune to her. What man wouldn't be? With her vibrant red hair, rosy lips, and creamy skin, she'd be considered exotic on their home planet. Where the women of Trilor tended to be tall, with long lines and a more athletic build, by contrast Daniella was small boned, softer, and seemed more vulnerable. Her fragile state, and what she must have endured at the pirates' hands, stirred his protective instincts.

Considering those same instincts came as natural as breathing to his dominant twin, he knew they coursed fiercely through his veins at this very moment.

*Shit! He predicted this would happen.*

"This is Malik." Jaylin's introduction pulled him out of his study of their guest. Her big green eyes framed with fans of thick black lashes shifted their focus to him. "He cooked for you and will tend to your injuries when you have eaten."

"You can trust I know what I'm doing, Daniella. I'm the ship's medic."

"Among other talents so I hear, like blasting dangerous pirates to the far corners of the galaxy. I must express my thanks for the opportune rescue. They were about to…" She looked down at her hands, the fingers laced so tight her knuckles had blanched. "Since the ransom didn't come through, they intended to sell me at auction and needed pictures, naked ones." Retelling the events obviously rekindled the terror and brought a tremor to her voice.

Moving toward her, Jaylin took her into his arms.

She accepted his embrace without hesitation, trusting him after such a short time. Dread made Malik go cold. *Dammit to eternal hell!*

"Did they harm you more than the bruises show?" his brother asked gently. "I know it's hard to speak of, but to treat you, Malik will need to know the full extent of your injuries."

"I wasn't raped—" Her voice broke on the awful word. "Although Nestor meant to do so. If Cobb hadn't stopped him..." She trailed off into a whisper. "He didn't do so to be kind. They were cruel, all of them; I had no idea such evil existed."

Jaylin's lips pressed to her temple. "I'm grateful we arrived in time."

"Not more so than I." She glanced up at him, face bright, eyes gleaming, clearly smitten by the gallant hero who had saved her. And his brother delighted in her adoring expression, especially when she caught her bottom lip between her teeth and shyly glanced away.

Malik knew in his bones this mission was doomed and their beautiful passenger would be their undoing. Her guileless innocence and womanly curves a challenge to any man's fortitude. And her mouth, he imagined it became more tempting when turned down in a pretty pout. If she belonged to him, he'd never get enough of it, whether nibbling on its softness at his leisure, or watching as it wrapped greedily around his cock.

When the erotic picture popped into his head, that part of him stirred to life, semi-hard by the time sanity jolted him back to the here and now.

What was wrong with him? The girl had been through a trauma. And hadn't he been the one who warned Jaylin about keeping his cock under control and in his pants?

Malik shifted, and faced the counter, his back to them both, hiding the uncontrollable reaction of his body, something he hadn't had to battle in years, not since Mahlia.

"Your meal is hot. You should eat now." His words came out sharper than intended. He addressed Dani, nodding his head toward the table. "If you'll sit, I'll keep you company while the captain lays in our course for Earth. We should have you home in five days, no more."

He looked pointedly at his twin while Dani moved to the table in the open galley.

*Don't be an ass to her, brother,* Jaylin's warning rang inside his head. *She's had it rough and doesn't need your crap piled on top of it.*

*She also doesn't need to be seduced by you after what she endured, not to mention after surviving nearly twenty-five years as a virgin.*

*I've got it under control.*

*Ha! If I wasn't standing here, you'd be carrying her to your bed right now.*

When his eyes narrowed and he moved into his space, Malik knew he had gone a step too far. Although he was taller by an inch, Jaylin outweighed him due to his greater muscle mass. Broader, stronger, a more skilled fighter, his brother could take him, not readily, though if they came to blows,

Jaylin would win. His twin had a long fuse, but when riled, a dangerous, even lethal temper. Malik didn't fear him, although regretted piquing his ire with his taunts.

*Caution, little brother. Test me at your peril.*

Not prepared to fight him over a woman he had no intention of sharing, he backed down, dipping his head slightly. *I'm just doing my duty and reminding you of our mission.*

*One I negotiated. I'm unlikely to forget it.*

*I know.*

*Then don't bring it up again.* The biting command sounded as crisply in his head as if he had spoken it.

Malik nodded.

After holding his steady stare for another moment, Jaylin stepped back, glancing at Dani, although he addressed him when he spoke. "I'll be on the bridge." Some of the tensile strength had abated from his demeanor when he looked at him again. "Call me if you or Daniella need me."

\*\*\*

With both fear and fascination, Dani had observed the intense stare down between Captain Jaylin and his crew of one. Although neither spoke a word, it seemed as if they knew what the other was thinking. The air around them crackled with electricity, making the fine hairs on her arms stand on end. She feared they would come to blows, and if that happened, she had no idea what she would do except move out of their way and hope she didn't get caught up in the melee.

She assumed the captain won the standoff when Malik backed off. An expected outcome, she supposed, since Jaylin commanded the ship, but the entire interlude, though fascinating, left her feeling awkward, and like she'd witnessed something she shouldn't have.

Afterward, when the sparks had abated, and she could breathe again, the golden-haired Adonis who had handled her so gently, protected her with his body, and held her in his strong, supportive arms just moments ago excused himself, leaving her alone with Malik.

Also, strikingly handsome, he was much different from Jaylin. Where his leader had thick, bulky muscles, Malik was whipcord lean. He had dark-chocolate hair, and his eyes, which had appeared gold from a distance, up close were a deep brown with golden flecks—gorgeous. He seemed brooding and much more serious than the captain who had a warm, teasing manner about him.

She worried the issue between them involved her and couldn't keep from asking him about it. "Is my presence here a problem?"

"No." He didn't elaborate beyond his succinct reply. A bit leery of this large man, she moved back, giving him a wide berth to pass.

He noticed, and his frown intensified. "Please, don't shy away. I mean you no harm. Like Jaylin, my goal is to see you safely home." He motioned to the small table and waited until she took a seat before moving to the food prep area. When he removed a steaming, fragrant plate of food from the unit, her stomach rumbled, and she almost got distracted from her next questions.

"What if that isn't my goal?"

His head came up, smooth brows quirked in surprise. "You don't want to go home?"

"Things aren't good there," she admitted. "What if...?"

Her hesitation came from not knowing him. Could he be worse than what she faced if she returned to her father? These men worked for him, it they disclosed her idea and he found out it might make matters worse — if that was possible. Still, she had to try.

"This isn't something ethical, by any means, but I'm desperate." Her teeth worried her bottom lip for only a second before she blurted out, "What if I hire you for a different mission? I can double my father's offer."

He said nothing for a moment. "Our fee is one hundred thousand credits. Do you have twice as much?"

Her jaw dropped open. It was almost a quarter of her entire inheritance. "I, uh, don't have it yet, although I will very soon. In twelve days, in fact."

"What happens then?"

"I turn twenty-five. It's the age of legal majority on Earth, and I will come into my trust fund and inheritance from my late grandmother."

He set the plate down and took the chair across from her. She could tell from the tightness of his expression, he was skeptical.

"I can pay, I promise."

"Dani..."

Tears sprung up, stinging her eyes. "I'll triple your fee if that's what it takes."

"Your father also held the deed to the Renegade which was an advance payment. It is worth ten times our fee in credits. The last time we worked for him, we fulfilled the contract, and on a technicality, he cheated us out of our ship. I can't image his reaction if we don't follow through on this deal."

*One million credits – her entire small fortune. Holy crap!*

Stunned, she stared at him in silence. She could live comfortably for years on the money. Hiring them would free her from her father's control, but she'd be left without a credit to her name.

She didn't know what to do.

Struggling to hold back her tears, she bit her bottom lip to keep it from quivering. She knew she wasn't successful when his gaze dropped to her mouth and his frown intensified.

"Did you speak to Jaylin about this?"

"No. The idea just came to me."

"Hasty decisions rarely end well, Dani."

She pushed to her feet. "I'll go talk to the captain now."

"He's busy, and you need to eat. Sit down." Although he ordered this firmly, he didn't raise his voice. She hesitated, considering testing him. "I may not be in charge of the ship, but you are a guest which means I outrank you." He pushed out her chair with his foot and tipped his head toward it. "Sit. While you eat, you can explain 'things aren't good.'"

She bit her lip, chewing on it in indecision.

"Dani…" Her name, though said softly, held a clear warning. He intended to get his way. Instead of quivering, her bottom lip curved into a pout as she did what she was told and sat. He waited, watching, until she picked up her fork and took a small bite.

She expected bland-tasting ship-board food, not the mix of bold flavors and a zing of spice exploding on her tongue. Her appetite kicked in, and she scooped up more.

"This is really good," she said around the next forkful.

"I'm glad you like it."

Mid-chew, she caught a hint of a smile and the amusement lacing his tone. It was a small break in his somber demeanor. She would have pushed for more if she knew him better, and, if she wasn't so darn hungry. Unconcerned about manners, she began shoveling it in.

Without another word, she ate every morsel then reached for her glass of sparkling water and drained it. After she folded the cloth napkin he'd supplied and set it beside her now-empty plate, she looked up at him for the first time in several minutes. "Sorry. Three days of the brown stuff they called food left me starved."

"I could tell, but you don't have to apologize for doing what I asked you to do. Do you want more?"

"Oh, no." She patted her belly and shook her head. "If I take another bite, I might pop."

"We can't have that."

Dani didn't miss the not-so-subtle twitch of his lips. "You're not what you seem."

Appearing startled by her comment, his dark brows inched upward. "What do you mean?"

"Outwardly, you're cool, with an air of aloofness, although I suspect underneath, you are full of…well, more. I'm betting there is fire in you, but it's buried deep." All signs of animation fled, and his face reverted to its previous impassivity. "Oh, I didn't mean to insult you," she rushed to explain. "Me and my big mouth."

"It's fine, Dani."

"Is it? I mean, I saw the silent exchange with the captain. You seemed ticked, then you shut it down, conceding the argument. I do the same with my father, who is overbearing and dictatorial. Most times it's easier to give in than fight a battle I can't win, but it gets old."

"Jaylin is nothing like Daniel Alltryp."

She stiffened at the sharpness of his tone, afraid she'd offended him again. "I didn't mean that he was." This discussion wasn't going at all well. "You've met my father?"

"I regret to say I have, and it's no reflection on you."

The brief flash of anger vanished so fast she questioned if she'd misread him, which, with Malik, who was turning out to be an enigma, wasn't easy. She was more convinced there was a depth to him he didn't let on. Having just met him, and already insulted him twice, she decided she'd keep further observations to herself.

"Maybe we should change the subject."

"If you wish, except I want to make something clear. Jaylin is my superior, Dani. I trust and respect him, and he holds the same regard for me. We are both ex-military, and despite this being a private vessel, we follow a hierarchy because it's how we were trained, and it makes sense. He outranked me then, too. I'm used to following his orders. It doesn't mean I do so blindly and don't question them on occasion."

She arched a brow, recalling how he'd pushed out the chair and commanded her to sit. "You seem to have no problem giving orders, yourself."

"To a slip of a girl who wants to argue instead of filling her empty belly of three days? I'll take charge of that situation every time."

"God forbid this happens again. If it does, I'm going to remember your bossy streak and snap to." While she teased him, she managed to suppress her smile. She couldn't do anything about the heat creeping into her cheeks when he winked at her, however.

"Are you finished eating, Dani?" This came from Jaylin who exited the lift on the far side of the circular space.

"Yes. It was delicious."

"Good. Then it's time for Malik to have a look at those bruises over your ribs."

"I'm okay, really."

"A kick from a boot can do serious damage." He glanced down at his own large booted feet then met her gaze. A hard shot from one of those would cave in half her chest. None of the pirates had been close to his size, but they had all worn similar boots, pretty much standard-issue for space flight these days in case of a zero-gravity event. The trick was the electromagnets inlaid in the soles. When switched on during weightlessness, rather than floating free, they allowed for easier maneuverability around the ship. The hard, sturdy boots also came in handy in a fight, or when dealing with an uncooperative captive. Rondo and Nestor had taught this lesson well.

"I suppose I am a bit tender."

"You're more than tender," Malik observed. "You are guarding your right side. I noticed you ate with your left hand although I can tell it isn't your dominant one. I'd like to examine your bones and run a few internal checks."

She didn't like the sound of anything internal. "What do you mean, exactly?"

"He'll use a scanner, sweetness."

That was encouraging, as was Jaylin coming to stand beside her. He slipped his hand beneath her hair, curving it around the nape of her neck. His presence reassured her, especially when his fingers flexed and he lightly squeezed.

"Malik is very good at his job, Dani, and has a gentle touch. He also has some magical equipment which works without him having to lay a finger on you."

"The exam will only take a few minutes," their medic added, which she figured meant doctor in their world.

When her gaze shifted to him, and she took in his concerned, yet professional expression, the same as any other doctor she'd been to, she calmed somewhat. He seemed knowledgeable. Besides, if the examination was noninvasive what harm could it do?

Decision made, she nodded and let Jaylin help her up from her chair. The hot shower had done wonders for her stiff joints and tender places, but the temporary effects had worn off long ago.

In the medical room, she didn't need any help hopping up, the table doing everything for her. With a few swipes on the wall-mounted control screen,

Malik adjusted the table into an upright position. She only had to place her feet on the two pedals near the floor, and, with a low hum and a slight shimmy, it moved, tilting horizontally with her on it. When it stopped, she lay face up on the elevated surface waist-high to her doctor. He ran a blinking wand over her body from her chin to her toes. As Jaylin had promised, it didn't touch her, hovering about two inches above her while Malik watched the readings on the screen. He paused at her chest, gaze narrowing, as his jaw clenched, before he grunted and moved on.

"Did you find something wrong?"

"You have several severe contusions and hairline cracks in two ribs on your right side, but your lungs are intact."

"So, what do you do about it, tape them or something?"

"Tape?" He looked perplexed by her suggestion.

"Yes, bind my ribs to ease the pain while I wait for them to heal? Isn't that the usual treatment for broken ribs?"

His grunt this time sounded more like a scoff. "Earth is woefully behind on medical advancements. There is no waiting to heal with us. I'll have the cracks mended in seconds, and the bruises will be gone."

"You can do that?"

"Yes, and have been able to for years. Jaylin, if you'll assist her, I'll program in the settings."

Moving to her side, the captain complied, ready to assist in whatever capacity. Malik went to a metal cupboard with double doors and opened them. Clearly, this was his domain, and his captain understood it. Curious as to how he'd work this healing magic, she strained to see inside the cupboard. Around the doctor's broad back, she saw several shelves holding different-sized towels and folded blankets.

"Sit up, baby. The treatment is applied to bare skin."

"What?"

"Your tunic needs to come off so Malik can make you better," he said patiently.

"But, I'm not…um, I don't have anything on underneath."

"Good. Less to remove and sooner for the healing to begin." His arm beneath her shoulder lifted her to a seated position. He grasped the hem of her top and eased it up. She grabbed his wrists.

"Turn around."

"I've seen you naked. No more delays." He pulled it up a few more inches before she jerked away. The sudden jarring movement had her hissing in pain. Jaylin frowned, quite ferociously. "You're shy, I understand that, but I won't have you injuring yourself further. Off with this now, and no more fussing."

When she lifted her arms as high as she could without causing more discomfort, he had her tunic over her head and off in a blink.

Malik came back holding one of the larger blankets. "Help her lie flat."

Now she had both men standing over her near-naked body. "Can I cover up with the blanket first?"

He looked down, understanding dawning. "This isn't a blanket, Dani. It's a healing accelerator. For it to work effectively, I need you to lie on your back, be very still, and you must be completely unclothed." He looked at his captain and told him, "The leggings need to go, too."

"Why?" she squealed. "You're healing my ribs."

"Jaylin said you have bruises on your hips, too."

She shot her silver-eyed rescuer an accusing glare. Apparently, he'd been talking to Malik about the extended eyeful he'd gotten.

"You're being silly, Dani," Jaylin muttered while he eased her back. "I've seen you, and, as a medic, Malik has treated hundreds of naked women. We aren't going to think anything of this. You're hurt, our priority is to see you better." His fingers curled into her waistband, next. Carefully, he lowered her leggings, pulling them over her hips and down to her ankles. "Lay it on her, doc."

Dani's eyes cut to Jaylin, who winked. It did nothing to calm her nerves.

"Hands by your sides," was the next humiliation.

Closing her eyes, she put her arms down, feeling cool air blow lightly across her breasts. Her nipples hardened, and she almost leaped from the table. Malik moved swiftly before she could, and spread the device on top of her, covering her from her neck to her knees. Beneath its weight she relaxed a bit, not only because it concealed her nudity, but from being toasty warm against her skin.

"There now," he said, while leaning over her, his dark wavy hair falling forward and framing his face. The remote and distant man had disappeared, replaced by a healer with a comforting bedside manner. "That wasn't so bad, was it?"

"No," she admitted, embarrassed for making such a fuss. "Will this mending, hurt?"

"Most patients find the experience relaxing. You'll experience a tingling in a moment, which means it's working. There should be no pain. Lying still will help us achieve the best result, all right?"

She nodded, wanting to get it over with.

As he moved away, Jaylin took his place at the head of the table, except on the opposite side. Smiling down at her, his big hand smoothed her hair away from her face. "I know a lot of this is new to you, but you have to trust us."

"I'm sorry, this is my first time away from home, and it's been one awful experience after another. I keep waiting for the next shoe to drop."

"Which is understandable," he murmured, bending to touch his lips to her forehead in a light kiss. "You don't need to apologize for being afraid, but neither will I when I step in for your own good."

She gave him a small smile. What was one more time being naked in front of him? And they had both been acting out of concern, nothing else.

"No more talking," Malik said. "I'm starting the healing cycle."

Dani held her breath, waiting for the tingling he spoke of. The blanket began vibrating. It started out slow. After a few seconds, the pace quickened. It tickled in spots, yet felt good in others, like her nipples, which contracted into hard buds. And the buzzing made the place between her thighs come alive. She pressed her legs together to keep from getting too turned on and embarrassing herself further.

"Lie very still, Dani," Malik urged.

"Sorry," she whispered. Attempting to change her focus to anything else, she concentrated on her sore ribs, which had started to prickle, not painfully so, but more intense. And it seemed to be increasing. "How strong will this get?" she asked, a little alarmed.

"Are you hurting somewhere?" He leaned in, his face over hers and alongside Jaylin's. Both handsome men gazed down at her with twin looks of concern.

"It's my sore ribs. The tingles seem focused there. Not hurting, exactly. It's more like hundreds of tiny hammers tapping against my skin. Though if it becomes any more intense it will become uncomfortable."

"It's more concentrated there because of your injury. Breathe and relax. Being tense can amplify the prickling sensation."

"Deep breaths, Dani," Jaylin murmured, and bent closer, his hand coming to rest on the top of her head. "Close your eyes and concentrate on breathing in through your nose and out through your mouth. Pursing your lips will help. I'll do it with you," he said. "Breathe in, one, two, three, and blow out three, two, one. Try it with me." The warmth of his breath caressed her cheek while he counted and did the exercise along with her. "Concentrate and breathe in...and relax when you blow out... Good girl," he praised. "And again."

Malik was right. Her focus on something else made the hammering decrease, and, thanks to Jaylin's guidance, the focused breathing dialed it back to a not-unpleasant tingle once again.

"It's better," she whispered.

"A few more minutes to make sure," Malik urged as he moved to the foot of the exam table. When he removed her shoes, and pulled off her leggings the rest of the way, her eyes popped open. He was quick to explain. "I'm going to wrap your ankle. The shackle abraded your skin, in addition to leaving a ring of bruises."

"They used iron," Jaylin muttered under his breath. "Fucking bastards had her chained to the wall. I'd gladly kill them all again if I could."

"If I had to do it over, I'd toy with them longer before I blew them to bits," Malik growled with equal intensity.

His touch was gentle, as he used long strips of the same material draping her body on her ankle. It tingled just like the larger accelerator, thankfully, not reaching close to the intensity of her ribs. Soon, the discomfort disappeared, and the sensation penetrated further, like a deep tissue full-body massage. Her eyes drifted shut again while she continued to breathe slowly in and out in the rhythm Jaylin had taught her. Soon, she didn't even need that because she was floating, completely relaxed, and pain-free.

"Dani," a low voice nudged, trying to rouse her. She ignored it, not ready to wake yet.

"We're all finished, sweetheart." Malik's announcement coincided with a waft of cool air as the warm blanket disappeared. Her lashes fluttered open. Jaylin was there, and without missing a beat, wrapped her up in something soft.

"I fell asleep," she stated, coming more fully awake.

"You did. Not surprising after three days without any." His strong arms slid beneath her thighs and upper back, and he lifted her from the medical table. "Let's get you into your bed."

This sounded like a fine idea to her, so she didn't object. "I'm all better?" Her voice came out muffled where she lay curled into Jaylin's chest, her face pressed to his shirt.

"Malik says you're good as new."

"Thank you, Malik," she called in a sleepy voice.

"You are more than welcome, Dani. Get some rest."

She moved, or at least the captain did, carrying her swiftly. In wasn't long until he stopped and lowered her, his warm, safe arms releasing her body. She almost asked him to stay, but the softness of a bed beneath her and the blankets being pulled up to her chin drew her back into a drowsy lethargy.

"You're a very nice man," she murmured as he tucked the comforter snug around her shoulders.

"I have my moments." He pressed his lips to her forehead. "It's easy to be nice to a down on her luck girl who's had a rough go of it lately. Sweet dreams, beautiful."

Those lovely words were the last she heard as sleep overtook her.

# Chapter Five

Ghostly blue fingers reached for her while others, filthy with grime, held her arms down, legs spread wide. The sound of cloth ripping muffled a maniacal laugh in the distance. She looked down and saw Ivar kneeling between her legs. He gripped his cock, a deathly blue shade like his fingers.

"You're mine, bitch, at last. To fuck and breed at will."

But the crude voice didn't belong to Ivar. It had morphed into Nestor's, and he leaned over her naked body, his foul breath wafting over her face. He poked between her legs with his dirty fingers, and she realized he now knelt between her open thighs.

"No!" she cried out in panic, becoming breathless from her struggles.

"Yes, and there's no one here to stop me this time." His harsh, caustic laughter chilled her blood. "Spread her nice and wide, boys. I'm gonna make the cunt pay for what she's done."

Harsh hands pulled her legs apart, pushed her knees to her chest, rendering her completely vulnerable to Nestor's cruelty. His gaze dropped between her thighs while he licked his lips. As he moved closer, she watched in terror as he stroked his cock. It was huge, and she knew it would tear her apart. She went wild, thrashing against the hold on her wrists and legs as she screamed.

"Dani—"

"Please, don't hurt me."

"No one's going to hurt you, baby. Wake up."

Coming from far away, the voice seemed oddly familiar. Too far to help her when Nestor and his oversized cock were looming, his horrible, ugly face leering down at her. The maniacal laughter continued, settling heavy over her, surrounding her with evil.

"Stop!" She pleaded raggedly, twisting against the hands on her shoulders. She covered her ears, trying to block out the awful laughter. "Make it stop!"

"Daniella," a stern voice called, low and insistent. "Open your eyes and look at me."

They flew wide, and instead of the bulging yellow leer that haunted her, she saw Jaylin's silver gaze narrowed with worry.

"It was a nightmare," he assured her. "You're safe."

She broke down, sobs pouring out along with her tears. His strong arms encompassed her, pulling her against his warm, bare chest and held her tight.

"Shh," he whispered, his mouth pressed to her hair. "Everything's all right. It was only a bad dream."

Except the tears wouldn't stop, coming in a deluge while she clung to him, soaking his skin.

"A sedative." This came from Malik half suggestion, half question. She hadn't heard him enter the room. How could she with all the blubbering she was doing?

"Bring it," Jaylin ordered.

She didn't protest. Drugged, she could rest and not worry about Nestor, or Ivar, or hearing her father, because it had been his maniacal laugh. She shuddered as she felt her clothing adjusted and cool air waft over her back and bare bottom. Next came the hiss of an injection gun diffusing the welcome medicine beneath her skin.

"It will take effect in a moment." A hand gently cupped the back of her head. It had to be Malik's because Jaylin's arms hadn't relinquished his grip.

She wanted to sink into blessed oblivion. At the same time, she fought it, trying to linger in his embrace, relax into the wonderful glide of fingers through her hair, and listen to their whispered words of reassurance. Sounds and sensations soon faded, and with them, her consciousness.

\*\*\*

Groggy and heavy-headed, she awakened, unsure of her surroundings. She stared at the gray tiled ceiling above her, cast in shadow from the dim floor-level lights it didn't clue her in on where she was. Neither did the soft, wide bed beneath her, or the wall of heat inundating her on one side.

The thick blanket was warm, though nowhere near the furnace behind her. She snuggled into it. As she did, arms came around her. Her lashes fluttered open, her vision filled with golden-hued skin and a smattering of dark-blond chest hair. She tilted her head and looked up into sleepy silver eyes framed by fans of long silky black lashes.

"Am I still dreaming?"

His lips kicked up into a sleepy smile. "If you are, I am, too. And I don't want to wake up."

His words sent a wave of warmth sweeping through her.

Twin vertical lines appeared between his brows. "You had a bad night, Dani. How are you feeling this morning?"

"Much better, but…" Pausing as the nightmarish images returned, she bit her lip.

He shifted, his hand coming up to sweep over her cheek. When he cupped her face, his thumb slid along her lower lip until her teeth released it. "But what, baby?"

"Do you think the nightmares will haunt me long?"

"Not if I can help it," he murmured. One strong arm flexed to pull her closer. "I plan to sleep right here every night and ward them away."

The thought of him beside her, holding her while she slept, battling her demons, and keeping her safe made her already-heated skin grow hotter. She tingled all over, the idea of Jaylin in her bed, half-dressed aroused her despite the horror of the night before. It occurred to her half-dressed might not be true, except she didn't have the nerve to explore whether he was as bare below the waist as above. Her nipples stood up hard and tight in reaction, and liquid desire drenched the pulsing place between her thighs.

He couldn't be real. No man she'd ever met had come close to being this wonderful. Both caring and sweet, but also brave, determined, and smoking hot.

An idea popped in her head, something more daring than she'd ever done, and rather naughty. Since she didn't plan to wed Ivar, or anyone else her father chose, why not go for it with Jaylin? He stirred her, and she could tell by the hard press of his erection against her thigh she had a similar effect on him.

"I'd like that," she whispered. "Falling asleep safe in your arms will keep the bad memories and dreams away."

"If not my arms, sweetness, then my kisses should wipe out the bad thoughts and leave only good." He demonstrated their power by dipping his head and claiming her mouth with a soft touch of lips and tongue. She'd had dry pecks and a few sloppy lip-locks in college, none of which had been pleasant. But this…? Pure heaven. And she wanted more, much more.

He must have sensed her eagerness because he took it a step farther, tracing his tongue along the seam until she opened for him. When she did, he swooped in, searching, tasting, and tangling with hers. His fingers slid into her hair, his big palm cradling the back of her head, angling it just so while he rolled her onto her back. Heavy, but not overpowering, his chest pressed her down into the plush mattress as he devoured her—there was simply no other way to describe it. Not sloppy, too hard, or the least bit unpleasant.

It was sublime, and she loved every moment of it.

A clearing throat broke through to them. Jaylin raised his head, though only a fraction, staying close enough for his breath to graze her wet lips lightly. Neither looked away from the other, however.

Malik's voice cut through the fog of desire created by Jaylin's potent kisses. "The morning meal is ready. If you two can drag yourselves out of bed, we can eat while it's hot."

***

Breakfast confused Dani. Not the bacon, pancakes, and warm maple syrup, like back on Earth, but the way Malik was acting.

After inquiring if she'd slept well and had no lingering effects from the sedative, he hadn't joined them to eat. Instead, he moved around the small galley kitchen, cleaning up, doing so noisily by slamming drawers and banging cupboards. She thought he might be angry, although his face didn't show it. In fact, it revealed no emotion at all, as if he wore a mask.

This didn't go on long before Jaylin had enough. "Are you planning to show your ass all through breakfast, or are you going to tell me what has crawled up it?"

He stiffened, his back to them, but he didn't stop wiping the food prep area. "I don't know what you mean. All is well. We had a successful rescue, and soon, Miss Alltryp will be back home, safe and sound, and unharmed--the same as when she left." Although his voice came out flat, beside her, Jaylin flinched like he'd shouted.

"If all is well," he growled, "quit slamming things. Dani jumps every time you do. I think she's had enough commotion in the last few days, don't you?"

Posture rigid and jaw held tight, he turned, his golden eyes dull, without the glimmer from the day before. He surprised her by bowing formally. "My apologies, Miss Alltryp. I never meant to add to your distress."

"Oh, but you didn't," she hastened to say, not wanting to make him feel bad when he had been so helpful.

"Don't excuse his rudeness," Jaylin snapped, his temper flaring in contrast to Malik who remained unemotional.

"I don't recall saying anything which could be construed as rude, captain, sir."

Dani's gaze darted his way when she thought she heard sarcasm in his "sir," so subtle she'd almost missed it. Jaylin had no such oversight. With a crash, his fist came down on the table, making the plates and silverware dance. Dani had to make a grab for her juice glass to keep it from toppling over.

"Captain, you're startling Miss Alltryp with your commotion."

So much for subtle. He'd leapt from barely detectible sarcasm to deliberate baiting yet did so with the same flat tone and inexpressive face. Jaylin surged to his feet, sending his chair skidding across the floor.

"Either say what you must, or find something productive to do."

"Since I have nothing new of import, I'll go above and check our course."

"Good idea."

For another tense moment, their eyes clashed, Jaylin's narrowing while a muscle flexed in his cheek. Then, without any reaction at all, Malik stepped aside, nodded to Dani, and walked with a stiff, measured stride to the lift.

"Was it something I did? Yesterday, he called me Dani, now I'm Miss Alltryp. Perhaps my screams disturbed his rest?"

"It wasn't you. It's his nature. Cool and perfunctory, like the automaton he is."

"Automaton," she echoed, puzzled by his implication. "You mean as in a robot?"

"Exactly. Outwardly, he's a living, breathing man, but inside he's a machine, going through the motions. And the living part is still up for debate."

Dani looked after him, considering their odd interchange, and the captain's description. Suddenly, it clicked. "You're saying he's a cyborg?"

She saw the tall, handsome man from a new perspective. It explained a lot, yet confused her. At times, though mostly during interactions with Jaylin, he seemed to show emotion. "I've never met one before, though I've heard it's hard to tell them apart from real men."

Jaylin gave a short bark of laughter. "Organic yet with biomechanical parts. Cut him and he bleeds, stroke him and he feels pleasure, if his programming allows it. Isn't that so, Malik?"

He didn't react, only said in the same remote voice, "Whatever you say, Captain."

"Well, he certainly fooled me." Amazed was more like it. "So, he's capable of emotion? Yesterday, I would have thought so. Today, however, he's much different."

"Cyborgs are sentient, and many have evolved to show a wide range of emotions. Sadly, Malik has a narrow spectrum, limited to the extremes. Except when it comes to more subtle qualities and those requiring a heart, I'm afraid he hasn't quite figured it out."

"Oh, that's too bad. Maybe one day," Dani offered.

"I have work to do." Malik had turned, his attention on Jaylin, his eyes narrowed a fraction she thought. "Perhaps you can finish your inventory of my abilities without me. Or maybe you and I could do so in private, later, Captain."

If he'd been a man, Dani would have said he was irritated, but someone would have had to program him for that, which made no sense to her. "He seems put out with you, and you argued yesterday. Is it normal for a cyborg to have disputes with his leader?"

"Malik and I have been together for a long time. He knows me and the way I think, which encourages him to take more liberties than an ordinary crewman would."

"Yes, he mentioned something about not following blindly. I suppose it's good he interacts with you on different levels. Otherwise, you'd be alone which would make extended voyages dull and seem longer, I'd think. Perhaps you need to work on his softer side. Maybe program him to smile, laugh, and lighten up a little."

She thought she heard a low growl coming from Malik's direction, then decided it was the humming of the auto-lift doors opening. Although, she couldn't be sure, because Jaylin found something she'd said very amusing and his laughter drowned out everything else.

# Chapter Six

With the awkward breakfast done, Jaylin took her on a tour of the ship. At least he started to, but they became distracted whenever their eyes met or their bodies touched, which happened often. It led to kisses, first on her knuckles, which was so gallant and romantic her knees turned to jelly, then to soft touches of his mouth to hers.

In the coolness of the cargo hold, when she shivered and he put his arms around her, things soon got out of control. Dani found herself against the wall, his long body next to hers, while his tongue delved between her lips. She clung to him, not protesting when searching fingers slipped under her shirt, and splayed over her back. More slid lower, curving around the fullness of her bottom, molding it with his large palm. Her head tipped back as she gasped for air, which allowed his mouth to sear a path along her cheek to the ultra-sensitive side of her neck. The broad hand at her back swept up and in, cupping a breast. When his thumb swept over the crest the edge flicking her nipple, she arched into his touch, and a groan escaped his throat.

It seemed to snap him out of the state of lust surrounding them. He pulled back, and, with the heat of their passion reflecting in his eyes, stared down at her.

"I hate to end this here, but I have to get to the bridge. I've left too many of my duties to Malik of late." He said this with as much reluctance, as desire showing on his face.

Jaylin led her back to the main area on the lower level and excused himself. Though not before touching his lips to hers one more time. Sweet and light, not the sizzling, all-consuming kisses of earlier but equally stirring.

Left alone, she tried to find something to occupy her time. He'd said to make herself at home, including using any of the recreational equipment. She eyed the exercise room, but gave it a quick no. Although Malik had declared her ribs healed, she figured it wise to take it easy for a few more days.

The library was also out. Feeling too antsy to concentrate on a digital book, she would probably nod right off with an audio version. She looked to the room with the large screens and the black recliner. Immersion Reality, Jaylin had called it. A new technology on Earth, she'd never had the opportunity to try it. Mostly because the units were located in malls and public places she wasn't allowed to go without her security team. This brought back bad memories of the few times she'd gone shopping with friends. The armed men with communicators, following and watching her every move garnered strange looks and whispers from the other shoppers, and her friends found it awkward. She hadn't gone again because they never invited her back.

Their private booth was her best chance, so, why not? Especially when Jaylin had encouraged her to try it, thinking it might be a way to help her relax.

"Sit down, put on the gear, and let it take you wherever you want to go, present, past, or future," he said. "Think of a favorite spot from your childhood or a place you've always wanted to go.

## The Renegades' Reward

You can lie on a sandy beach at home or be a fighter pilot defending a battle cruiser, or a real princess marrying the handsome prince of her dreams. The best part, whatever you decide, it's safe because it's a fantasy — your fantasy. And because it's attuned to your brain waves, it will be detailed specifically to you."

She entered through the heavy glass doors and paused for a moment, taking it all in. It seemed harmless and relaxing, like the black recliner which molded to her body when she took a seat. The headgear, however, was big and bulky, covering her ears, and had a visor that flipped down over the upper half of her face. It also flattened her hair, something she had a lot of, but she was relieved to find it lightweight and fully padded.

"Unit on," she said, as Jaylin had instructed. Now she only had to lie back and decide where she wanted to go. She had no favorite places from childhood because her father had never taken her anywhere. And being a fighter pilot held no appeal. But she loved the beach, the smell of the ocean, feeling the warm sand between her toes and the waves rolling in and out, washing over her skin when she walked in the surf.

The next thing she knew, the heat of the sun spilled onto her face and she could taste salt on her tongue. She blinked then had to squint against the rays of light reflecting off the water, now fully immersed in her beach fantasy.

A wave rolled in, and the frothy foam tickled her toes. She looked down at the shifting sand beneath her feet, and noticed her clothes were very different, and skimpy. The IR interface had created a sexy, black bikini which fit her perfectly.

She'd never worn a two-piece suit before, not seeing the point when no one was around to notice while she swam alone in the pool on their estate. This one, with its halter top and neckline that plunged low between her breasts, was more risqué than anything she would have ever chosen for herself. It tied up the front, baring the inner curves of her breasts. Threaded through the laces were small white conch shells which contrasted with the dark fabric. The back stayed together with a single string tie, leaving her bare except for the itsy-bitsy bottoms. In front, a shockingly small scrap of diamond-shaped fabric preserved her modesty, though barely, since the sides were nonexistent, with nothing more than three gathered laces at each hip. If she wore this on a beach for real, she'd never come out from under a towel or cover-up.

As she made her way down the strip of white sand, Dani sensed eyes upon her that she knew couldn't exist. She walked for a while, soaking up the tropical beach experience, until she came to a red cabana, set back from the water. Somehow, she knew it belonged to her. After veering toward it, she picked up the pace when the dry sand away from the water's edge became so hot it stung the bottoms of her feet. She was running by the time she reached the tent. Laughing at all the oo's and ah's and ouch's she'd made, she flopped on the blanket spread out under the cabana's shade. Taking a deep breath, she sighed, making plans for a beach getaway to celebrate both her birthday and her freedom in two short weeks. With the sun still warm on her legs, only her upper body in the shade, she rolled onto her front, pillowed her head with her arms, and closed her eyes.

"With such fair skin, you need protection from the sun," a voice said out of nowhere. Hands began massaging lotion into her back. Of course, this had also been conjured up by the IR and her head. But it felt wonderful having strong fingers working the tension from her muscles as they rubbed in sunscreen. She tried hard to summon up one of those tropical drinks to sip on, the kind with fruit and a paper umbrella, which would make it perfect.

One didn't magically appear, sadly. Instead, her massage heated up as her virtual reality man moved to her shoulders, then kneaded along the length of her spine all the way to the top of her bikini bottoms. The fingers went away for a moment, and she heard the squirt of the bottle. Instead of the cold she expected, warm hands rubbed the coconut scented lotion onto her thighs. And on her back... At the same time.

Confused, she opened her eyes, seeing sand, sun, and the shadow of not one, but two men leaning over her.

*Great day!* The machine had dug into her subconscious and found a recurrent fantasy she'd had for years. It started in college, though she hadn't told a soul, not even her roommate the night they'd been drunk on wine and revealed their deepest, darkest secrets.

She felt a tug on both her bikini top and bottom at once. The strings disappeared, and the bottoms peeled down. The sensual massage resumed, now rubbing places that hadn't ever needed sunscreen before.

"It's a shame to cover such beauty with cloth," one of the men whispered near her ear.

"And a crime to bury the best parts in the sand," said the other.

Flipped suddenly to her back, she gaped up at the men, one dark headed, and one light. The massage continued to her breasts and thighs. Fingers pinched and rolled her nipples, while others parted her thighs and stroked lightly on the tender skin in between. As the caress moved higher, his fingers grazed places never touched by a man.

Her body vibrated with shock and pleasure, and she almost forgot how to breathe, especially when the dark head bent to her breast, at the same time the blond pushed her legs further apart and settle between them. Twin spirals of warmth drifted over intimate places a moment before lips and tongues, swirling and sucking, made her back arch off the sand.

In seconds, a wave of incredible pleasure engulfed her body. It had to be the fastest orgasm in history. Her breathing became rapid. No, it couldn't be.

Before she could think, or breathe, they moved her again. She found herself on her hands and knees, her dream lovers taking their places in front and behind. Then, they took her right there on the beach.

The man at her thighs parted her with his thumbs, slid the smooth tip of his cock through her wetness and drove inside, filling and stretching her until she cried out with intense pleasure. This gave the man in front the opportunity to slide between her parted lips, and along her tongue. Two at a time, they fucked her, until she moaned around the hard shaft in her mouth, while clamping down and orgasming around the one in her pussy.

They didn't stop there, building it again within her. Instead of four hands, it seemed like a dozen. Slightly rough fingertips plucked and tweaked her dangling nipples, while a hand slid around to her front, locating the nub that she alone, in the darkness of her bedroom at night, had ever stroked, circled, and rubbed to a hard peak.

She let out a cry for more. And they gave her what she asked for, one large cock gliding persistently to the back of her tongue, as the other of equally impressive size began pumping hard into her from behind. Dani screamed, but to her it came out muffled, the simulator replicating how it would sound if she really did have a hard shaft wedged in her throat.

A hand on her shoulder made her jump at the same time she heard her name called with urgency. She sat up, tearing off the headgear to find the captain and his cyborg first mate standing over her, with identical looks of concern.

"You were screaming," Jaylin stated. "And you're out of breath."

"Her heart is racing," Malik observed. "I can see her pulse fluttering in the side of her neck."

She couldn't answer, not yet. And if they wanted details, they'd be waiting forever. With trembling hands, she wiped the sheen of sweat from her brow.

"This is a relaxation device, meant to help, not send you into a panic." Brushing the damp hair back from her face, Jaylin leaned in and asked, "What did the simulator bring up for you? Bad memories?"

"I, uh, don't recall. I must have fallen asleep," she lied, badly, earning doubtful looks from them both. She didn't care. No way was she disclosing anything about her erotic fantasy, particularly how it starred both of them!

"Something isn't right. Let me check the settings." Malik went to the wall and flipped open a recessed panel. After making a few swipes and punching a few buttons, he glanced up at her, surprise in his golden gaze.

Dani cringed, flushing hotly. Was it possible he knew what she and the machine had contrived?

"I think I'll go lay down," she announced, bolting out of the chair. Except when she stood, her knees wobbled and she had to grab onto the arm to keep from hitting the floor.

They reached out to catch her.

"Don't touch me," she hissed.

Startled, they both froze. Dani didn't apologize, though she should, but with her body still on edge, if they laid hands on her—anywhere—she was afraid she'd orgasm on the spot, number three in a matter of minutes.

"I need a moment is all." Somehow, she managed to walk out, her chin high, acting as though nothing was amiss. Except she moved stiffly, sore in places where she really shouldn't be from a mere fantasy program.

\*\*\*

Malik watched her cross the main floor and turn down the hall to her room, his brother's gaze aimed the same way. A second later, the whoosh of doors opening and closing drifted back to them.

"I'm concerned she's having residual stress from being held for so long by those thug pirates."

He gave Jaylin and sidelong glance, unconvinced. "I don't know. She looked embarrassed more than afraid. I think it's something else."

"What?"

Malik didn't answer. Instead, he swung back to the control panel and punched a few keys. "Although it violates her privacy, I think we need to know for the nature of her session for her welfare."

"Certainly, Dani's well-being takes priority," Jaylin growled. "But I'd prefer you tell me what you're talking about, so please, spit it out."

"I'll do better. Watch."

Then the floor-to-ceiling screens replayed the last few minutes of Dani's immersion fantasy. Malik hardened at the sight of her pale body bowed, her head tossed back, stunning red hair tumbling down her back. But what aroused him most, the three sets of arms entwined, six hands feverishly touching, and two male heads bent to her, their mouths leaving wet trails along her skin.

Beside him, his twin's husky murmur oozed with blatant arousal. "The naughty little imp was screaming for us."

He tried to remain objective. "I suppose there is a small resemblance."

"Small! That's you sucking on her nipple and my head between her thighs." Jaylin grinned from ear to ear. "Now are you convinced she was meant for us? I have been hesitant to broach our ways with her. Although Earth women are known to be adventurous sexually, not all are comfortable with multiple partners. They are still primarily a monogamous society."

"This convinces me of nothing."

His steely glare zeroed in on him as he snapped, "Must you be so obstinate?" His arm swept toward the screens surrounding them. "You can't deny what is before your eyes."

"This is sex, Jaylin. It doesn't equate to the connection a twin pair establishes when joined with their destined third. A special bond like that comes around once in a lifetime."

"Says who?"

"Me! Don't you think I know how I feel? You must face the fact, as I have, our one was Mahlia. Take Dani if you must, but it will be solo, brother. I'm not interested."

"Liar! Your cock is rock-hard the same as mine. Admit it."

"I'll admit to having a physiological response to a beautiful woman, yes. But I'm not ruled by the often-indiscriminate part of me between my thighs, Jaylin."

"And you're saying I am?"

"It is your nature. As the first, you have an instinctive need to seek out and provide a mate for the both of us. In this case, I'm not willing. We've been there, and I won't go back."

"You're denying your true nature, brother. Your first has found our mate. It is up to you to follow my lead, to help form the bond of our triad."

"No. I'm sorry. Take her and enjoy her. She is interested, obviously, and her eager response to you this morning shows she is willing. Find your happiness without me, brother. And leave me alone to find my own way."

"I cannot, Malik. We are twins. You can't sever the bond."

"I must or risk losing myself in grief again, something I won't do."

"Are you clinging to Mahlia or your grief? Has it become so ingrained in you, you can't remember life without it? I understand your reluctance, brother, but you can't let fear condemn you to an isolated, unfulfilled life. And me with you."

He stiffened, a wave of guilt rushing over him. He'd felt it often before. His inability to move forward was unfair to Jaylin, yet he couldn't. He swore to himself he wouldn't, not ever again.

"I'm done with this argument." He stalked past him on his way to the door. "Go to her, Jay, with my blessing. I'll stand by you until the end of this mission. Afterward, I'm going home."

"Mal, you can't—"

"You're wrong. I'll rejoin the army where I have structure, purpose, and there is no temptation for me to betray my vow of faith." He looked once more at the frozen screen, and the expression of pleasure on Dani's beautiful face. "What I can't do is this. Not anymore.

"A vow you made to our dead wife five years ago. Do you think she'd want you to grieve for her this way, to never love again, or be loved? You know she wouldn't, and you wouldn't want it for her if the situation was reversed."

His voice raw, he met his brother's stormy-gray eyes when he uttered, "I loved her."

"As did I, Malik, but this isn't right."

"It's the only right I know. I made a vow."

"That vow was unto death, man! She's gone. You've spent five years, missing her. It's time to let her go."

"You're wrong," he whispered. "The vow I made was forever, and I made it to myself. Never again, brother. It hurts too damn much."

He walked away, not hesitating when Jaylin called his name. Nor did he stop or so much as flinch when a violent bang and a crash, followed his twin's frustrated curse.

***

Seething with a whirlwind of emotions—anger, frustration, and sorrow—he spun and, needing an outlet, punched the wall. A profound error in judgment because, rather than meeting the wall, his fist went through glass and one of the video screens exploded. He didn't feel pain, only regret, as the crystal shards and internal components rained down around him.

"Fucking hell," he growled.

"Are you hurt?" Her soft voice cut through the rawness clouding his vision. He blinked and looked down, seeing the back of her head as she took his hand in her own. Bending close, she ran her thumb lightly over his knuckles, examining it. "The skin isn't broken," she whispered. Her head tipped up, and the cloud of vivid red curls was replaced by pools of deep green.

"The Creators protect idiots, evidently," he muttered.

"We have a similar saying on my world. What happened?"

"It's nothing."

She shifted slightly, glass crunching beneath her boots. This time, they both looked down. He immediately wished he hadn't because wisps of her soft hair brushed his face. The fragrance of his shampoo, a light herbal scent, smelled different on her—seductive and alluring. As if he needed more stimulation after seeing her fantasy of the three of them, in glorious, clear crystal color on every wall in the room.

"Let's get you out of here," he announced abruptly, moving his hand to her lower back to firmly guide her out. After the automatic doors closed behind them, he hit the locking mechanism by the ceiling. "I'll get this cleaned up. Until I do, this is off limits."

She angled her chin up. "You're very bossy."

"I'm the captain, Dani. Bossy is a prerequisite for the job."

"I don't mind, although it seems to rub Malik the wrong way, despite his programming. I saw him storm out in one of his extreme modes. He looked angry."

"You flew out of here earlier, just as upset. Do I rub you the wrong way?"

"No." Her response came out on a breathy sigh, which stirred both his blood and his mounting need for her. "I kind of like how you take command and wield your authority. I'm sure there will be instances when it will set my teeth on edge, but so far, so good."

"In general, I'm easy to get along with. There are times, particularly while on a mission, when my instincts take over. If so, do as I say and you'll be fine."

"What times?"

"If we are under threat, or there is imminent danger, or if someone I know is being stubborn as hell."

"Me?"

He smiled, taking in her expression, wide-eyed with curiosity and a touch of regret. Noting an out-of-place tendril of hair clinging to her eyelashes, he lifted it away, tucking it behind her ear before he answered. "You aren't stubborn, Dani. Not that I've seen. You're very agreeable and sweet natured."

"I have my moments."

His own words echoed back to him from the night before made him chuckle. But as he stared down into her upturned face, seeing the becoming smile and the glint of humor in her stunning green eyes, his amusement faded, becoming a burning, aching, need. If Malik was so stubborn to deny the gem who had fallen into their laps, so be it. He had no such qualms.

He captured her mouth, reveling in her quickly indrawn breath and the press of her body against his. She didn't hesitate to kiss him back, and it was all the encouragement he needed to take over. Threading one hand through her thick hair, he angled her face to take things deeper. The other, he swept down her back to curl around her ass. He lifted her, and while her legs wrapped around his hips, he carried her across the pod, down the hall, and into her room.

"Tell me you want this, Dani. If you don't, I need to know now."

"I want this. Twenty-five, well, almost, less a few days, is too damn long to stay a virgin. And I'd like my first time to be with someone gentle, like you."

Humming his approval, he didn't correct her or explain he planned for all her times—not only this one—to be with him, and Malik, when he brought him around. Which he fully intended to do with her help.

Instead, he crossed to her bed and sat down with her in his lap, drinking in her sweetness. While he reveled in her taste, his hands sought the roundness of her breasts, her soft convex belly, which pleasantly cushioned his hard body, then his fingers slipped between her thighs encountering the heat permeating her clothing. Erect from witnessing her full-screen fantasy earlier, his cock jerked with anticipation.

He wanted to toss her on the bed and consume her, but forced himself to be gentle, as she deserved. He stroked her body, listening to the whimpers of delight rising from her throat and feeling the tug from her grip on his hair. Too far gone in the headiness of claiming his woman, he refused to think of the ramifications of what he was about to do. Warm, willing, and already precious to him, Dani was his. He'd be damned before he handed her over to the son of a bitch who called himself her father. Their debts he'd worry about later, once he thoroughly sampled her lips, her full breasts, and sweetly rounded thighs. And after he introduced her to the joys of lovemaking, made her come apart in his arms a time or two, and long after his body was spent alongside her own. Later, he'd think about the future and what came next.

Busy fingers made their clothing disappear, hers, opening the buttons on the front of his shirt, stopping when he impatiently pulled it over his head. He did the same for her, whisking her tunic off in one smooth movement. Moving her hands to his waistband, he encouraged her to finish the job which she did with a few fits and starts, and several low moans, because he was unable to resist the temptation of her pink-tipped breasts staring him in the face. Drawing one into his mouth, he sucked, nipped, and nibbled, as he worked her tights over her hips and down her legs. He muttered a frustrated curse when thwarted by the fasteners on the side of her boots, but made fast work of those, too.

Lifting her, he deposited her naked in the center of the bed. He had to stop to take in the lovely picture she made, cheeks flushed, hair in disarray, the red waves tumbling around her shoulders. Despite her obvious shyness as she sat with her hands clasped over her breasts, fingers tightly interlaced, he could read the unbanked fires of desire in her eyes.

He moved in, leaving his pants on for the moment. Clasping her beneath her arms, he moved her up the bed and laid her back on the pillows. Next, he followed her down, so they lay chest to chest, hips aligned, his face hovering over hers.

"Last chance, sweetness. I intend to take you now, unless you say no."

"I want this, Jaylin." She raised her head so her lips touched his. "I want you."

He knifed off the bed and removed the rest of his clothes, stripping in mere seconds. When he returned, pressing his naked body to hers, he kissed her until they were both breathless. Without breaking the connection, he nudged her thighs open and settled between them, making it so the length of him slid along the glistening seam.

Near ready to burst from wanting her, Jaylin stared down at her intently. "I can do gentle, baby, but don't know if I can manage slow, or long on this first round. I want you too much. I admit it's been a while for me."

"It's been a lifetime for me, and I don't want slow, either."

Eager to be inside her, he propped on his forearm, and guided his cock to her entrance. Gliding the head through her wetness with firm steady pressure, he slid into her tight sheath. In far enough to go hands-free, he wrapped his fingers around the back of her neck, his thumb along her jaw, supporting her beautiful face. As he advanced, he watched how her lips parted, and she sucked in a breath when he hit resistance.

"A little pinch then pleasure. I swear."

"I'm ready," she whispered as she braced, her face squinching up tight.

He almost laughed at her brave sacrifice, but that would have spoiled the moment. Instead, he murmured softly, "Look at me, Daniella."

She peeped at him between her lashes, opening them fully when he remained still. With her green eyes locked on his, bright with excitement, and, yes, some trepidation, only then did he move. With a controlled, steady thrust, he broke through the barrier and sank in to the hilt. She didn't look away, eyes big as she stared up at him in surprise. He remained still waiting for her to adjust to having him inside her. It took a moment for her features to soften, as she began to relax.

Only then did he move. With care, he eased almost all the way out before sliding back, going as slow as his control would allow. He repeated the motion, watching for the slightest sign it wasn't good for her, too. When he didn't see her flinch or grimace in pain, he picked up the pace a bit.

As was her habit, she bit her lower lip. He almost stopped, but her fingers curled into his shoulders, her nails digging in, as one of her legs moved to encircle his hips. She arched to meet his motion, and he knew she felt the connection.

Like he'd promised, he made it all about pleasure, his mouth once again opening over hers, involving tongue and, when hers matched his motions, reveling in her response. Her moans were like an anthem, spurring him on. Determined to give before he took, he found the nerve center at the front of her sex. With his thumb, he circled it, rubbing back and forth until she pulled away, arched her neck, and cried out.

"Yes, Dani," he urged, in a husky groan of encouragement. "Give in to the pleasure."

Her body tensed beneath him, the muscles inside her, rippling around his cock and gripping him fiercely. He didn't stop fucking her, but he did raise his head to watch her find her release. So damn beautiful, his only regret that Malik wasn't there to witness and partake in it, too.

After a moment, the nails in his shoulders eased, and she softened beneath him. "Now it's my turn," he murmured, thrusting faster. "Feel free to join me for seconds."

His thumb working again, he drove her to the precipice of another orgasm, and since he knew what she looked like when about to soar, his head came down, mouth sealing over hers when she found it again. As his own orgasm gripped him, something more than pleasure overcame him. A feeling like he'd felt only once before, a feeling of rightness, of coming home. He had suspected, but as it washed over him, he knew without a doubt Daniella was made for him. It also meant she was the perfect woman for his twin, his second, his incredible, maddeningly stubborn brother, as well.

# Chapter Seven

In the aftermath, Dani snuggled up against Jaylin while he dozed, amazed at the amount of heat his body produced. Big, strong, protective, and a phenomenal, caring lover, he seemed too good to be true. Maybe she was stuck in an immersion reality session and couldn't get out. If so, she didn't want to.

With the notion of a perpetual sex fantasy with Jaylin bouncing around in her head, she giggled softly, nuzzling her cheek into his chest.

"What's amusing?"

Uncertain she wanted to express her silly thoughts, she gave him a fact, just not the answer to his question. "Your chest hair is tickling my nose."

He shifted, hauling her up his body until she lay on top. As she came up on her elbows to look down at him, a thick swathe of her dark-red hair slid over her shoulder into his face. He wrinkled his nose, and she laughed when it twitched. With a toss of her head, she shifted it all to one side, watching it mingle with his dark blond. "Together, we have a lot of hair."

"On our heads." His hands slid down her back to her bare behind. There he cupped both cheeks. "Your body, unlike mine, is smooth—everywhere. I hadn't heard this about Earth women. Is it true of all your species?"

"No, our females have body hair, except most of us laser it off."

"Really?" His perfectly arched brows shot up his forehead. "Isn't that painful?"

"Heck, yeah, especially the first time." She shrugged. "You get used to it."

"You lasered your skin more than once? And you did this everywhere?"

She flushed, knowing the "everywhere" he referred to.

He grinned. "This calls for further exploration."

He rolled them, gave her a short yet thorough kiss, then began to slide slowly down her body. The thick mass of his hair trailing his lips as he moved lower, tickled, making her squirm.

"Jaylin!" she squealed, turned on but also giggling from the light sweep of the silken strands.

At her thighs, he spread them wide, his mouth sliding over the smooth, denuded skin. Immediately, her giggles evaporated, changing to hitching inhaled pants when his thumbs parted her outer folds and his tongue licked into her.

"Exquisite," he murmured, the heat of his breath stimulating her clit an instant before he sucked on it. She arched off the bed, sensation rocketing through her body. Needing more, she gripped his head, her fingers twining into his hair, and she pulled him in closer. After wantonly spreading her legs, she went a step further and draped them one at a time over his broad shoulders, offering him whatever he wanted to take.

"Mmm," he hummed, not letting up while he swirled his tongue in a slow torturous circle. He flicked it back and forth and few times, finally dropping lower and dragging the flat of it from her weeping entrance up to the bud again. Next, he opened wide and sucked it inside, letting go after a three count with a wet pop. "Mm, mm," he repeated in a low, hungry growl. "Sweet like *pershada* nectar," before he went back for another taste, making her quiver.

"What's...that?" she asked between ragged gasps.

"A native fruit from Trilor." He gave her another slow lick. "It's very expensive...because it grows...in a remote location." He punctuated his words with slow licks and flicks of his tongue. "It's well guarded by treacherous terrain." When he applied sustained suction, she bowed off the bed. Releasing her again, he finished with another slow swirl, this time in reverse. "However, the risk is well worth the reward."

"Please..."

"Isn't this what I am doing, *pershada*? Pleasing you?" he whispered, teasing the bud with his tongue.

"Yes, although I can't bear much more of this deliberate torment."

"Ah, Dani," he murmured, and slid a finger into her soaked channel. "Don't you know anticipation makes the reward all the sweeter? Like waiting to harvest the succulent berries only at their ripest, or teasing you to climax." He added another long, broad finger and, while pumping at an unhurried pace, went back to lashing and sucking her clit. But he relented on the stopping and starting, not letting up until her hips arched, and, with her legs clamped around his head, she cried out in ecstasy.

Breathing fast, with the rapid beat of her heart thudding in her ears, she twitched as he pressed one more kiss on the top of her mound, and then he rose over her. He positioned himself, and, unlike the first time, slid in all the way with one thrust. There was the same stretch and wonderful fullness, without a hint of discomfort.

He covered her with his body, and lowered his mouth to hers. He tasted of her, not at all like berries, but the mix of her and Jaylin on her tongue she found pleasantly erotic.

"You enjoyed tormenting me," she accused without any bite to her words.

"Damn straight," he replied, his grin like the cat who lapped up some cream. When he began to move, all teasing vanished from his face, replaced with intensity, his silver orbs dark from unquenched desire.

"Wrap me up, Dani. This time is going to be neither slow nor gentle. I want you too bad."

With all four limbs, she encircled him, locking her ankles behind his hips, her arms around his neck. She hung on while he moved above and within her, his hips driving harder and faster than before. Although it seemed impossible, in a few full strokes, a quiver started low in her belly, and the throb in her clit rekindled, intensifying every time his body melded with hers. Breathless, when his tongue drove into her mouth, it made her more so. Jaylin's power and passion surrounded her as he took control. The room filled with groans, slapping skin, and sensual wetness, the same sounds at any other time would have been mortifying. Now, she found it hot.

Then she couldn't think because another shattering climax raced through her. Her moans were drowned out by his discordant, yet sexy masculine cries. He slammed into her once more, hard body going rigid, while his chest left hers, and his head arched back. She latched onto him, clinging to his shoulders, lips open along his corded throat, tasting the salt on his skin, and feeling the tension inside him as his climax took hold.

In that moment, with his shaft embedded fully, his ragged groans vibrating beneath her mouth, his large body shuddering in her arms from the force of his release inside her, Dani realized the power of her femininity.

Her heart swelled with the knowledge she could inspire in him the same exquisite pleasure he'd given her.

He inhaled, his chest expanding against her breasts when he blew it out slowly. His head dropped forward, eyes meeting hers, crinkling at the sides as he smiled, before touching his lips lightly to hers again.

"Is it always like that?" she whispered in wonder.

His face smoothed out, the laugh lines gone. "No, Dani," he whispered back, in all seriousness. "It is rarely like that."

He came back for another, more thorough kiss, sending the rest of her questions out of her head. A few moments later, Jaylin rolled off her, which meant he slipped out of her, but he gathered her close, tucking her under one arm. She settled against him, her head on his chest, in the same position she had started out in, with his chest hair tickling her nose. This time, she nuzzled against him, not minding at all.

"It seems as though I'm always saying this, but I need to go relieve Malik. I've left him the brunt of the work since supper last night."

When she lifted her gaze, she tried to hide her disappointment. "Okay."

"Don't sound so down. We're on a ship, *pershada*, how far can I go?"

She pushed up on an elbow, not trying to mask her frown. "I'm not sure I like the nickname. It makes me think of sex."

"And this is bad how?"

"Others, like Malik, will guess how I got it."

"Then it won't be a secret you taste like a rare succulent berry."

"Jaylin!"

"I do not lie, Dani. Your flavor is still on my tongue." He was above her again, his handsome face alight with mischief. "Have another sample and see for yourself." He swooped down and claimed her mouth. She still didn't taste berries, only Jaylin, warm and delicious.

"I must go," he groaned, before breaking free. "Stay, rest, lounge, whatever you like. I'll see you later."

When he rose and gathered his clothes, she rolled on her side, pulled the sheet over her nakedness, and propped up on an elbow, head in hand, watching the show. She caught a glimpse of tight, muscled male ass before snug-fitting black trousers blocked her view. More like a flash, really. Still, it was quite nice. She sighed.

"Don't start again, Dani. I really must go."

"What did I do?"

"You're being cute, which arouses me. I don't have time to go another round."

"Like you could."

He twisted, his brows shooting up. "Is that a challenge?"

"Uh, well, no. It's biology. You already, um, twice, well, you know…"

He grinned. "Came deep inside of you?"

She plucked at the sheet, not meeting his gaze. "Yes. And if you count last night. It's three times in twelve hours." Without warning, a horrible thought entered her head, and she forgot her embarrassment, her eyes flying wide to stare at him. "You're not a cyborg, too, are you?"

He stilled, the amusement fading from his handsome features. "About that—"

"Jaylin, I need you on the bridge." Malik's voice over the speaker interrupted what else he would have said. "I've picked up a ship approaching fast."

He walked to the wall and flipped up a recessed panel she hadn't noticed before.

"Any communication?"

"No, and I've tried. The computer can't get a fix on its origin, either."

"I'm on my way." He flipped the panel closed, and returned to the bed where he put on his boots.

"Do you think they mean trouble?" She rested her hand on his back.

"Likely not, still, it pays to be cautious." His eyes met hers when he rose to tuck in his shirt. "Get dressed. I may need you to come up and strap in if we have to make a run for it, or engage."

Neither option sounded good to her.

He bent to her, his hand in the mattress by her hip as he leaned over and kissed her brow. "Don't worry. It's probably nothing, but come upstairs when you're ready, so I can keep an eye on you."

She wrinkled her nose. He sounded like every other man she'd encountered, thinking she needed a keeper.

"For your safety, Dani."

"What trouble can I possibly get into while lying in bed?"

"I'd rather not find out."

"Uh!" she grunted.

"I'm teasing about the last part, baby. The first, however, is an order. Get dressed and come up top."

She liked when he called her baby much more than a strange alien fruit, and because of he did — not really, she would have done it because he was the captain, and had asked — she agreed.

"Okay, fine."

"That's my sweet *pershada*."

She scowled at his teasing; it only broadened his grin. Then he brushed his nose alongside hers, stood, and strode from the room, chuckling as he went, the low, sultry sound making her tingle.

***

When Jaylin got to the bridge, he found Malik in the pilot's chair. Coming to stand beside him, hands on hips, he scanned the variety of different screens on the control console. "Is it still on course for us?"

"Yes. I've changed our heading twice in the last thirty minutes and it does as well."

"They're tracking us. Damn. Dani still has the homing chip in her thigh. How could I have forgotten?"

"That's not it."

"Of course it is. We've got to get it out and deactivate the signal."

"There is no signal. I neutralized the chip when I healed her ribs."

Jaylin twisted his head and stared at his brother. "You didn't mention it."

He shrugged. "I figured it would come up soon enough. I saw it on the scan, and didn't like the idea of Alltryp chipping her like a pet."

"Good man." Jaylin smiled as he turned back to the screen. Taking initiative, being protective on her behalf, caring; all small steps, but it showed progress.

"Don't think more of it than it is, brother."

"I'm not thinking anything at all, except how to get rid of this ship," he replied.

Malik grunted, clearly not believing him.

Jaylin put thoughts of his promising reaction aside and focused on the looming threat. "Can we outrun them?"

"I've increased speed. They're keeping pace, so probably not."

"We need to outmaneuver them." He moved into the co-pilot's chair and pulled up the star chart on the navigation panel. Before studying it, he flipped on the intercom. "Dani, get up here and get strapped in." He resumed scanning, searching for a solution to their current dilemma. As he did so, he asked Malik, "Why didn't you call me sooner?"

"When neither of you appeared for the morning meal, I figured you were otherwise occupied."

"I was," he answered, ignoring the dig, "but you know my priorities."

"Dani isn't at the top of the list?"

"Don't be an ass. Her safety is my prime concern, as is yours, and the Renegade."

"I'm honored you remembered me and our ship in your answer," was his caustic reply.

His eyes cut to his brother. "What the fuck is your problem? You say you don't want her, yet complain when I do and take action about it."

Malik scowled, but when he opened his mouth to reply, Jaylin cut in before he could utter another word. "Are we going to do this now?"

His twin's golden gaze narrowed before snapping to the view screen. "What do you suggest?"

Studying the maps, it took several moments for him to decide. "There's a nebulae cloud not far away." He plotted the new course. "On its edge sits a series of asteroids. The nearest one is large. We'll come around to the far side. Between the rock's density and the ionization of the cloud, the interference should impede their ability to scan us."

"The same will apply to us."

"Yes. Except we'll cut power and activate our cold shields, which will eliminate any infrared capabilities." He brought up the map on the main screen, pointing to four closely spaced minor planets that formed an arc around the edge of the cloud. "We'll follow the first until we're in line with the next, and so on, while keeping undercover. When we get to the last, if we haven't lost them, we'll set an alternate course and come around the back side of Earth. If we're lucky, they'll think we have a different destination."

"You're convinced they're after Daniella?"

"What else could they want? We have no cargo. She is all we have of value onboard."

"Who do you think it is?"

As one, they turned to see Dani standing behind them, neither having heard the lift or her footfalls while arguing and plotting a defense.

"Get strapped in," Jaylin ordered without answering her question. There would be time for answers once she was safe.

She didn't move, her attention fixed on the screen. "Is it my father?"

"I want you strapped in now, Dani," Jaylin intoned when she still didn't move to get secure.

"He sent us to retrieve you, remember?" Malik replied. "We sent word of our success. Why send another ship?"

"You sent word?" Her brows gathered, and her gaze flicked from Malik to him, before going back to the screen. "Prince Ivar, perhaps?" she guessed next, her voice low and constrained.

His frown eclipsed the intensity of hers. First, over the sudden rasp in her tone, and, second, the fear in her eyes, but more importantly, because she still stood in the same spot and had not obeyed his order, now issued three times.

"I don't think so," his twin told her. "They don't have a space fleet."

"They could hire someone, couldn't they? Like my father did the two of you?"

That's all they needed. Other paid mercenaries after the would-be princess. The idea enraged Jaylin who was already on edge.

"We don't have time for guessing games," he ground out as he spun in his chair and leaned toward her, hands on his knees. This time when he spoke, it wasn't as the lover who had so recently left her bed, rather, the pissed off captain of the Renegade tired of being ignored. "When I give you an order," he snapped, "I expect it to be obeyed. Not in a minute, or perhaps in an hour, or whenever the hell you feel like it, but immediately." He barked this last word at considerable volume. When she stiffened, and her eyes flared wide in surprise, he knew he had gotten through. "Now, for the last time. Get your sweet ass in a seat, strap in, and do so without arguing. I need quiet to concentrate."

"He gets like this when he feels threatened and needs to focus, Dani."

"I don't need you to explain my actions to her," Jaylin snapped without looking away from her pale face and the plump lower lip which she'd once again caught between her teeth. He'd figured out she did this when uncertain, or afraid, and, in this case, most likely, that her feelings had been hurt. Unfortunate, yes. But in a serious situation like this, he didn't have time to hold her hand and explain — that could come later — and he damn sure wouldn't tolerate any insubordination. "What I need is for you both to follow orders without giving me lip so I can get us out of this mess." Although he used a more modulated tone, his message left no room for argument.

Without another word, she walked to one of the chairs set behind and to the side of the helm. When she began putting on the harness, Jaylin faced front again. He'd have to do damage control with Dani, later — of that he was certain. Right now, he needed to focus and keep them all safe.

"Now who's being an ass?" Malik muttered.

\*\*\*

She sat in her chair for the next two hours, quietly fuming. Jaylin had ticked her off for so many reasons. If told to make a list in order, she would be hard-pressed to pick the one to top it. But even while she stewed over his coarse speech and manner, she found what was going on in front of her, fascinating.

Jaylin piloted the ship skillfully, maneuvering around the asteroid while avoiding debris in the outermost edges of the ionized cloud, without entering it which would have been like shining a spotlight on the Renegade, making it a beacon for the other vessel. Once behind the airless rocky world, they slowed, activating the cold shields that would protect them from infrared scanning. They caught a brief heat signal of their pursuers once, but they were headed in the opposite direction, as they'd hoped.

By the time they flew past the last planet in the row, and veered around the trailing edge of the molecular cloud, there wasn't a sign of them. And through it all, no one said a word.

As they worked, the two men looked at each other on occasion, one or the other would nod, then flip dials or switch screens. It was as though they could read each other's minds. It kind of freaked her out, and also ticked her off further. Off to the side, out of their way, hushed to silence like a bothersome child, she felt excluded. And after the way Jaylin had barked orders at her, it made her already-wounded feelings hurt more.

They had their hands full, she knew that. A threat loomed out there, likely against her. They had a job to do, including protecting her, but did he have to be so mean? He'd morphed into Captain Jaylin Sin-Naysir, renowned mercenary badass, and class A jerk, nothing at all like the man she'd come to know. Not the kind, considerate man who'd rescued her, handled her with care when she'd been hurt, and held her close when she'd been terrified by her nightmares. And he in no way resembled the man of last night and this morning, who had claimed her innocence with tenderness, ensuring she was wholly satisfied, and then some.

What really hurt her, though, considering what they had shared, was that he hadn't changed his plans to return to Earth. This could only mean one thing—he intended to complete the job her father had hired him to do. Malik couldn't have told him what they'd discussed. Or maybe he had, and Jaylin had decided against it. Her last offer had been triple. Hell, she'd pay it all if she had to. A million credits should tempt him. Weren't they, by definition, soldiers of fortune, their skills sold to the highest bidder?

She snorted. Leave it to her to find mercenaries with work ethics.

"Do you have something to say, Dani?" Jaylin's question was the first words spoken aloud in some time.

"Oh? Do I have permission to speak now, Captain?"

"I don't need your sass, sweetness. We're a long way from being out of the woods. If you have something to say, speak up now, or keep the sound effects to a minimum."

"I wanted to ask if your services were for hire?" This got his full attention, and he once again spun in his chair.

"You did not just ask me that," he snarled.

Upon seeing the fire in his eyes, she understood the services he assumed she referred to.

"I meant the Renegade's services," she explained in a hushed voice, her gaze darting to Malik, who stayed busy at the controls. She glanced back at Jaylin. "I would like to hire you. And buy out your contract to my father."

"To what end?" he asked, less bite to his tone.

"To the end of not becoming an Elzorian bride, which seems to be a death sentence. I'll do anything to avoid such a fate."

He stiffened, his jaw clenching so tight a muscle twitched in his cheek. Something she'd noticed Malik did as well. Interesting. Except she couldn't dwell on it now.

"Dani…" Her name from his tense lips came out like a growl.

Before he could spout more orders for her to sit by mutely obedient, or to cease and desist bothering him while he worked, she spoke over him. "Malik didn't tell you."

His head came around briskly. "When did I have time?"

"Time for what?" Jaylin demanded, getting riled again.

"I will be twenty-five in ten days and will come into some money. I proposed to double what my father is paying, but he said you ship is worth ten times as much. I'll pay it—one million credits. Keep me safe out here in space somewhere, well beyond his reach until my birthday, and when you return me to Earth, it's yours."

"And your plans beyond that?"

She didn't like the sudden coldness in his tone, but she hadn't liked much about him since he'd left her bed this morning. "I don't know. I hadn't thought much beyond getting away. Perhaps I'll open a gallery out west somewhere."

"On Earth," he drawled.

She threw her hands up in frustration. "Where else would I live? I'm from Earth."

"Dani…" This subtle warning came from Malik, who looked at her, shaking his head.

"Was this your plan when you first spoke to Malik?"

"Well, yes."

"And you thought to sweeten the pot by spreading your legs for me? To convince me to break my contract with your father."

She gasped. Appalled he could think her so conniving as to sacrifice herself. "How dare you! I wouldn't do something so…so…mercenary." Her chin snapped up sharply, and she watched his eyes narrow as her barb hit home.

"You said a moment ago you'd do anything to get out of marrying Ivar."

"Well, I didn't mean…that."

While he stared at her for a moment, his mouth settled into a hard line and the silver of his eyes changed to flat, dark gray. Before she could defend herself further, he spun back to the controls. He dismissed her coolly, doing so through Malik. "Take her below, and see she stays there. I don't need the distraction right now."

Her throat tightened with tears. Before they broke free and she embarrassed herself in front of him by blubbering like a smitten fool, she stood up — or at least tried to. The harness, still latched in place, prevented her from moving.

She ripped at it with her fingers. "I'd love to be out of your presence." She tried for a harsh, biting undertone, except her breath hitching gave her jagged emotions away.

Without looking at either of them to see if they noticed — how could they not? — she pulled at the clasp. It wouldn't release. Frustrated and a second from collapsing in a torrent of self-pitying sobs, she grasped the straps and tugged hard.

"You're only making it tighter, Dani. Stop."

"Don't tell me what to do!" she shrieked, losing control.

Long fingers moved her hands aside.

"Don't touch me." Her words came out in a hiss as she smacked Jaylin's hands away.

"Sweetheart, let me help you."

She stopped, realizing Malik leaned over her, and he was the one she had slapped. "I'm sorry I hit you."

"It's okay."

He easily opened the latch and would have helped more, but she shrugged out of the harness and surged to her feet. With her eyes averted, she bolted to the lift, waving her hand over the sensor. When it didn't come fast enough, she waved it again, and again. Knowing it wouldn't make the unit arrive any sooner, it at least gave her something to do.

Hands on her shoulders made her tense.

"You don't need to escort me down. I can find my own way."

"He gave me orders, same as you."

"And you're his minion, so you always obey?" she shot back, lashing out at him angrily. "He won't find me as subservient."

The door opened, and she scurried inside, Malik crowding into the small unit with her. She didn't look at him or toward the bridge, averting her eyes as the half door closed and they started to move.

"He didn't mean what he said, like you, he was angry."

"I hate him."

"You don't mean that, either."

"He makes me furious, and I definitely meant that."

"Things got heated back there, but think on this. For Jaylin to become volatile, so quickly means he doesn't hate you, either. Far from it."

"I want to go home in a week and a half and forget all of this happened."

"A girl doesn't save herself for twenty-five years, find a man she trusts enough to gift her innocence to, then practically overnight, want to forget it. Jaylin will realize this when he calms down."

"He's an asshole."

"He can be. He's also very kind, caring, and extremely protective. I warned you he gets this way when threatened. All he can think of is eliminating the danger and keeping everyone safe, to the exclusion of courtesy, kindness, and pretty redheads whose feelings he otherwise wouldn't hurt."

Blinking back frustrated tears, she glanced up at him and asked, "Why are you defending him?"

"I know him. This is his nature. Later, when we're safely away from whoever is pursuing us, he'll regret being so harsh and come find you. Wait and see."

"I won't hold my breath," she grumbled. "If I do, I'll be as blue as Ivar."

The door opened to the lower level, and she rushed out. She couldn't outdistance Malik's long strides, however, and he caught up with her at her bedroom door.

"Dani, let me tell you a little story."

"I'm not in the mood for fairy tales. And I realized today, I'm much too old to believe in them, anyway."

"Don't—"

Emotionally wrecked, she cut him off. "I'm sorry I lashed out. Jaylin deserves my sharp words, not you. And, please, Malik, understand when I say I need to be left alone right now."

He stared at her a moment, and she thought she saw a flicker of something in his distant eyes, but, if she did, it vanished as quickly as it appeared. Or perhaps in her pique, she'd imagined it.

He inclined his head. "I'll leave to your thoughts."

The next moment the doors slid shut and she was alone. And, although she'd lived most of her life that way, she felt the loneliness more completely than ever before.

# Chapter Eight

Never one to sulk, despite having a lifetime of reason to, it turned out she had an aptitude for it, staying in her room the rest of the day, brooding over Jaylin's behavior, and replaying their ugly scene in her head. The only realization Dani came to, when disappointment felt this devastating, it deserved a good pout.

She refused Malik's invitation for dinner, leaving the tray he brought in untouched. Jaylin obviously didn't care whether she passed out from starvation, because she didn't see the first sign of him by the time she crawled into bed. She did so with a bruised heart. Tossing fitfully, it took a long time before she could relax enough to drift off.

It was dark when her eyes popped open again, except for two floor lights bracketing the bathroom and the main door to her quarters. Wide awake, she didn't feel at all rested. She could have been asleep minutes, or hours, on board ship it was hard to tell because day and night ran together. She rolled to the side in search of a clock, but didn't get far due to the heavy weight around her middle.

Glancing down, she saw long, broad fingers, neatly trimmed nails, attached to a masculine hand and thick wrist. Following it up a sinewy forearm to biceps which bulged despite his relaxed state. Wanting him after what he'd said and done would be crazy. Next, she tried to imagine why Jaylin thought he would be welcome in her bed.

Steaming with unspent anger, she lifted the heavy arm, made weightier from sleep, and eased out from underneath it. On her feet, she stared down at her nemesis, again struck by how beautiful he truly was. Features softened by sleep, he looked like the man she had developed a fondness for. She'd let him kiss her and take more liberties than any man, ever. But he had morphed into some arrogant, autocratic monster earlier today—or was it yesterday?—and, on top of it, hadn't so much as blinked when he told Malik he'd plotted a course for Earth and her even more autocratic father.

His motto seemed to be get laid, get paid, and forget both the job and the woman once he was done.

"Big jerk," she hissed, clapping a hand over her mouth when he stirred.

Holding her breath, she waited for those long lashes to flutter open and his unforgettable silver-eyed gaze to catch her standing over him. Seconds passed and he didn't move. She counted to ten, then to twenty, before she relaxed, and dropped her hand.

In the silence of her room, on a ship in the middle of the galaxy, she came to a decision. She wasn't going back, not until she could be free and clear of her father's control, and all other self-important patronizing men and their authority—like Jaylin Sin-Naysir.

She bent and picked up her shoes, leaving the room before she smacked him for being such a dumbass, and a big fat heartbreaking disappointment as well.

As she crept down the hall, she tiptoed by Malik's open door. She could see his still form on his bed. She stared at him a moment, watching him breathe, his dark wavy hair mussed and falling over his forehead. He looked so human in sleep. This was something else she found interesting, expecting him to be plugged in, or in some sort of recharging chamber overnight. But she guessed she'd watched too many sci-fi shows.

Shrugging if off, she moved to the lift, abruptly bypassing it when she decided it would make too much noise and wake them. She knotted her shoe strings together, then hung them over her shoulder and quietly climbed the ladder to the upper level.

With the lights from the control console blinking green, yellow and red, and flickering on a host of other equipment lining the perimeter of the circular room, she had plenty of light to explore the bridge level, really taking it in for the first time.

Not as big as the lower floor, windows made up a quarter of the walls of the room, and revealed hundreds of stars in the pervasive blackness. She stared at the view, surprised to see the nebulae they had edged around all afternoon was gone. Searching for something other than stars, she saw nothing. Taking a seat in one of the four flight chairs on the edges of the room, she put on her half boots and laced them tight.

She didn't know what she was doing up here, except than to be far away from Jaylin.

Dani eyed the control console. What she knew about operating a ship of this kind could fit on the head of a pin. She'd ridden in shuttles and gliders countless times back home, and sat beside the pilot more often than not. Always inquisitive, she'd asked about every button and switch and panel, though she didn't expect a star cruiser like this would be quite the same.

She stood and walked to the bank of maps on the far wall. All lit in a series of blue, green, and red. Earth was the center point of the first screen, and red dots delineated their flight path, the flashing one about midway representing their current position, or so she guessed. Out of curiosity, she touched the screen, and it shifted, zooming in slightly. Like with any other touch screen, she could use two fingers to expand and shrink the view.

After doing this several times, a window opened. With the same flashing red dot in the center, this view brought planets and moons and other large bodies into focus. And, unlike the smaller view, they had labels. Leaning in, she read the names. Only one or two sounded familiar, though didn't jog her memory enough to recall anything specific about those worlds.

As she continued to scroll and shift the screen, a line of yellow dots popped up, then some in green. Unsure what it meant, she looked for a legend, but didn't find one. She zoomed in on one good-sized planet. When she had it enlarged to double, a text box appeared.

"Nusapphra," she murmured. "I've read something about this one."

She scrolled past the lengthy physical and scientific descriptions to the section on the inhabitants and culture. There she paused and began reading aloud.

"Settled in 2217, nearly ten thousand refugees from the war-torn planet Sapphra formed an all-female colony. Rich in natural resources the population eschewed fossil fuels in lieu of plant-based energies to establish their fuel-efficient, energy-independent colony."

Intrigued, she continued. At the end of the summary, she grinned. "Woman president...all female Army...city-state league of governors—all women. Now we're talking."

Enlarging it further made a blue box with coordinates pop up. They meant nothing to her, although, underneath was something of interest—a button labeled Travel Time to Destination. She clicked it and read: 12 hours, 35 minutes. She searched for a clock--almost 2 am.

If she changed course now, they would be halfway there before they finished breakfast. She clicked the next button that read Plot Course. A new screen came up with some bulleted details—speed, nearby conflicts, restricted areas, and threats. All in green, the last bullet labeled Warnings was marked None.

A red button located below the box said in bold print, Set New Course.

From a map? No, this was too easy. Her finger itched to press it. Did she dare?

If Jaylin had been angry before, she could imagine what he would be like when he found out she'd changed their course. She laughed softly, picturing the big bad captain of the Renegade dealing with an all-female government who wouldn't be swayed by his high-handed ways and his arrogance.

Her anger, which had never dissipated, bubbled over. Use her like a loose woman only to toss her away. Screw him. It would serve him right.

She moved her hand over the screen, index finger extended, but she hesitated, hovering over the red triangle that could very well engage the new course. She closed her eyes, wishing she had the nerve, but even she wasn't so foolish.

A beeping sound made her open her eyes. On the screen in big bold letters appeared "New Course Engaged." Suddenly a progress bar popped up.

"No! I didn't press it," she cried softly. She whirled, staring with dread at the bridge and the two dozen or so more blinking, flashing lights which hadn't been blinking and flashing moments ago.

"Crap," she cursed. Spinning back to the map, she looked for an abort button, an arrow back, or an undo… something. There was nothing.

She raced to the command console, stopping beside the pilot's chair. She searched the panels, slide bars, and buttons for something that appeared to be able to take her back to five minutes ago, but she didn't recognize anything remotely similar to the shuttles she'd been on.

Looking up at the view screen, she picked out a star, a red one, and watched it. Nothing happened, which gave her hope she hadn't actually changed course. It was at a map, after all.

She heard a beep, followed by a series of buzzes, and the star began to move—though she knew it was the Renegade doing the actual moving. She'd expected it to happen slowly, which would give her time to go get Malik to undo whatever she had done, but the star shifted and seemed to race across the screen. She felt the rotation of the ship beneath her feet, which she hadn't before, not in the days she'd been aboard.

Shit! What had she done?

When the controls started to hum, and the floor vibrated, she ran for the lift.

"Shit! Shit! Shit!"

Waking Malik became her prime objective.

The vessel jerked suddenly almost knocking her off her feet. She looked back, expecting to see smoke and flames. All seemed normal, except for the buzzing and flashing lights. Finding the red star took a moment because it now twinkled on the far side of the screen—opposite to where it had started. Her heart leapt into her throat.

"We've come around too fast," she whispered in horror.

An alarm began to scream, and a red button lit up below the control panel. It was on a slide-out drawer all by itself with a plastic cover over it, as if to keep it from being accidentally pushed. It had some strange marking on it.

"Dammit. Isn't this just my luck when everything else is in AUL?"

Alliance Universal Language was used on all thirty-seven planets. Taught in school, it's how she could communicate with Jaylin and Malik without a translator, although they both knew a good deal of English—Jaylin's command of Earth slang and swear words particularly impressive. The intent of AUL, to standardize language across all Alliance planets, to promote communication between worlds and their people, and most important, for use during space travel to prevent barriers in emergency situations like this.

Okay, the last bit was mostly bullshit. Never had it been intended to help an Earth girl who'd accidentally changed course on her rescuer's alien ship.

Staring at the red light, her throat closed around her heart, still wedged firmly in place. All the shuttles at home had a similar button, an emergency shutdown in case of an engine fire. Did she risk the assumption alien ships were equipped the same way? If she hit it, and it worked, she could run and fetch Malik.

Except what if she gambled, and lost?

She moved forward, her hand extended, hovered over it for a second then she snatched it back, vacillating whether to do it or not.

*Do it,* a little voice told her. *If you don't correct what you started, Angry Alpha Captain is going to be up here in ten seconds, ready to beat your ass.*

The decision was made for her when something hissed and a little ribbon of smoke started rolling up from the center panel. Figuring her fate had been sealed either way, she flipped up the plastic cover, squinched her eyes tight and, while holding her breath, pushed it. Then she prayed.

Before she uttered the words Dear God, her ass hit the floor. Shocked, she could only stare at the spot where she had stood and the thick cloud of smoke now billowing out of one of the seams around a screen with a shower of sparks.

"Mother of God, help me," she whispered. Rolling to her stomach and onto her hands and knees, she scanned for a way to extinguish the fire. After a moment, and coming up with nothing, she screamed in frustration, "How can they not have a fire extinguisher?"

With the alarm still shrieking, the ship began to shimmy, and emitted a loud *ka-thunk*. Climbing to her feet, she spied one of the men's jackets draped over one of the chairs. Snatching it, she swatted at the flames, hoping she hadn't signed their death warrants with her stupidity.

As she tried to contain the fire, the auto-lift behind her creaked. She couldn't abandon the fire, and take the time to see who it was.

*Please, please, please, let it be Malik.*

Her luck — always bad since the day she'd come into the world — failed her again.

"Daniella!" Jaylin's roar eclipsed the pounding of his boots and all the alarms combined. "What the fuck have you done to my ship?"

"Does it matter, right now? We're on fire," she screeched.

But his question, apparently rhetorical, didn't require an answer. His hands encircled her waist and he lifted her, bodily moving her out of his way. Then he hit a yellow button on the wall which made the lights dim and the console blink off. Next, he bent and retrieved a fire extinguisher from a low cupboard nearby — one she hadn't seen. He aimed it at the console, and, after dispensing a cloud of an orange powdery substance, the fire was out.

For a moment, he stood still, his shoulders back, and his spine rigid as if forged in steel.

"You better run and hide if you know what's good for you," Malik whispered in her ear.

She jumped, not having heard him come up in the commotion. Taking his advice, she whirled, following a direct path to the lift. The only trouble, Jaylin had finished perusing the mess she'd made.

His glare hit her like daggers piercing her skin. With a sudden change of plans, she veered right, toward the ladder.

Four feet from the round hole in the floor, and ready to dive head first through it, his roar stopped her in her tracks.

"Don't you dare take another step," he bellowed.

She chanced a glance back and saw his utterly livid face, eyes glittering with fury, nostrils flared. His mouth a thin slash in his bearded face — something new from the day before — and his jaw was held so tight she thought it might break.

"I'm so sorry," she whispered.

His hand came up, palm out. Wisely, she remained silent.

When he spoke again, long moments later, his voice held an icy chill. "I'm too furious to even ask what the hell you were doing up here in the middle of the night. But it doesn't matter. There is no excuse for this." He swept his arm toward the destruction.

"I—"

"Silence," he ordered tersely. "This cannot go unpunished."

She sucked in a ragged breath, and nodded. Whatever he decreed: keelhauled, boiled in oil, strung up by her toes, she deserved. His sentence, however, stunned her.

"Malik, take her downstairs, put her in her room, and lock the door. And, before you leave her to think about what she's done, that she may not have merely crippled the ship with this stunt, but could have very well stranded us in the middle of nowhere vulnerable to whatever lowlife parasites might happen across our path—"

"Jaylin, please let me explain," she cried in desperation, but he continued as if she hadn't spoken.

"Spank her mischievous little ass, and make every swat count. Fifty should do for a start."

"Fifty!" she squealed at the same time Malik shouted, "Spank Dani?"

Then, they replied in unison, "No way!"

He ignored them both and went right on issuing orders. "Once you're done, send her to a corner to wait for me. I'll join you to give her the rest when I get this cleaned up and fix whatever components she has fried. And," he added further, "I want her hands on her head, her spanked ass on display when I walk in."

"I can't spank her. You know how I feel about that. I'm sure this was all a mistake."

"How can this be a fucking mistake, Malik? She crawled out of bed in the middle of the night and sabotaged our ship."

"Not with intention," she cut in weakly.

His eyes burned into her with such fury, she jumped back, as if they might scorch her skin.

"You"—he pointed at Malik—"will follow orders. My word is law on the Renegade, and I stand as judge and jury. Her carelessness has threatened not only our livelihood, but our very lives if I can't do the repairs and pirates happen upon us."

"Wait until after, then you can carry out your own damn sentence and spank her yourself."

They squared off, nose to nose, two large, angry men, light versus dark, captain against first mate.

Shame filled Dani as the ripples of her colossal blunder widened and engulfed everything and everyone around her.

"Stop!" she cried out, unable to stand by and watch them argue. And she couldn't allow Malik to get in trouble for disobeying his captain when this was all her fault. "I'm the one who screwed up. Don't be angry at him because of me. I'll take the punishment."

Two sets of angry eyes flicked her way. Silence reigned for a moment. Malik's face relaxed as he gazed at her, his body visibly releasing its tension.

Not so with Jaylin, who still stood rigid, still humming with rage.

"She realizes this is warranted, and you have your orders," he said in a deadly tone. "Take her below, now, before I do something I will regret!"

Malik's long fingers curled around her upper arm, guiding her to the auto-lift.

"He'll calm down, Dani. He just needs time alone to do so."

"I don't think so. I saw murder in his eyes."

"He isn't going to kill you," he reassured her as he closed the gate.

When they began to descend, she caught a last glimpse of Jaylin, head bent, hand wrapped around the back of his neck, body vibrating with anger as he stood alone amidst the shambles of his bridge.

\*\*\*

Like a death row inmate taking the last long walk before execution, she moved forward, her feet dragging.

"I've never been spanked before," she told him when they came to a stop in the open doorway to her quarters. The navy comforter was thrown back, the linens mussed, and the thick pillows indented from where she and Jaylin had lain not thirty minutes before. Oh, why hadn't she stayed in bed beside him? He'd been resting so peacefully, his arm around her, as though protecting her while she slept, much better than having the full force of his fury aimed at her in condemnation.

"I'm not surprised," Malik replied. "You seem like a good girl, Dani. What were you thinking?"

"I wasn't, obviously." She glanced up at him, though stopped at his chin, stubbled like Jaylin's with a scruff of beard. She couldn't meet his gaze and doubted she ever would again. Not after this. "I'm sorry you have to do this."

"It won't be the first time."

Proven wrong, just like that, she looked him in the eyes and asked in surprise. "You've done this before?"

"Plenty of times."

"On Jaylin's orders?"

"Sometimes. Other times on my own account."

"To who? Other passengers?"

"Once before, but also on Trilor. It is a common punishment."

"Oh."

He guided her inside, coming to a stop by the bed.

"Will it hurt?"

"Yes, it's meant to be a punishment. Except you won't be harmed. It will sting, and your bottom will be sore, though nothing long-lasting. I promise."

"But fifty is so many."

"I'll be careful with you, Dani. And though I disagree and think Jaylin should do this himself, you've earned every swat. You should have come for one of us right away, not tried to fix it on your own, or cover up your mistake."

"I know," she whispered, looking away.

He turned her to face him. Like Jaylin often did, he nudged her chin up to his, searching her face for the truth. "Tell me the reason you went upstairs in the middle of the night."

"After the scene with Jaylin yesterday, when I awoke with him beside me…"

"I didn't know he went to your bed."

She nodded. "Still angry, I got up to get away and think. I didn't want to wake either of you and went up to the bridge. It was innocent at first, then I started exploring. Your maps are really too easy to use."

He blew out a breath. "That explains it. There is something wrong with the interface. We don't set course from there because of it. It sends us into hyperdrive. The sudden increase in speed and to such a high rate always overheats the engines."

She blinked. "If you know it's a problem, why don't you deactivate it?"

"We could, but saw no need since Jaylin and I know of the defect." His fingers tightened, and lines around his mouth made him look angry. "We didn't expect anyone else to change course from the maps, especially a guest we rescued, who wandered up where she didn't belong while we slept."

She flushed. Guilty as charged. "Please, can we get this over with before I dig a bigger hole for myself?"

"Smart idea." He sat on the edge of her bed and patted his thighs. "I want you facedown, right here, Dani."

"Can I ask a favor first?"

"What's that?"

"After, can you, um...well, erase this from your memory? Because this is really embarrassing."

He stared at her a moment, his expression puzzled, then his lips flattened into a hard line. "Is that why you're going along with this so easily? Because you see me as a cyborg, rather than a man?"

"Oh, please, don't be offended. But Jaylin, if he did this, I don't think I'd be able to face him ever again. If I wanted to, that is. He deserved to be angry tonight, but I'm not over yesterday."

"Good, don't let him off the hook, just yet."

"So, will you?"

"Erase your spanking from my memory banks?" He stared at her, and for a moment she thought he might erupt, but this was Malik, not Jaylin. His features relaxed, the glimpse of anger she thought she'd seen gone, his usual impassive expression in its place. "I'll see what I can do."

She breathed out slowly. "Thank you."

"Let's get these tights down and see this punishment done." His fingers dipped beneath the hem of her tunic, and into her waistband. He pulled the stretchy fabric over her hips, hooking her panties with them, and tugged both down to her knees. Before she could blush at being so exposed, he upended her over his lap.

"This is a lesson, Dani. I want you to remember it well so you never repeat such a reckless act again."

"I've learned my lesson, Malik. I promise."

"Unfortunately, that's not quite true, however, it will be soon enough."

She couldn't speak any more, because the spanking began.

His large hand came down swiftly on the fullest part of her cheek. When the flat of his palm met bare skin, the loud crack resonated in the small room. It stung, a lot, much more than she'd expected. The intensity built with each successive swat as one after another fell on the exact same spot. She counted to five before he moved to the other cheek, and repeated the process.

For the next set of five his hand moved lower, swinging in an upward motion which made her fleshy bottom jiggle. Mortified, a whimper escaped when she hadn't made a sound over the sting. Five more repeated in similar fashion on the other side then he switched it up, applying one smarting spank at a time, back and forth on each cheek.

She'd lost count by the time he paused. "Halfway there."

Twenty-five more to reach Jaylin's decreed sentence and already her bottom burned and stung. Tomorrow she wouldn't find sitting easy.

When Malik's hand returned, it was to rub lightly over her hot skin.

"Your skin is very fair," he murmured, his voice so soft she wondered if he was talking to her, or merely making an observation. On the verge of telling him to get on with it, so she could begin trying to forget, his fingertips grazed the seam between her cheeks, near her thighs. She sucked in a breath as a tingling spark shot straight through to her clit. She knew what would come next, a surge of wetness.

Mortification consumed her. Here she lay getting a bare-bottom spanking from a cyborg — pretty much a machine — and she was becoming aroused. The only thing keeping her from groaning in utter humiliation, the unexpected yelp she let out when he shifted. She rocked on his thighs, which tipped her head down toward the floor. Gripping his leg, her other hand flew out reaching for the floor, hoping to catch herself before she landed on her head.

Maybe she'd be knocked unconscious and get a case of situational amnesia.

"I won't let you fall, Dani. I'm simply broadening my canvas."

She noticed, although she dangled close enough for her hair to touch the floor, he held her securely with an inflexible arm around her waist.

His comment about a broad canvas penetrated as the spanking resumed. Two by two, he peppered her lowermost curves catching her upper thighs in the process. Knowing he would see her wetness, and guess what it meant, she clamped her legs together. Unfortunately, this made her butt cheeks clench too, and being spanked while tense hurt twice as much. Who knew?

"Relax, tightening up will only make it worse."

Okay, Malik knew. But then he'd done this before, as he'd said.

"Just get it over with," she told him, her voice breaking on the last word.

"Not until you unclench your muscles. You'll bruise."

"I don't care," she sobbed.

"I do. Spread your legs, a bit. It will help with the final ten." When his hand slid between her knees and began moving higher, she couldn't bear any more.

"Stop!" she shrieked, while kicking and squirming, no longer willing to take what she knew she deserved, not if Malik would see it aroused her.

"Dani, stop this, now," he said sternly, "before you get hurt."

"Like you care. You're spanking me, remember? Isn't that your intent?"

He shifted her again, dropping one of his legs over both of her own to keep her still.

"My intent is you learn to never do something so foolish again. My intent is also for you do what you're told. Now stop this nonsense. You have ten more swats, afterward, we'll talk."

"No. I won't stop. I hate this, and I hate you, and I hate this fucking ship."

"What in the name of the Creators is going on in here? I could hear the commotion above. I said spank her, man, not kill her."

*Great, now Jaylin is here to witness my shame.*

"I was going easy, I swear. Out of nowhere, she went wild. I've never had a woman react this way before."

"Let me up," she demanded, while pounding her fist against his leg. "I said, let… me… up!"

His hands fell away, while others slid under her arms and pulled her upright. Before she could blink, she stood on her feet, her hair in disarray over her face. She tossed her head, sending it flying then all she could see was Jaylin's shocked expression.

"What's come over you?"

"He was spanking me, that's what."

"I know, I told him to, but I've never heard such carrying on from a few little swats."

"Little swats! Obviously, you've never been spanked by a cyborg.

"This is really starting to get old," Malik grumbled behind her.

Jaylin spun her around and bent her over his arm. "Baby, you're barely pink."

"I told you I was going easy. She acts like I took a strap to her."

His big hand stroked over her tingling skin, like Malik had. Moisture flooded her pussy, so much a little trickle meandered down to her thigh. She clamped her legs together again.

Neither man had noticed yet. When they did, she'd have no choice except to launch herself into space down the refuse chute. No way could she spend the coming days with them knowing she became aroused by having her bottom bared and smacked.

Jaylin picked her up and sat beside Malik on the bed, with her perched upright on his thighs instead of over them. She squinched her eyes shut. It was only a matter of time before her wetness transferred to his trousers, and her embarrassment would be complete.

She tried to remember if she'd seen the trash receptacle. It had to be in the galley, or close by. Maybe she'd use the air lock in the cargo hold and eject herself into the nothingness of space, it couldn't be worse than this.

A tear escaped and rolled down her face. Great. Now they'd see she was also a big cry baby. Would her humiliation never cease?

Tenderly, one of them wiped the wetness from her cheek, and a warm hand brushed back her hair. She didn't dare look to see which of them—or if both—were responsible for the comforting touches, she couldn't.

"Dani, sweetness, are you really in such discomfort?"

"I've never hurt a woman, Jaylin. You know that."

She couldn't let him go on thinking he'd done her harm. She shook her head, still not looking at either one of them. "It wasn't you, Malik. I mean it stung, but more so my pride than my bottom."

The bed shifted, as did she, and she found herself in Malik's arms which held her tight against his chest. "Then what happened?" His hand stroked up from her knee to her hip, the gentle touch so close to where she ached it made her need burn stronger.

"Uh, Mal. I think I know."

She cracked an eyelid and, as she feared, Jaylin stared at the wet spot on his buff-colored pants where she had been sitting.

With another mortified whimper, she tried to sprint from Malik's arms, but he anticipated it and held her fast. "Becoming aroused by a spanking is nothing to be ashamed of. Many women react the same way."

Unable to run, she decided to hide, burying her face against his chest. "Can we not talk about this, please? As in ever, again?"

"I'm sure Malik can tell you the physiological response behind it." Jaylin went right on dissecting things as if she hadn't said a word. "Proximity to a lot of other nerve endings, and then there's the carnality of it all, and, to some, being dominated, stripped naked, and made to submit is very arousing."

"Not the technical terms I would have used, but he's right, Dani."

"I find it hot."

Hearing the grin in his voice, she peeped at him with one eye, the other and most of her face still hidden against Malik. "What?"

"You're drenched, Dani. Your bottom is pink, not to mention bare." He inhaled. "And you smell fucking fantastic."

"I thought you were furious with me for damaging your ship."

His face went taut, and she regretted bringing it up, since he had appeared to have mellowed with all the sex talk. "You made a damn mess, that's true. But I put out the fire before any of the vital parts went up in flames. I replaced a few components, and we're back online. I have a few more tweaks to do, and there is the orange residue on everything to deal with." His head tilted as he contemplated her. "You, sweet Dani, have a mop and bucket in your future."

She sat up, feeling a glimmer of hope well up in her chest. "Can I swab the deck instead of taking the other swats?"

"Absolutely not."

She scowled at him, feeling her lower lip curl down and stick out. He leaned in and kissed her. "Finish up, Malik. When you're done, send her on up with the mop." Once he stood, he looked down at her, his thumb gliding over her pouting lips. "Afterward, we'll take care of your wet spot."

Her jaw dropped open and a soft gasp escaped.

He didn't say more, only winked at her, before striding out the door. After she stared long and hard at where she'd last seen him, she turned and asked Malik, "Any chance we can pretend you gave me the rest?"

"No." His answer came with a tilt to the corners of his mouth.

"You two are cut from the same cloth."

He choked on a laugh, which surprised her.

"What's funny?"

"You'll find out soon enough." He firmly guided her back over his knee and without further delay, delivered the last ten swats. His broad hand and rapid pace reheated her skin, and the sting resurged as though she hadn't had a reprieve at all. It only took four smacks before she pleaded for forgiveness, and by the time he stopped, she'd promised to never set foot on the bridge again.

When he set her on her feet, he helped set her clothes to rights, including pulling up her tights. The heat coming off her singed behind got trapped in the clingy fabric making the discomfort worse. She rubbed, except it was tender and only made it hotter.

She didn't suppose she could go around with her bright-red, steaming butt taking the air, and she certainly didn't plan to ask. He didn't give her time to anyhow because he took her hand and led the way to the storage area where they kept the cleaning supplies.

"You'll have to make at least one more appearance on the bridge, sweetheart, in a command performance by the captain."

"It just keeps getting better," she muttered.

Then, with a bucket in one hand, and an old-fashioned rag mop in the other, he put her on the lift with a light pat on the ass. When she twisted, and looked back, she was stunned to see the twitch of his lips and the amused glint in his amazing eyes. Both remained in place as he watched her ascend to face the rest of her penance up top.

# Chapter Nine

By the time she mopped the orange fire suppressant agent from every nook and cranny of the bridge, Dani swayed from exhaustion. So much, she almost dozed off while standing, both hands curled over the top of the handle of her mop, her cheek propped against them.

"Daniella."

Though he spoke softly, she jumped, her head swinging around to find him. He smiled at her from where he lay flat on his back under the command console, tools in hand.

"It's time for you to go to bed," Jaylin announced. "You're dead on your feet."

He did an ab curl, and hopped up as if he hadn't been working for hours fixing the mess she'd made. Guilt, though she had done none of it on purpose, had been a near constant companion since the alarms had gone off.

"What about you? Aren't you tired?"

"I've got three more parts to replace then I'm for bed, too." He took the mop from her hand, set it aside, and taking her by the shoulders, aimed her toward the lift.

She glanced back at him. "I'm sorry. I didn't mean to change course, really."

"Yet you thought about it."

"Thinking something isn't a crime! Your controls are too sensitive. I swear I didn't hit the engage button." She bit her lip. "At least I don't think I did."

"Baby…"

Her heart skipped a beat. Was that amusement interlaced in his long-suffering tone. Noting the softer, more open expression on his face, she welcomed the return of the kinder, gentler version of Jaylin. He'd blown up, justifiably so, because she'd put them all at risk. He didn't appear to be holding onto his anger, as Malik had predicted. She conceded her fault. "I should have come and gotten you first thing, it was crazy not to."

"Not so much crazy as desperate. But we'll soon be good as new, your bottom paid for your crime, and, with a middle-of-the-night cleaning session, you fulfilled your sentence. Time to put this in the past and move forward."

"Okay," she said around a yawn so it came out unintelligible.

He grinned. "Get to bed, Dani."

Jaylin moved her along with a pat on her behind, just like Malik. This earned him a confused look, which he didn't respond to. What he did was stand watching her go with his hands on his hips, looking gorgeous despite working hard beside her the entire time. She entered the lift and disappeared below the floor, the whole time pondering how similar, yet different the two men were—near identical muscle twitches when angry, same pat on the behind. Chalking it up to a cyborg's ability to learn and mimic behaviors, she slogged to her quarters, pausing long enough to kick off her shoes before she flopped on the bed and was out cold.

Sometime later, she woke briefly when Jaylin stretched out behind her.

"Go back to sleep," he murmured as his arms came around her and he pulled her body into the curve of his.

It felt too nice to protest. She snuggled into him thinking tomorrow would be soon enough to hammer out their other differences. Then, she drifted off again.

\*\*\*

Dani's breath rushing warm across his chest brought him slowly awake. Before he opened his eyes, he savored the feel of her body resting snug against his side, her cheek pillowed on his right pec, one leg tangled between his own. An awesome start to the morning. The way to top it, seeing her smile. Better yet, with a kiss.

As the events of the day before came flooding back, he didn't think he'd get either any time soon. He'd been harsh with her and let his temper flare—a flaw Malik had harped on since they were children—but his mind had been preoccupied with keeping them safe from their unidentified pursuers. Her indifference after what they had shared and her callous talk about a future without him sparked his anger. It had cooled by the time he evaded the ship.

When he came to her bed, much later, she'd been asleep. Unable to resist slipping in beside her and holding her as he did now, he'd fallen asleep, intent on making it up to her when they awakened. Those intentions had gone up in smoke, quite literally, when he found his bridge in flames. He'd been enraged, rightly so, and didn't regret the punishment he'd ordered.

As he worked to correct the damage she had wrought, knowing his brother was punishing her below, his ire had abated. And his mind had settled on a new course for the next ten, now nine, days. He'd give her the protection she requested, keeping her safe from her father's reach, and during that time, he'd tie her so irrevocably to him and Malik, when she came of age in less than two weeks, she wouldn't be able to imagine a future without them.

The same went for his brother.

He knew how his mind worked, and what he liked. They might look different, but they shared many other traits. Malik wouldn't be able to resist Dani's allure any more than he could.

Throwing them into intimate situations like with the spanking, where he had to touch her silken skin, smell her sweet scent, and see how beautifully she responded, would have his twin hooked. He, like Dani, would realize how much they belonged together, and if he couldn't make this happen, he wasn't the dominant first he thought he was.

A sigh from her lips preceded her stirring beside him. He rolled to his side, pulling her flush against him, front to front. Hard and aching for her, his length nudged into her soft belly. Her head tipped back, face soft and still drowsy from sleep, but coming quickly awake. She stiffened before she could blink, and her hands slid up his chest to push against him.

Yes, repairing the damage to her would require more work than the Renegade.

"Good morning," he murmured, ignoring her resistance.

"You're in my bed," she grumbled, "so it's not starting out good at all."

"I see you're still angry."

"You yelled at me!"

"I have a temper and it tends to flare when I find my ship going up in flames."

"And, you ordered Malik to spank me."

"Something I won't hesitate to repeat if you do anything as reckless again."

She scowled at him, then averted her gaze.

"You've taken your punishment and are forgiven, Dani. Can you do the same for me?"

"No."

"Baby…"

"You hurt my feelings."

"I know, sweetness. My bark is sharp when I'm angry."

"So Malik says."

"And he would know. I'm trained by the military, used to commanding soldiers whose jobs are to take orders. That's not who you are. I promise to temper my responses with you in the future."

"No more spankings?"

"I didn't say that."

Her frown intensified, looking so disgruntled he couldn't keep a grin a bay.

"What do you say, Dani? Am I forgiven?"

When her eyes lost their angry glint and her mouth softened, he thought she would relent, but her next accusation revealed the wide chasm remaining between them.

"You intend to take me to Earth, back to my father."

"I've reconsidered."

She reacted with a slow blink. "You have? You'll accept my offer?"

"We'll keep you safe until you turn twenty-five."

Her face transformed, relief replacing the wariness, and she whispered, "Thank you." Her hand came to his face. "You don't know how glad I am to hear that."

"Your plans for afterward we will need to discuss."

"What?"

"That's for later," he whispered, lowering his head for a kiss. There were no more questions, at least none she could verbalize with his tongue tangling with her own. He rolled her onto her back and pressed her into the mattress, his knee insinuating itself between her thighs. When he propped on an elbow, ready to rid her of the tunic that was blocking access to the rest of her, she laid her hand on his chest.

"Jaylin, maybe this isn't a good idea."

He stared down at her in challenge. "You don't want me anymore?"

Her lips parted, as though she would disavow the strong attraction between them. He wouldn't allow it, moving his leg higher between her own, until his thigh rubbed against her center.

With his mouth almost touching hers, he dared her further. "You can't deny your body's response any more than I can, Dani." And he didn't give her the chance to, claiming her with a feverish kiss as he shifted over top of her, and he pressed the hard proof of how much he wanted her between her parted thighs.

Her fingers drove into his hair, as she kissed him back, her hips moving against him.

He wanted to shout in triumph, but it wasn't enough. He wanted her bare, to feel her smooth, silky soft skin everywhere. Her clothes disappeared beneath his hands, both her tunic and tights.

"You're good at that," she whispered as the material cleared her head.

"Easy off, why do you think I suggested it the first day?"

She stilled, her eyes wide with shock. "You didn't."

"Of course, I did. I wanted you from the moment I saw you."

Not giving her time to say more, he took her mouth again, while his fingers rolled and tweaked one hard nipple. His thigh pressed hers further apart, using his trousers to abrade, letting the friction build her need.

"It feels naughty being naked with you still fully clothed," she rasped, when his lips grazed her cheek and slid down her throat. Her hands moved to his back and tugged on his shirt until she could run her fingers down his spine.

Wanting more of her touch, he rose above her and stripped it off. As he did, he caught sight of Malik in the hallway, his scrutiny on them, though mainly Dani. He tipped his chin in invitation, although he hadn't broached it with her yet. He saw his brother's face tighten as he shook his head.

Inside, his frustration twisted in his gut, though outwardly he shrugged. Still early, he had time to put his plan into action. Let him watch, see Dani's beauty and how readily she responded to his touch.

When his hunger increased, and his longing for the woman his first had chosen, he'd come around — he felt sure of it. Shucking his trousers quickly, he returned to Dani and covered her again, but a better idea on how to hurry things along, occurred to him. He slipped behind her giving Malik an unobstructed view of her breasts, her slightly rounded belly, smooth mound, and sleek thighs.

His hands acted as a guide for his brother's eyes as he played with her body. First, coming up to her breasts where he teased both rosy nipples until they were hard points then, moving slowly down her belly, not stopping until they framed her sex. He draped her top leg over his hip before sliding his fingers into her wetness. Spreading her open with his thumbs, he let his index finger run over the slick pearl he'd exposed.

He heard an indrawn breath from the doorway at the same time Dani gasped, her stunned gaze fixed on the man standing there, watching.

"Do you mind, sweetness?"

"What, him watching us?" her voice quivered with shock, and what he knew was excitement.

"Yes, or we could invite him in."

At his suggestion, a small squeak escaped her throat, which he couldn't quite read, although it was not a denial. He swept his tongue along her neck and over her pulse point, pleased to find it thrumming rapidly.

"I don't understand. You mean you want him to join us? In bed?" Her voice became breathless on the last word.

"I know you fantasize about being with two men, Dani."

Her head twisted, and she gaped at him. "How could you know?"

"The immersion reality device stores your fantasies for replay, unless you erase them." While he explained, his lips slid across her shoulder, pressing a trail of kisses as he went.

"You could have mentioned this little feature before." She squirmed, attempting to sit up. Jaylin had other ideas. The hand at her breast slipped down to her waist, holding her firmly, while the other hand continued to play between her thighs.

"What arouses you is nothing to be embarrassed about. And your fantasy is a commonplace practice where I come from. So why not have Malik join us?"

"But, and I mean this as no offense, he's a cyborg."

A clicking noise from his twin's direction drew both their gazes. Dani appeared puzzled; he recognized the sound of Malik's teeth snapping together to contain his irritation. He waited to see if his annoyed brother would correct her. He didn't, for some reason not yet ready to abandon the pretense. He'd give him that play, and use it to his advantage.

"Many worlds create cyborgs solely for sex."

"Really? Are they, um, fully functional? I mean can they, um, you know…"

"Yes, everything works like any other man," he said with a grin. "Better, in fact. Their stamina alone can make a woman beg for mercy."

Her mouth formed a little circle of wonder as she looked back at Malik. "I'd never imagined such a thing."

From the corner of his eyes, he saw Malik cross his arms over his chest and send a dark glower his way. He ignored him, saying to Dani, "You've seen little of the universe, haven't you?"

"Elzor was my first trip."

His head came up, eyeing her, an innocent in many ways. This pleased him. "There is much you have to learn. Malik is well versed in the arts of pleasure. Let us teach you the joys of being with two." He bent his head, caught her earlobe with a little nip before he spurred her fantasy onward. "Imagine four arms holding you tight, twenty fingers gliding over your skin, and two cocks filling you and making you cry out with passion. All this from two men with one goal, to bring you to the height of pleasure."

She glanced between them. "I don't know…" she hedged, fixating on Malik who stood statue still.

"Fear not, Dani, I didn't come to join you. I heard a noise and came to investigate."

Jaylin chuckled as Dani's blush stained her cheeks.

"I, uh, didn't. That's to say… I wasn't referring to you."

Malik's clumsy stammer amused him more.

"You are not the least bit humorous, Captain. And, although I appreciate the invitation, I shall have to decline." Then, with a tight-lipped look on his face, he left.

When she glanced back at him, he tried to smother his grin, but he wasn't successful.

She arched a perfect red brow when she asked, "Do you usually, um, share, well…sex, with your cyborg?"

His gaze snapped to hers, searching and finding what he suspected, pupils dilated and her face flushed a rosy pink. She would have agreed if Malik hadn't skittered away. This was a good sign. And with the subject broached, he'd keep trying, damned if he wouldn't.

"I've been known to," he said at length.

When Dani licked her lips, his humor fled, and his thoughts turned carnal. He rolled them until she lay on her back. "Never mind him," he murmured against her throat as his cock found the warm wet cradle between her thighs. "Where were we?"

He shifted, pushing her legs wider and plunged into her with a swift, sure upstroke. She moaned, encircling his hips with her legs, the open position allowing him to sink deeper.

"Yeah," he whispered, moving up to catch her groans with a kiss. "This is how I remember it, too."

# Chapter Ten

Over the next few days, Jaylin implemented his plan, playing with Dani's curvaceous body, and with Malik's head. It wasn't a hardship for him by any means, touching her often, and making a point to do so in front of Malik whenever possible. He held her cuddled in his lap at nearly every meal, joined her in her bed, insisting they sleep skin to skin, and he made love to her with the door open.

All of this put his brother in a foul mood. Unquenched desire, or what they called blue balls both on Trilor and on Earth, easily doing that to a man.

With Dani, he kept laying the groundwork for establishing a future together. When he wasn't taking his fill of her gorgeous body, or bringing her to heights of passion with his own, they talked. Of her hopes, dreams, and he learned of the harshness of her childhood, something harder for her to tell.

Her father was a cruel bastard — not physically so, but she spoke of growing up isolated, surrounded by servants, with few friends, and without love, something unheard of for a Trilorian child who had three doting parents.

It would be impossible to erase her past, but he and Malik would shower her with more affection than she'd ever imagined, if he could only get through to his stubborn twin.

His strategy seemed to be working, Malik's frustration mounting and his unchecked desire growing by the day. He thought he would cave the night before when he came up to relieve him on the bridge. He'd brought Dani with him to keep him company, while he monitored the systems, scanned for nearby ships, and made several planned course changes ensuring anyone out there was kept guessing. Otherwise, there wasn't much else to be done, space flight exceedingly dull for the most part. Dani made it anything but boring on this trip, however.

After he programmed in another set of coordinates, the last scheduled in his shift, he pulled her into his lap for more kisses and cuddles. Things quickly got heated. With her shyness ebbing as she grew more comfortable with him and with sex, her touches became bolder, even daring. Jaylin didn't discourage her when she opened his pants and began to explore. Soon, she took a position between his spread thighs and swapped out stroking fingers for tentative licks with her tongue.

What she lacked in experience, she more than made up for with enthusiasm. Her small, soft hands and pretty, pink lips wrapped around his cock as she learned a new way to bring him pleasure, nearly made him end their spontaneous session long before either of them wanted to. Her innocent exploration had him so enthralled he lost track of time and didn't immediately notice Malik's presence.

He found him staring at Dani, his twin's eyes locked on her mouth working him. After taking it in for a while, his gaze moved, traveling down to her round bottom clad in form-fitting tights. During their cuddling, Jaylin's hands had gravitated to her curvy hips, his fingers slipping beneath the long hem of her tunic. It had migrated to her waist and remained there, bunched up. Now, with her backside pointing outward, covered by nothing more than clingy thin fabric, Malik couldn't keep his eyes off it.

Jaylin divided his attention between Dani's warm, wet, agile tongue and watching his brother, noting the tension in his body, how he shifted restlessly, his hand at his groin, adjusting the ache of his constrained cock. He wondered what his breaking point would be.

Malik swallowed, the muscles in his throat noticeably tense as he dragged his focus away from Dani. Then, without a word, he shot Jaylin an angry glare and whirled, ready to storm out, except the mental message his twin sent halted him mid-stride.

*Her mouth is divine, so is sinking into her tight, unbelievably wet pussy. But she's more than a beautiful woman and a mind-blowing fuck. She's gentle-natured, giving, witty, cute as can be, and as eager to be loved as she is to give love in return. Though she's shy, she's responsive, and her fantasy – you saw it – is to be with us. Dani is our perfect third, Malik. Stop denying what is in front of your face.*

He didn't respond, instead, moving stiffly and silently to the ladder.

*Don't be a damn stubborn fool,* Jaylin called after him. *She'll heal your shattered heart, brother, and burrow under your skin. Mark my words, because already, she's worked both of those miracles on me.*

\*\*\*

The next morning, Jaylin stepped up his game.

Knowing his twin was a creature of habit, he woke Dani early and had teased her to a heightened state of arousal when it was time for Malik to leave his room for the kitchen to start breakfast.

His door stood crossways from the guest quarters, and if he glanced left when he exited, he'd have a direct view of where he sat naked on the edge of the bed with Dani sprawled in his lap. When he heard the swish of the door, Jaylin tugged on a taut nipple and slid two fingers into her silken heat. She moaned, as he knew she would, and Malik's attention was caught. His eyes zoned in on his hands, holding beauty in his palms. The timing couldn't have been better. He had her back to his front, her head resting against his shoulder, glorious mane of hair streaming across his chest, and thighs spread wide as they draped over his own.

*Look at her, brother, what do you see?* He projected his question into Malik's head.

*Pink lips, fair skin, fiery-red hair, and a stunning round, curvy figure.*

Surprised he'd responded after not speaking to him even through their link since the day before, Jaylin couldn't miss the glazed-over look on his face, like someone hypnotized or inebriated. Indeed, a man could easily get drunk on Dani, and that's what he hoped would happen to his twin very soon.

*Yes, and what do you feel when you take in the beauty before you?*

Malik shook his head, though he didn't look away or leave.

Jaylin pushed him further. *I'll tell you, you feel alive. Looking at her makes your heart beat faster. Your blood heats, expands, and races through your veins, thawing what has been frozen. The breath of desire stirs within your chest, and your cock, asleep these past five years surges back to life.*

*No.*

*Yes!* he shot back. *I know this because I feel it, too, every time I look at her, more so when I touch her.*

*I feel nothing.* From the obvious hard-on tenting the front of his pants, his denial was unconvincing.

*Liar.* His response ricocheted in his head like a shot. Malik flinched, hearing it, too. Dani shifted restlessly, although her response he suspected was caused by his hands playing over her. *I heard every thought, felt every feeling you denied. She's the one, brother, trust me on this.*

*Mahlia…*

*Is gone. I miss her, too, but I swear, she wouldn't have wanted this isolated, lonely existence for you. She'd want you to be happy, and to move on, with me, to have the family we are destined to build with Dani.*

Almost as if she knew they were mind-speaking about her, Dani whimpered, her body trembling against his. When he looked at her, she was watching the man at the door.

"Malik," she whispered. "What is it? You seem…tormented." Concern made her voice husky as much as her desire.

Jaylin's gaze traveled back to his brother, and sensing he teetered on the edge of indecision, he nudged him hard, hoping he'd fall on the side where he and Dani waited.

"He wants you, baby. And not being able to have you when you are so near *is* torment."

She sat up, her head coming off his shoulder. The movement rubbed her soft bottom over his own hard, aching flesh, and he fought to contain a groan when it nestled between her thighs. Malik, who hadn't taken his eyes off her, noticed, lost his own struggle, and let out the agonized sound for him.

"Is it true?" she asked in a quiet voice. "You want me?"

"Yes." His one word reply came out raw, intense.

Still uncertain, she glanced at Jaylin, who nodded. "It's okay, Dani. We are Trilorian. This is our way, but you must ask him to join us. It has to be what you want, above all else."

Her head swung back, tilting to the side as she considered what to do next. With his cock wedged between, he felt the heat and wetness bathing her thighs, and knew her answer before she did. When Dani extended her hand to Malik, knowing his twin's long self-denial neared an end, he almost came. His brother didn't know the control he was exerting on his behalf.

But this pivotal moment, which he felt in his gut would be a turning point took priority. "You saw, as Jaylin did, my secret desire for you both." Dani spoke softly, her flushed cheeks stained crimson with her admission, but it didn't stop her. "You don't have to wait any longer, Malik."

He staggered forward a step as if unable to keep from it.

"Brave girl," Jaylin groaned, his hand leaving her breast to bury in her hair. Tugging her head back, his mouth slid along the arching length of her throat. "And so fucking sweet," he added with a growl.

Malik did as well, the sound of his surrender rumbling in his chest. In a few long strides, he stood before them.

"Taste her," he urged. "When you do, you'll understand what I'm telling you is true." He hesitated, and Jaylin had had enough. "On your knees, now."

He heard the hitch in Dani's indrawn breath as Malik obeyed, and sank to the floor. Once there, his hungry gaze swept from her face, down her quivering breasts and belly, to her smooth, creamy thighs, which Jaylin spread so he could see her glistening clit and drenched entrance.

"Kiss her," he ordered next, but his dark head was already descending.

\*\*\*

Malik's mouth covering hers wasn't the soft, slow exploration she'd expected, rather a fiery possession filled with impatience. His tongue traced the seam of her lips until they opened, then swept inside, sending shivery spirals of desire racing through her body. It was enough to make her heart flip-flop and send every thought except "more" skittering out of her head. Add to the mix Jaylin's hot tongue sliding up the side of her neck, while his hands glided over her thighs, stroked her hips, and moved up to her breasts to tease her nipples to aching hardness. As the myriad sensations set off a chain reaction of pleasure, Dani closed her eyes and surrendered to the sensory overload.

Desiring two men at once and letting them do these wicked things to her body was something she'd never dreamed would come true. And never did she believe she'd be so bold to ask for it. But with Jaylin's encouragement, his easy acceptance of this as natural, and something he strongly desired, too, and the need gleaming in Malik's golden gaze, she'd gone for it. And why the hell not? She only had a few more days before this idyllic escapade alone in space with two seriously hot men ended. And once back on Earth, she didn't know what would happen.

She put everything from her mind as Malik raised his head and stared down at her. Dark, to Jaylin's light, he was equally beautiful. Her tongue flicked out to catch the taste of him which still lingered. His gaze followed her movements, and with the ice broken, and no longer needing his captain's commands to continue, he took control of the kiss, his tongue delving hungrily inside. Just as quickly it was gone, as he moved down her throat and beyond to her chest. He veered to the side, claiming a breast which Jaylin held in offering.

She cried out when he latched on to the crest, the incredible heat of his tongue lashing from inside while he sucked hard. Through half-open lids, she watched his dark head shift to the other breast, treating it to the same swirling suction.

Cool air claimed both sensitized peaks when his insistent mouth went away, on the move again, going lower. A riot of sensations swept over her all at once, her wet nipples tightened further, almost hurting, and the muscles in her belly rippled as his lips traversed it, opened on her navel, hot tongue circling briefly, then licked over the slight roundness of her tummy. When he reached his goal, he knelt between her legs almost reverently, the slightly rough rasp on his jaw abrading her tender skin sending drenching heat coursing to her center. Hands, four at once, moved over her, capturing her breasts, plucking at the hard peaks, curving around her inner thighs, and parting them.

Malik's words fanned over heated skin, as he breathed out, "She's soaked, Jay."

"I know," he growled. "I'm surrounded by her scent, and it's all I can do not to toss her on the bed, spread her wide, and devour every creamy, delicious inch of her."

"Sorry, but you'll have to remove me bodily from this spot first," he countered.

Before she could think, which was near impossible with these two big, powerful men focused on her, large hands at the back of both knees lifted her legs. She glanced down and saw golden eyes, molten with desire had homed in on her splayed sex. It was Malik's hands holding her legs apart, the same ones who now draped them one at a time over his broad shoulders. With his mouth so near her center, his hot breath drifted over her even hotter flesh, and she trembled in anticipation of his next move.

"Stop!" came the growled command by her ear.

Malik's face tipped up, his gaze travelling up her body to fixate over her shoulder. Following where he looked, Dani twisted her head until her eyes collided with Jaylin's. He stared back at her as his hand slid down her front, two fingers sliding through her soaked slit to her entrance, and glided inside her.

On a quick rush of indrawn air, she somehow stifled the groan of pleasure his possessive motion aroused in her. It was as though he—no, they—had every right to play, command, and dominate her body. This notion roused her most of all. She'd asked for this two-on-one, and her willingness gave them rights they were ready to claim, both, at once. Her heart pounded and her back arched within their hold, ready for them to get on with it.

The fingers stretching and filling her stroked once, twice, pumped for a third time then left her. Her cry of disappointment was replaced by one of shock, as Jaylin's fingertips, glistening wet with the proof of her desire rose to her mouth. Next, in a move so erotic she almost came on the spot, he ran the wet tips over her lips, painting them with her taste and scent.

He growled again, still scary, but not from dominant orders, rather, because the hungry look on his face said he intended to feast on her whole. Except he didn't, not yet, instead saying to Malik, who watched with fervent desire on his face, "Your first taste of her we'll savor together."

Her heart pounded from the overpowering intensity of the moment, and, from the periphery of her vision, she saw Malik smile. His hands slid around her thighs, holding her in place as he bent toward her. Dani watched, unable to look away as his mouth opened over her achy, needful, pink flesh. She would have cried out the moment his tongue licked her clit, or when he began feasting hungrily if Jaylin hadn't curled his hand beneath her chin and raised her face to indulge in a simultaneous searing kiss.

Her mind reeled, shocked by the taboo nature of two men making love to her at once. At the same time, her body screamed it was so very right—especially, when she went soaring at light speed toward a nerve-shattering climax.

\*\*\*

Never had Malik had such sweetness. He wanted to gorge himself on her nectar until sated but also to slide his straining cock between her plump lips, and while her tongue licked and teased, spend himself down her throat. It had been so long, and Dani an exquisite temptation.

As usual, Jaylin, directed where they went next. *We'll come together. Stand up.*

Malik rose without needing to be told twice, ripping open his trousers.

"Take him into your lovely mouth, *pershada*," Jaylin urged as he lifted her by the waist.

Dazed with pleasure, she obeyed. Leaning forward, her tongue slipped out, wetting her already-glistening lips in invitation. Trembling with need, Malik guided himself into position while his twin took his place at the entrance between her thighs. Their eyes met, and as one, they joined with her.

He took care, which after so long shouldn't have been possible. In consideration of her newness to all of this, he exerted the utmost control when he slid inside. Dani wouldn't have slow, however, and sucked him deep, enveloping nearly half of his length as she eagerly closed around him.

When she eased back, circled the head slowly with the tip of her tongue without losing him then engulfed him again, drawing him in further, his body shook violently. But it was more than a physical response—although it was intense—this went beyond carnal. A calm settled over him, the same as he'd felt whenever he returned to Trilor, a sense of coming home. Despite his body's yearning to plunge into her again and again until he came, this calmness, and rightness, was something he wanted to make last. His gaze fell to the lips around his cock, the lovely face angled to his, seeing trust there, and an overt desire to please him.

He hadn't felt this way since…

*Heavenly Creators, it's true.*

His head came up, and he connected with his brother, who stared intently back at him.

Jaylin smiled. *I told you she was our third.*

A conflagration of mixed-up emotions exploded in his mind, yet his body, too long in need, answered Dani's call. His hands plunged into her hair as he glided farther along on her tongue. Once he saw she could take him, and did so greedily, he gave into his desire and fucked her mouth, at the same time Jaylin took her pussy.

Two masculine groans filled the room, along with Dani's muffled cries. Their first joining, one so incredibly raw and intense, and with Malik too edgy to prolong it in any way, the three of them rose to a fast peak. Once there, they hung on the precipice for one glorious second then, as a triad, they convulsed and came—together.

He shuddered and spilled on Dani's tongue, while she took every drop as her body tensed. Her eyes never left his, but went unfocused, her climax overcoming her. And Jaylin, not to be outdone, surged upward, planting deep, also finding his release.

"Never," he whispered in awe. "Not even..." What he'd done struck him abruptly, and he pulled out, stepping back.

"Don't," Jaylin snapped, his bliss-filled expression of a moment ago, gone, replaced with stern authority and burgeoning anger.

Dani jumped, blinked at him, then glanced over her shoulder, confused. "What's wrong?"

"I'm sorry," Malik murmured.

Her face angled sharply up to his. "Sorry?" she squeaked, growing pale.

He could see her shutting down, stiffening in regret. And by Jaylin's response, his arms tightening protectively around her, he saw it, too.

"Stop being a damned fool," he demanded.

Malik couldn't keep the all-encompassing guilt from claiming him, however. "I must go—"

Jaylin cut him off, his anger booming inside his head. *So help me, if you take another step I will beat you, if only to knock some fucking sense into your head.*

"I don't understand," Dani whispered. "Did I do something wrong?"

"No!" Jaylin uttered harshly. To settle her, his hand came up to her jaw, his thumb stroking her cheek, while his other arm flexed and gripped her tighter.

His brother's harshness wasn't meant for her, but directed at him. Tears of uncertainty pooled in her eyes. When one spilled over, and another, sanity returned.

"No, Dani," he uttered hoarsely, falling to his knees. His hands pushed Jaylin's aside and he cupped her distressed face between his palms. "This took me by surprise, as much as you, and I reacted poorly. You did everything right—so right, sweetheart." He watched the tension ease from her face, then looked up into silver eyes that were rapidly losing their intention for violence. "And Jaylin is correct, as usual. I'd be a damn fool to walk away from both of you."

A series of beeps interrupted what else he may have said.

"Approaching spaceport," the ship's computer announced.

"Damn shitty timing," his captain bit out.

He agreed, but his focus was solely on the woman in front of him. "Forgive me, Dani?"

"You had a mini freak-out," she said with a tremulous smile. "It happens to everyone. There's nothing to forgive."

He glanced as his brother, a brow arched, wordlessly asking him the same.

"You reeled it in. I'm with Dani, nothing to forgive." Silently, Jaylin added, *just don't do it again.*

Malik nodded, and brushed his lips over the twin tracks of her tears, and gently touched his mouth to hers.

"Incoming communication. Requesting identification."

Sighing over yet another interruption, he rested his forehead against hers, but said in a low tone to Jaylin. "Someone should go up top."

"Because we're stopping?" Dani asked.

He sat back, searching her face, relieved to see her distress had been replaced with curiosity. "We have to replenish the backup fuel we used with the cold shields when we evaded the pursuing ship."

"Do they have more than fuel?" she inquired further.

Jaylin chuckled while he lifted her off him, and they all rose to their feet. "Yes, and you're in for a treat if you like to shop. Would you like to get something else to wear?"

"Could I?" She looked between them, her features bright with anticipation.

Although still raw from the experience, Malik got caught up in her excitement and smiled.

"Of course, or I wouldn't have mentioned it." Grinning, Jaylin tapped her on the nose. "Malik will take you."

"What?" The prospect of a shopping expedition with a female who had only a tunic and tights to her name seemed suddenly daunting.

*It's your penance for not listening to me and being a stubborn ass for almost a week,* came Jaylin's response in his mind. He clapped him hard on the shoulder. *How you held out when I caved on day two, I'll never know.*

He sighed. "Get dressed, Dani. I will be honored to spoil you rotten."

She laughed with delight, stood on her toes, and kissed the underside of his chin. Next, she gave Jaylin a hug and a kiss on his jaw. Then she whirled and dashed to the bathroom.

"New clothes!" she exclaimed. "No offense... Your facsimulator may do the job in a pinch, but purple on gray is getting old."

When the door closed behind her, Malik stared at where she had been. Jaylin had moved to pick up his trousers.

"She *is* our third," he murmured, as if he still couldn't believe it.

"Yes, which I told you from day one."

"Don't rub it in."

"I was ready to pummel it in, brother."

He turned. "And don't sound so smug. We have a problem."

"What's that? She's happy. As you should be, after getting some for the first time in five years. You'd have had to lock me up."

"Jay—"

"And I'm damned thrilled I don't have to go shopping." He grinned while buttoning his shirt. "I'll gladly deal with the fuel."

"You're forgetting something."

"What?"

"You've got her convinced I'm a cyborg." His twin's golden skin muted as his head came up. "Yeah, you're in for a freeze out I think. I'll enjoy watching you squirm your way out of this one."

He closed his eyes when he uttered, "Fuck me."

Malik found this ironic and chuckled. "That's what you'll be begging Dani to do when she finds out. While things are frigid in space, a bed with a pissed-off woman can reach absolute zero."

"You're hilarious, Mal. And don't think you're off the hook and will be cozying up while I can't. You did nothing to dispel her misperception."

The truth in his observation sobered him. To get in after so long without, only to be shut down for

Jaylin's stupid slip, the prospect was maddening. "Damn your asinine automaton comment."

"Yeah, but your silences and sour faces did the convincing. Why didn't you explain?"

"I thought it would be easier to keep her at arm's length as a cyborg."

"It seems we both might be frozen out."

Malik's emphatic, "Shit," was uttered right as Dani walked back in.

"What's wrong now?" she asked. "I've never heard you swear before."

"Approaching destination," the computerized voice announced.

"I'll deal with docking the Renegade," Jaylin announced. "You explain."

"The hell I will," he shot back.

"Explain what?" she inquired, looking back and forth between them.

Jaylin spoke over her head, addressing him when he replied, "Then we'll both deal with it later."

Brimming with impatience, Dani demanded to know, "Deal with what?"

His brother shook his head and grabbed her hand. "We don't have time to get into it now. We need to dock." He towed her toward the door. "And while Malik gets dressed and prepares for your shopping spree, you'll come upstairs and strap in, just in case."

"But you'll explain this deal?"

"When you get back."

"Okay," she said more agreeably. "I'll let you work while I stay quiet as a mouse."

"No need, sweetness. This I could do in my sleep."

*You're stalling, brother.* Malik had to broadcast this to his departing back.

*I know.*

*You must tell her,* he insisted.

*I will in the morning.*

*Why morning?*

Jaylin stopped, glancing his way, seeming more determined than concerned over the outcome.

*Because I plan for the three of us to spend tonight in the captain's bed.*

Big enough to accommodate four, Malik had wondered why Jaylin hadn't introduced Dani to it before now. While hers slept two comfortably, in his brother's huge bed, they could spread out, roll around, get adventurous. His body stirred as he imagined the possibilities.

*And that's why I saved it until you got your head out of your ass.*

He glared at his twin.

"Excuse me, but you're doing the thing again," Dani announced. "Is Malik programmed for silent communication mode or something?"

He stiffened, then his head snapped around, and he looked down at her, wanting to shout he wasn't a damn cyborg. Except this was Jaylin's hole to dig out of. He rolled his lips inward to keep silent. Dani's essence still lingered, deliciously sweet, very much like the succulent pershada berries back home. His tension faded away as his twin's unusual nickname for her suddenly made sense.

His cock hardened, ready for more of her, despite having spent himself minutes ago. Malik's thoughts echoed Jaylin's from earlier, although unlike his brother, his were groaned in his head. *Fuck me!*

"Arriving at destination in five minutes," the computer announced. "Incoming communication requesting identification."

"Let's go," Jaylin said while pulling her with him to the door.

"Can 'later' include an explanation of this weird head thing you two have going on 'cause it's freaking me out."

"*Pershada*, what happened to the quiet mouse?"

"We're not on the bridge yet!"

He stopped and curled her into his chest. "Shall I make you hush in another way?"

"Arrival in four minutes. Prepare for impact."

"Impact!" Dani echoed in alarm. "Shouldn't you do something about that? Like now?"

"Yes, except you keep interrupting me."

"Squeak, squeak," she muttered, gesturing as if she'd locked her lips and tossed away the key. It didn't work because she added, "Now, can you stop the Renegade from plowing into the spaceport, please?"

Malik chuckled. As Jaylin had claimed, she was cute as can be.

His brother grinned, too, but did so while crossing to the communication panel on the wall. He opened it, switched on the audio command, and gave his orders. "Slow to impulse speed. Provide ship identification and request docking slip coordinates."

The computer immediately responded. "Initiating slow down. Request for docking coordinates sent."

"You could have told me it was so simple," Dani muttered, her brow wrinkled and her mouth in a pretty pout.

Jaylin bent and caught it in a hard, quick kiss, before he advised, "Or, you could trust your captain to know what he's doing."

"I could, and I do."

His head jerked back in surprise. "Then why are you baiting rather than obeying me?"

She glanced at Malik and winked. "Because baiting you is more fun."

Jaylin's jaw dropped. "You're teasing me, on purpose?"

"Absolutely. Like you do to me."

Watching them and listening to their banter, he smiled. "In you, Dani, our captain may have met his match."

Her soft laughter filled the room. His brother merely grunted as he moved to the door, their adorable redhead following behind because, with her hand in Jaylin's bigger and stronger one, she had no other choice.

"After we dock, I think we'll to discuss your teasing me further, perhaps with you draped over my knee."

"What? Wait?" She dug in her heels, resisting, although not too aggressively. "I thought Malik carried out the discipline."

Jaylin's grin reappeared, wolfish in appearance, his tone husky with intent when he replied, "Who said anything about discipline?"

She blinked in surprise. "But we arrive in three minutes."

"True, it doesn't mean we have to disembark right away."

He watched as she bit her lip, cheeks flushed, eyes bright, clearly torn between two tempting pleasures. Next, she said in the most conflicted voice he'd ever heard, "But, Jaylin, there's shopping to do."

Their third was a delight, and Malik felt more lighthearted than he had in years. He laughed, not just a chuckle, rather, a full-throated, head-tossing, belly laugh that brought tears to his eyes. Jaylin gaped at him, obviously in shock after not hearing the sound from him in years. His dumbfounded expression made him laugh harder, until he bent double.

When this went on for a while, she became concerned. "Is he all right?"

Jaylin, who had recovered by now, gathered her into his arms and hugged her, lifting her off her feet as he buried his face in her hair. When he answered her question several moments later, his voice was gruff with emotion. "He's going to be, Dani. Thanks to you."

# Chapter Eleven

All did not go as expected with the docking. Word had not gotten out the Renegade had been deeded back to the rightful owners, and security had demanded to board as soon as the mooring arms had snapped onto the hull, and the oxygenated hangar had sealed around the airlock. Jaylin, displeased by the questioning and the delays, dealt with the extra paperwork, and subsequent refueling, while Malik escorted Dani into the spaceport and out into the shopping hub.

Dani's shyness had reemerged—never having expected to take on two lovers at once, let alone aliens, and never one who was half man, half machine. Thinking about what she'd done to them, and what Jaylin and Malik had done to her in return made her blush and her heart stutter in rhythm. It also tested her morals forged by years of conservative private tutors and the practically puritanical all-girls college her father had decreed she attend. Not that Daniel Alltryp was the pillar of decency and decorum. Far from it, with a different woman on his arm every time the media photographed him, but he had a different set of standards for his only daughter.

To the world, he seemed doting and concerned; Dani knew better. She put it aside, however, as she took in the spectacle before her.

The spaceport's cavernous central hub consisted of multiple levels, some offered services ranging from a hair salon to a medical clinic, but most were exclusively for shopping. While any woman's nirvana, it was every man's nightmare. Malik, in an easygoing mood for a change, took it all in stride. The reason behind his current disposition not escaping her, it was also the cause of her cheeks heating every time she came close to meeting his eyes.

"You're going to set fire to the oxygen inlets with your blushes," he teased when her gaze darted away from his for the umpteenth time. "You have nothing to be embarrassed about." His hand tipped up her chin, giving her a light, yet tantalizing kiss—their first, if she didn't include the searing kisses he'd laid on her body, or she on his. The memory made her flush even more furiously, and he laughed softly. "More exposure to what we shared will take care of the problem."

"Sounds like a technique I learned in a psychology class."

"You studied psychology?" he asked, while leading her out into the flow of traffic circling the first ring of shops.

"A required class among others intended to make me a well-rounded student. My major, however, was art history."

He nodded, his attention divided between her and the patrons—aliens of every size, color, and skeletal structure, most beyond her wildest imagination. She couldn't keep from eyeing one tall, thin purple creature, who stood taller than Malik. It had large dark eyes, in an oversized head, and not a hair in sight. The oddest thing about her—she couldn't be sure of its gender, female being simply a hunch—was she lacked lips or anything resembling a mouth.

The strangely beautiful creature glanced at the tall man beside her, who nodded as if agreeing to something she'd asked. Before she could inquire about this exchange, Dani heard a soft, feminine voice in her head. "Greetings, Earthling, your mate is very attractive. I applaud your choice."

She stopped dead in her tracks, her jaw slack, staring rudely at the being as she passed. Dani clutched the strong arm she held even tighter. "I think that alien woman just spoke to me without— No, I must be mistaken!"

"You aren't wrong. She is Artruvian; they are telepathic. They used to have mouths, many millennia ago, but preferred not to speak. Evolution took care of it."

"Wow."

"Indeed. Makes me want to use all of my parts so nothing falls off."

She grinned, thrilled by his spark of humor. "Such a cool superpower," she whispered, drawing an odd look from Malik. "Except how do they eat?"

"By osmotic absorption of nutrients. It sounds unpleasant, but they live nearly two hundred years and are the healthiest species I know. They are obviously on the right path. Me, I'd miss chewing, and the flavor of foods. Like a grilled steak, or the delicious milk chocolate produced on your planet."

"No chocolate!" she gasped. "Why, that's a crime against nature."

His grin transformed his handsome face to gorgeous. "I couldn't agree more."

She twisted, looking after the creature while repeating "Wow!" still incredulous. When she did, she learned the Artruvian wasn't the oddest alien in the vicinity, case in point the green lizard-like creature with antennae who passed.

"You're staring, sweetheart." Malik put a finger beneath her chin and closed her mouth for her. When he took it away, it gaped right back open. She couldn't help it.

He shook his head, though his golden eyes gleamed with amusement. "There is a shop with Earth clothing on the other side of the pod. Let's go there before you insult someone with your gawking."

She followed where he led, glancing over her shoulder for one more look at the strange lizard man, a being straight out of sci-fi books from her youth.

"So, Dani," Malik said, also squeezing her fingers to capture her attention. "The study of ancient works—paintings and sculptures, and such—was it your calling?"

"Hardly," she said with a huff. "I wanted to go into medicine."

Surprise registered on his face before he asked, "Why didn't you?"

"Becoming a physician wasn't on the Daniel Alltryp approved list of careers for a mere woman."

His dark brows snapped together in an infuriated frown. "Your father is a real piece of work."

Her head tilted his way, eyes big, then she laughed.

"What's funny?"

"The way you and Jaylin toss around Earth slang, curses, and phrases, I forget you're from another world, sometimes."

"We have worked closely with your kind for years. I suppose we've picked up a saying here and there."

"By osmotic absorption?" she asked.

His expression softened as he grinned, his handsome face becoming more so when he smiled.

"You need to do more of that."

"What? Learn more Earth phrases?"

"No, smile."

Pausing at the door to the shop, he clasped her hand more firmly. "With you around, I believe I'll have reason to."

Her heart melted, and she marveled over having such strong feelings for a man, who really wasn't.

"Come on," he said. "We need to get a move on. Jaylin doesn't like to be kept waiting."

"And we wouldn't want to upset the big, bad alpha captain."

"You're learning," he observed, with some amusement. "Although most often his bark is much worse than his bite—which is another Earth expression, I know. Jaylin can be intense, but has reason to be while on a mission. He'll do whatever is in his power to keep you safe." His suddenly serious gaze caught and held hers. "As will I, Dani. Don't think because I'm a second, I won't bark like the captain when the situation warrants. And, you learned firsthand, I can also bite. Now, let's hurry and buy what you need. After this, we'll need to restock our fresh food and get a few other provisions."

Malik stood guard while she made her selections. The store, she was pleased to see, had a little of everything. She picked out two tops, a pair of loose-fitting wide-leg pants—which were a new style back on Earth—a comfortable dress, and even found a pair of vintage Levi's, something she practically lived in while in college. Also available necessities like makeup, a hairbrush, and hair bands. When she came to the lingerie section and was sorting through a table of bras with matching panties, Malik pulled the pretty pink satin-and-lace pair from her fingers and tossed them back on the table.

"Hey!"

"You won't be needing those, and we need to get back."

"But I don't have any underwear. Can the facsimulator make me some? Is that what you mean?"

"No, Jaylin doesn't like them. He would just throw them down the expulsion chute."

"You're joking."

"Have you met Jaylin Sin-Naysir?" He chuckled when she rolled her eyes. "The dress, he'll love. The pants, not so much, but he'll tolerate them. Panties blocking his way when his mind is set on something else? No."

"Has he ever read Earth history? If not, he needs to learn what happened to cavemen. They became extinct a few million years ago."

Malik added a grin to his chuckle. "I'll let you educate him all about that, sweetheart."

"What do you prefer?"

He tugged her close, his voice dipping low as he answered, "I like bare, but we can work you up to it."

Her mouth dropped open, and his laughter turned heads.

Still grinning, he led her—speechless, her body humming with sudden arousal—to the console where he paid with a thumb scan on a touch screen. After the green light appeared, indicating the purchase had been approved, he gathered her bags in one of his big hands, and caught her much smaller one in the other. Then, he guided her out into the crowded pod.

He paused, looking left before he turned right. "I think the food market is on the next level up."

Someone bumped into her, and, before Dani realized what happened, Malik crumpled to the floor with a thud. She stared at him a fraction of a second before she bent to see what was wrong. A sharp pain stabbed her neck and stopped her midway. Malik's prone form wavered in front of her eyes. Everything started spinning and she started to fall, except something hard caught her around the waist.

"Nighty-night, little princess," a male voice uttered low. "Next stop, home to Daddy."

\*\*\*

Fifteen more minutes.

Leaning against the cargo bay doors, Jaylin watched the gauge tick upward. The primary fuel cells on the Renegade were uradion-based, a radioactive material found on only four of the thirty-seven alliance planets. Easily mined and requiring only a small amount to power the engines in his medium-sized cruiser, it meant it was also cheap, considering it had a half-life of at least one thousand years and wouldn't have to be replaced in ten times his lifetime. All combined, it had become the most relied-upon energy source for space travel.

Unfortunately, the fuel cells weren't all they required. The spherical thrusters which enhanced maneuverability used standard combustible fuel stored in tanks. This slow-burning energy source had to be replenished every few months. He'd expended more of it than usual while eluding the unidentified space craft on their tail. It also powered their cold shields — a technology he wasn't willing to travel without. The conversion process from the spaceport stores to the Renegade took over an hour, however, and was about as much fun as watching hair grow.

Next time, Malik stayed and he played escort to their beautiful third.

He checked the gauge and time remaining — thirteen more minutes.

After he finished refueling, he planned to join Malik and Dani. Imagining her modeling her new clothes, something snug and formfitting or flowing and feminine, was enough to require adjustment of his suddenly snug trousers.

*Bang! Bang! Bang!*

Jaylin started. Instantly alert, he moved to the control panel, and activated the external viewers. Cursing at what he saw on the screen, he pressed the emergency button and opened the cargo hold.

"What happened?" he barked, as soon as the interlocking sliding doors separated enough to reveal the two security guards holding Malik's limp form. He moved forward, cupped his brother's jaws, and eased his head back. With his thumbs, he raised his eyelids—both almost black with the pupils widely dilated. Jaylin scanned his neck, rolling his head to the side as he searched for what he suspected he'd find—a puncture mark. After checking his pulse, which was slow, but steady, a growl rumbled in his throat.

"He's been tranqed. The woman with him," Jaylin demanded of the guards. "What happened to her?"

The two, thick-necked Roukars looked at one another and shrugged. Known for their strength and size, not for their brain power, as a species they were followers, gravitating to service jobs, better at taking orders than giving them. "He was alone when we found him," the bigger, uglier one said.

"Bring him inside," Jaylin ordered while moving back to the control panel. He brought up the data screen. "What is the code for your security feeds?" When he heard a thud, he turned in time to see his brother's head connect with the hard floor. "Careful with him, dammit."

The smaller one, although twice Malik's size, muttered meekly, "Sorry, Captain."

"Feed code?" Jaylin demanded once again. He entered the numbers he was given and waited for the Renegade's computer to connect with the spaceport. "Sector?"

"8-3."

As the video ran, he watched his twin and Dani exit a shop. Next, a single attacker came out of the crowd, incapacitating Malik first. His blood boiled as the assailant jabbed a needle into his brother's neck, and did the same to his woman. Human by the looks of him, the man caught Dani before she fell, put his shoulder in her belly then slung her across his back and disappeared. Jaylin became further enraged that he did so without earning a second look from the hundreds of patrons milling around them.

"I want a list of all departing ships in the past thirty minutes."

"Yes, sir," one of the guards said as he tapped his blunt finger against a handheld device. A moment passed. "There were two. A Stetrig supplier which only took on fuel, and an Earth Delta class vessel that docked a few minutes after you arrived."

Delta class was a newer model with a more powerful engine, one step above the Renegade, and ridiculously expensive. Jaylin's suspicions were instantly roused. "Who is the vessel registered to?"

Again, he waited. "It says here an Earth corporation called Alltryp Universal owns it."

"Fuck!" Jaylin roared. "Get out."

In the face of his rage, the Roukars bolted. Hurriedly, Jaylin ended the fueling process, and locked down the bay. "Prepare for departure," he barked aloud as he bent to Malik. With more care than the ham-fisted aliens, he lifted him, and strode to the medical room as the on-board computer updated him on his orders.

"Departure in three minutes. Disconnecting from hangar sleeve. Hull clamps will disengage in sixty seconds."

Jaylin laid Malik on the table, then pulled out the medicine stores. He searched the injector pods for the depressant antagonist, thankful his brother had drilled the emergency protocols into his head.

Spotting what he needed, he pulled it out and loaded the diffuser. He pressed it against Malik's inner arm as the computer counted down from ten.

At zero, he bent over the exam table, gripping the edges, holding his twin's unconscious form in place, and secured himself, prepared for what came next.

"Commencing to disengage."

The ship lurched, then pitched to the side as it came about. If he'd been at the helm, it would have been executed with more finesse, but he didn't have time. His muscles strained to keep them both from falling on the floor, not an easy feat with their combined weight near five hundred pounds. Ordinarily, they'd be strapped in, but neither Malik nor Dani had time to wait.

"Set course for Alliance Planet 22," he ordered.

An instant later, the computer answered. "Course set for Earth. Arrival in seventy-two standard alliance hours."

The erratic course he'd set to evade the unknown ship, and the detour Dani had accidentally sent them on had taken them far afield. Three days ordinarily would have been fine, but her abductor's ship with its superior engines would make it in half the time. With Dani, and their triad's future in the balance, he didn't have time to waste on less than FTL speeds.

"Calculate arrival time using hyperdrive."

"Not recommended with proximity to star in Earth's system."

If they got too close to the solar system's massive sun, its gravitational pull would yank them from hyperspace and they'd burn up. Not using it, they risk losing Dani. The other ship would have the same obstacle and, like them, stop short of their final destination to be safe.

"How close can you get us?"

"Eight hours out."

"And the Delta Class?"

"Will arrive two hours ahead of us."

He made a split decision. "Do it. Engage hyperdrive in ten seconds!"

"Unadvised. Personnel are not secured."

"Override safety protocol," Jaylin ordered. He pulled a strap across Malik's chest and another across his hips.

"Hyperdrive initiating in ten, nine, eight..."

This time, Jaylin climbed on top of his twin and wound his arms beneath the straps, interlocking his hands on the opposite wrist. He wrapped his legs around the edges of the table and held on.

The engines hummed, and the ship began to tremble.

"Six, five..."

"Daniella?" Malik asked weakly, appearing dazed, though with the rapid-onset drug coursing through his system, each time he blinked he looked more alert.

"Taken. But hang on, brother, we're going after her now."

"FTL in three, two, one..."

Malik's angry roar came near to deafening him as the engines engaged, and they accelerated to faster-than-light speed.

# Chapter Twelve

After the space jump takes them as close as safely possible, the remaining hours drag interminably by. While Malik, who believes he failed Dani, broods in a guilt-ridden silence, Jaylin couldn't keep the scene where she'd been drugged and carried off from playing in his head. Imaging what occurred thereafter caused an icy fear to gnaw at his insides. They were both ready to tear both the planet and her father apart when they arrived on Earth.

Protocol required they deactivate their weapons before entering Earth's orbital sector and docking at one of the spaceports—not a good experience for either man considering the outcome when they had done the same only two hours before. Once the Renegade had been secured, and both men passed through Global Security with the appropriate credentials and visas, they were allowed to shuttle down to the surface.

All went smoothly until they stepped off the small craft at the New York arrival center. A team of eight armed guards surrounded and arrested them. The bogus charge—kidnapping.

By a quirk of fate, Dani was still in processing at the center and witnessed it all.

"No, it's a mistake," she cried, struggling against the hard fingers banding her upper arms. "They didn't kidnap me, they're my rescuers. You've got the wrong men!"

No one listened, especially the police who slapped titanium shackles around their wrists, and, without a word to her of where they were taking them, hauled them away.

Daniel Alltryp's hired man — yes, she'd been kidnapped by her own father — did much the same to her, minus the cuffs, dragging her off in the opposite direction.

\*\*\*

After being shoved by her less-than-gentle, barely communicative captor into the back of an awaiting air glider, they'd merged into the crowded commuter traffic over the city, arriving at her father's sprawling mansion overlooking Noyack Bay. She'd been taken straight to his office, rarely used in the almost twenty-five years Dani had lived there, except when she had a lecture coming, and when receiving orders or bad news.

Today, she expected all of the above.

She paced the thick, expensive rug in front of his desk, too anxious to sit down, wringing her hands with each agitated step. At the sound of the digital keypad beeping, the door swung inward and her father appeared, followed by a smaller, much slighter man, with blue-tinged skin.

Daniel Alltryp didn't deign to look her way as he strode into the room. His guest did the opposite, staring down his blue nose at her as if she was filth stuck to the bottom of his shoe. She dismissed Prince Ivar and his rudeness, choosing to face off against her father instead.

Rushing to his desk, she gripped the edge with her trembling fingers while she demanded, "You must drop these ridiculous charges against the

Renegade's captain and crew. You know they aren't true."

"And how would I know that?" he drawled, still not looking at her as he unlocked a drawer. He withdrew a stack of papers and tossed them onto the empty desktop, sending them sliding across the shiny, polished wood. "This is the contract Sin-Naysir signed. You were due back days ago. When they didn't show, with you, safe in hand, but were sighted at a spaceport on the other side of the galaxy, in their custody, what was I to think? Surely you didn't break an engagement to the Prince and run off with those two mercenaries."

"Doubtless you know pirates captured the Titan and kidnapped me when I left Elzor."

"Yes, but the kidnappers' ship exploded in space nearly two weeks ago. Plenty of time to complete their contract and return you, yet they didn't for some odd reason. What did you offer them, girl?" Only then did his head come up, and he sent her a scathing look. "Your trust fund?"

She didn't answer, but glanced at Ivar. "I refuse to marry the Prince, something you neglected to inform me I was being considered for when I left for Elzor. Information clarifying the reason behind why he would be interested had come to light. I will not be used to further line your pockets, Father, and marrying anyone for the sole purpose of begetting an heir is unacceptable."

His fist came down on his desk with a loud bang. She didn't jump, expecting his reaction. "What is unacceptable is you gallivanting across space with a known seducer. Everyone knows about Sin-Naysir and his twin. You spread your thighs for them both, didn't you?"

She didn't dignify his crude accusation with a response. Instead, she focused on one bizarre thing he'd said. "His twin?"

"Yes, girl. They are Trilorian. It's a well-known fact the males come in pairs and they share everything — including their women. Being with them for an hour, much less alone for days, means your reputation is ruined."

"I don't understand."

"Didn't you pay attention during Universal Studies 101 in your damn women's school? I know I paid good money for you to do so."

She hesitated, a tumble of confused thoughts whirling in her head as she tried to jive what little Jaylin had told her with what bits and pieces she might have learned years ago.

"The planet is called Trilor, emphasis on Tri, for a reason."

She shook her head, still not following.

"All Trilorian males are born as twins. The females are single births. This means the men on their planet outnumber the women by at least two to one. Because of this, marriages in their world are always between two males and one female. And over time, since they've been procreating this way as far back as any of 'em can remember, it's become the only way they can conceive."

"I didn't know," she murmured. "They never said."

"What about all the head talking they do? As twins, the males have some kind of link. I've always found it disturbing. Didn't you think it odd?"

All the times Jaylin and Malik had stared at one another as if silently communicating came back to her. "I can't believe it." But she did, remembering the Artruvian woman who had spoken in her head at the space mall. Malik hadn't been shocked, not because it was common knowledge, because he had the ability, too. Dani knew what it was before he called it by name.

"They're telepathic."

It explained a lot, although not everything. "This is ridiculous. Jaylin didn't have a twin on board. I would have known."

"You're wrong. The police arrested Malik Sin-Naysir along with his older brother earlier today."

No! It wasn't possible. "It can't be true. They look nothing alike!" Except the pieces of the puzzle all began to fit, and she couldn't disbelieve her own denials.

"They wouldn't. One is dark, the other light. Did you notice one was in charge, and dominated the other? The elder, whether light or dark, is always in charge. That makes Jaylin the alpha twin, and his younger brother, Malik, his beta."

She began to feel sick.

"You act surprised."

Unable to stand as the room spun, she lurched to a chair and sank into it.

"What were you thinking?"

"They said, or led me to believe, Malik was…"

"Was what?"

She shook her head.

His fist came crashing down again. "Answer me, dammit."

"A cyborg," she whispered.

Silence pervaded the room, until her father snickered. "Oh, that's rich, and a new take on getting laid." Then he burst into laughter, something he rarely did, yet the same high-pitched cackle was unforgettable and straight out of her nightmare. "And you fell for it. You're a stupid bitch, just like your mother. So, did they fuck you? Both of them?" He shook his head. "Of course, they did, although it really doesn't matter. Whether you did or not, after being alone with them on their ship, everyone thinks you're a whore." With the press of a button on his desk a monitor popped up. He touched an icon and angled it toward her, revealing an ugly headline in large print.

"Daniella Does It All-Tryp and All-Ways!"

He queued up another.

"Mogul's Daughter Ménaged By Mercenaries."

She breathed deeply in through her nose, fighting back tears.

"This one is my personal favorite." He swiped the screen again and revealed another horrifying banner. "From Blue Prince to Interstellar Threesome, Dani Alltryp Gets Around."

Silence enveloped the room again, her mind reeling as she tried to make sense of things. Why would they lie to her? She felt like such a fool. A dirty, slutty fool.

"Well, Ivar," she heard him say around the pounding in her ears, "I'm guessing this nixes our arrangement."

"You guess right, Daniel. I did stipulate a virgin bride. This is very inconvenient." The prince's voice was cold and brittle. "You'll excuse me, but I must go send word of this to the king." The door closed just shy of a slam as he left in a huff.

"Well, ain't this fucking great. What am I supposed to do with you now?" Her father's voice dripped with contempt.

The steadiness of her voice surprised her when she replied, "Ignore me, same as you've done most of my life. Soon, you won't have to do anything with me, ever again."

"It's hard to ignore the millions of credits this is costing me."

"Of course, your only concern is your greed and the balance in your bank account."

"My greed has made it possible for you to live comfortably, to wear designer clothes, and get a fancy degree from a stick-up-their-ass, fancy university. Don't be ungrateful."

"Ungrateful?" she snapped. "Am I supposed to thank you for leaving me to grow up alone in this huge house, without family or friends, and the only people I had for any sort of companionship or the slightest bit of affection your paid servants?"

"Is that why you spread your legs the first chance you got because you were lonely? Pathetic. And to think, I spent a fortune keeping you intact for Ivar. What a waste."

Chilled to the bone, she didn't move, or react, or so much as look at him.

From the corner of her eye, she saw him signal to one of his guards. "I can't stand looking at her. Take her to her room and keep her there until I decide what I'm going to do now."

Movement on her other side made her look up. Barron, one of her father's longtime goons, stepped toward her. The knowing glint in his eyes made her feel like the slut her father made her out to be. Or rather, what Jaylin and Malik had turned her into.

She stood to go with the guard, wanting out of there, to be alone to think, and plan her next move. "Before I go, answer one question. Were you aware of Elzor's little problem? That they're in need of an heir, and if I didn't conceive within a year, they would have killed me like the others?"

"Those are rumors."

Surprised, she challenged him. "You're saying it's not true?"

Unblinking, he stared at her, neither admitting nor denying the appalling claims, which to Dani *was* an admission.

She found him repugnant, but her father seemed amused and snorted a short laugh.

"Why do you hate me?"

He considered her for a moment, before waving off the guard. "Leave us." He waited until the door closed behind him, then walked to the window. Pulling back the curtain, he let sunshine into the dark room. Crossing his hands over his protruding belly, he said absently, "I've mentioned you look like your mother."

"Held it against me every day of my life is more like it."

"Ella was a faithless bitch. Every time I look at you, I see her and am reminded of her betrayal." Afraid he would stop talking and she wouldn't learn what she'd waited a lifetime to know, she didn't make a sound. "She was beautiful, like you. Auburn hair, delicate features, and curves to make a man drool."

Okay, she didn't need to hear that.

"I had to have her the moment I saw her, and she appeared to feel the same way. I was older, forty-five at the time with her not yet thirty. Like a fool, I fell in love with her. I should have known she only wanted my money and the power it would bring her. I allowed her to lead me around by my dick for years before I saw her true colors." He paused for a moment, as if lost in memories. "I found her with my partner, humping like rabbits on my own goddamn couch. I asked why, as you did just now." He let the curtain drop and turned back to her, his face stiff with fury over two decades in the making. "She laughed, called me the fool that I was for thinking someone so young and beautiful could ever love an old man like me. I threw her out, and kicked his traitorous ass out along with her."

"I never knew you had a partner," she stated inanely, finding it easier to focus on a man she didn't know than her mother's calculated behavior.

"You wouldn't, since I bought him out, changed the company name, and erased any reminder he ever existed."

Shocked, Dani covered her mouth with a trembling hand, wondering the full definition of erased. "And my mother? Didn't she want to take me with her?"

He snorted. "Do you think she ever cared about you? She wanted to get rid of you from the beginning, afraid pregnancy would ruin her figure forever, but I wanted a little girl who looked like my Ella." His heartless gaze met hers. "I told her she'd never see you again, or a single credit from me. We had a prenup, thank God. Except she got the last jab of the knife in before I got rid of her. You aren't my daughter. She said so right to my face. And she didn't have a clue, of the hundreds of men she fucked behind my back, which one impregnated her with you."

"Oh my God." As though he'd punched her, she bent forward, her arms enfolding her middle.

"Yes, you're the daughter of a whore and an unidentified sperm donor. Consider yourself lucky I didn't throw you out, too. I figured, one day, my sacrifice would pay off and you'd be of value to me. Now, after what you've done, I have to come up with a new plan to make my years of sacrifice worthwhile."

"You are horrible," she uttered, in a suffocated whisper.

"I didn't sleep with two men while engaged to another."

"I never consented. There was no engagement."

"You didn't have to consent. The trip, spending a week getting to know your prince and his family, all of it was a show for the media. Until you're twenty-five, I decide. You could have sought emancipation if you'd gotten a job, moved out of my home, proved you were responsible, but you didn't. You continued to leach off dear old Dad, for money, food, shelter, everything, so you are subject to my parental guidance under the law. Which means you will do as you're told for three more days."

"I won't say yes."

"A formality. On Elzor, the ceremony doesn't even have 'I dos'. It's a moot point, however, unless I can convince the king and the prince to accept soiled goods."

"Let me go. I'll sign over my inheritance and never darken your door again."

"Your paltry million credits are nothing compared to what I have to gain from your marriage to Ivar. My contract is running out. If you marry, they renew it. If you produce an heir, it continues without expiration. It's a win-win for me. Your womb in exchange for unhindered access to the resource-rich north region." He actually rubbed his hands together, giddy like a child on Christmas morning. "And, when the research pays off, and it will, we're very close, the income the new energy will generate will be in the hundreds of billions."

He shouted for the guards.

"Take her away," he ordered when Barron and another equally scary-looking man walked in. "She's confined to her room. No one in or out without my express permission. I don't care if the president himself summons her, or if the place is going up in flames, the bitch is not to leave her room."

They didn't flinch, only nodded. Daddy paid well. Then, with their hard fingers digging into her arms again, she was hauled away. This time she went without a struggle, moving as if she were numb, though eager to leave his presence, perhaps forever. After the revelations today, being a pawn for Ivar, someone who wanted something she could give him, rather than rued her very existence, didn't seem all that bad.

***

The next twenty-four hours she spent as a prisoner in her room with a guard at her door.

Despondent, she paced. Unable to eat, the latest tray of food sat undisturbed like the ones before it. Brought in by wide-eyed household staff, she hadn't bothered to ask any of the unfamiliar workers for assistance. Paid well for their loyalty, it made sense to her now why there was constant turnover. She'd thought they left after short tenures because he was too critical and demanding. Now she knew why he rotated them through on a regular basis, none staying longer than a few months, a year at most. Because, heaven forbid, she developed a rapport or an attachment to any of them. Such an event would interfere with her father's diabolical plan to keep her isolated, so no one would question when he finally used his pawn for his own gain.

No... Not her father.

Never would she think of Daniel Alltryp that way again. Cruel, heartless bastard suited him better. But as she thought it, tears threatened, since she was the real bastard in the equation. Born to a mother who didn't want her, sired by God knows who, and raised by a man who despised her.

Heartsick, her stomach rolled every time she replayed their confrontation in his office, or thought of Ivar's calculated plan to breed an heir upon her, or thought of Jaylin and Malik's betrayal.

Was no man trustworthy?

Nusapphra, a world without lying, manipulative, selfish men, looked better with each agitated step she took.

She felt like such an idiot. To have so easily believed Malik was a cyborg, she had to be.

Though she'd had no experience with the human-like machines, she should have known by the way he argued with Jaylin, and his eyes flashed with emotion—no matter how fleeting. But even if she'd missed those clues, why hadn't she guessed when he smiled at her, and she felt his touch, his kisses, and when she had taken him in her mouth… Was her desperation for affection the reason she hadn't questioned an obvious flesh-and-bone man?

And Jaylin, her humiliation intensified when she thought of how readily she'd succumbed to his stunning good looks, his teasing grin, his charm. And, despite his volatile temper, how she had eagerly spread her legs and offered up her innocence like the slut she'd been accused of being. She wanted to kill him at the same time she wanted to curl up in a corner and cry. Because, worst of all, she'd fallen in love with the deceitful jerk.

When the door opened suddenly, and Daniel entered without knocking, she wiped her cheeks, not wanting him to see her weakness.

"Pack," he ordered.

"Why?"

"You leave for Elzor within the hour."

"No!"

Her denial went unheeded.

"You are going through with this marriage. Ivar and his family are so desperate for an heir, he'd breed with the town whore if she were compatible. The tests have been run; you're a match. That's all they care about at this point. You'll have to be tested to prove you haven't picked up something nasty from your Trilorian lover. Consider yourself lucky even the nastiest venereal diseases are curable these days."

"I'll refuse. I'll never say yes."

"As I've explained, you don't have to," he sneered. "You do as I say for two more days. And thankfully, afterward, I'll never have to look at you and see your mother's lying face ever again."

He hated her, she'd always known it. Still, his blatant animosity no longer held in check, hit her like a slap in the face.

"I'm not going with Ivar. You can't make me."

His humorless laugh bounced off the walls. "You think not? Shall I have Barron fetch a tranquilizer? It worked well enough the last time."

Reflexively, her hand rose to her throat. Her abductor hadn't used a diffuser, and the spot where he'd jabbed her with a needle remained tender days later.

"What's it to be? Conscious or unconscious? You've got three seconds to decide. I don't have time to play your games."

"Conscious," she hissed. If she were to have any chance to escape, it was the only option. "I hate you," she added, her voice shaking with emotion.

"The feeling is mutual, *daughter*." The last word contained such malice, she flinched. The slamming door punctuated the end of her relationship with the only father she'd ever known.

# Chapter Thirteen

Staring at the small window of his cell, Jaylin couldn't see through to the other side. The glass had yellowed and been scratched so badly it had become opaque. Not that it mattered. Lost in thought, he wasn't seeing anyway.

Anger and frustration warred for prominence within him, however, both were beaten out by remorse. He regretted not being honest with Dani about who he and Malik really were. He should have corrected her misperception immediately, instead of using it to needle his stubborn twin and letting the lie grow out of control for days. Now, as Malik had warned, he had dug a hole so deep and wide, he worried he might not be able to climb out of it and get to Dani.

As monumental a problem as it seemed, earning her forgiveness was the least of his problems. The primary issue being, stuck in jail with Alltryp on the outside, free to play whatever twisted games he wanted with Dani before tomorrow, the day she'd become both legally and financially independent, and free from his clutches.

He wanted to put his fist through the dingy window pane, like so many fools before him had apparently tried. Jaylin knew better. Similar to the glass used on the Renegade, it was impenetrable. Attempting to punch through it would do nothing more than shatter bones. It wouldn't get him closer to Dani, nor would it assuage the incessant worry gnawing in his gut.

A shadow at the door made him pause mid-pace. The door swung open to a guard behind him, Malik waited. Hair a mess with furrows from his fingers, and lines of stress around his mouth, his brother without a doubt as restless and agitated as he was.

"What's going on?" he asked sharply.

"Someone posted your bond," the guard informed him. Moving aside, he motioned him out.

"Who?" Jaylin stepped into the hall where his brother shook his head.

"Says it's a friend," the man answered, while he moved down the hall to another set of doors.

"Don't argue," Malik muttered. "Be thankful and let's get out of here. We need to find Dani."

"You've got to be processed first," the man called over his shoulder. "And if you're thinking of pursuit, your ship is impounded. To get her out will cost twenty thousand credits."

"You're joking!" Malik exclaimed. "Such an amount is usurious."

"Of course, it is," Jaylin griped. "This is Earth. There is always one barrier thrown up after another, and everything costs dearly." It seemed fate conspired against them.

"It ain't cheap to hold a ship in space dock, ya know," the guard grumbled in reply. "Especially an alien craft we don't know anything about—"

"Wait a moment," Jaylin interrupted, the pieces coming together into a picture he did not like. "Why would we need our ship to go after her?"

"Daniella Alltryp took off for Elzor this morning. News of a royal wedding always makes headlines. And when there's a sex scandal involved, it's all they can talk about."

"What sex scandal?" Malik asked, short of growling.

The doors now open, the guard turned and looked at them, curiosity arching his shaggy, graying brows. "You mean the three of you didn't, you know... Have a ménage a trois?" Except he called it "manage ay twah" slaughtering the French pronunciation which Jaylin, a visitor to the planet, knew was wrong.

"Quit talking to this idiot," Jaylin barked at his brother. To the guard, he said irritably, "You're wasting time with gossip when we need to focus on other important things."

Not fond of being called names, apparently, the man's curiosity fled, replaced by anger, as evidenced by his flushed cheeks and his mouth which took on an unpleasant twist. He opened the door to another room and gestured them in. "Wait here while this idiot processes your release. I hope you're not in a hurry to get anywhere. It might take me some time, since I'm such a moron." The automatic doors whooshed shut behind him. And though they were soundproof, Jaylin swore he could hear his laughter echoing on the other side.

Malik whirled to face him. "What the hell is wrong with you? We are at the mercy of the man you just pissed off, and so is Dani."

"Fuck," he exploded, lashing out at the nearest thing to him, a chair, which he sent flying across the room, courtesy of his boot.

"Calm, brother. Getting charged for property destruction isn't going to get us to Elzor to save her from marrying a cold, calculating blue prince."

He nodded, then closed his eyes while breathing deep. It worked to calm him a fraction, although his voice remained raw when he spoke. "If she's harmed in any way…"

"How do you think I feel? She was taken on my watch."

Jaylin grabbed his brother behind the neck and pulled him near, looking him in the eye. "We've both fucked up with her, but this isn't on you. Tranquilizing a target in the middle of a crowded spaceport is a ballsy move no one would have expected."

"We have to get her back."

"We will. And until we do, I promise to keep it together." When he received Malik's nod of acceptance, he moved his hand to his shoulder and squeezed in a show of support before releasing him. He couldn't stand still and wait, he had to move. Pacing the confines of the holding room, he started thinking aloud. "If what our ticked-off friend said is correct, we have less than a day to get the Renegade ready, travel to Elzor, find a way through their security onto the surface, and get inside the royal residence. Then we find Dani and do it in reverse."

"That sounds about right, which is not good."

"We've been in worse predicaments."

"With a payday on the line, brother. Never our woman."

"Which gives us extra incentive—"

They fell silent at the sound of door locks releasing. Jaylin expected to see the guard, but the double doors he'd left through remained shut. Instead, a man he didn't know entered through a single slider on the far side of the room. Older, close to fifty, wearing a blue suit with a lapel insignia, and a cap—not military—and he wasn't alone. Behind him, an old woman walked in, reed thin, hunched shoulders, leaning on a cane. She had to be ninety, at least—her wrinkles had wrinkles.

"Gentleman," she said in a surprisingly strong voice. She eyed Malik first, taking his measure, then green eyes, as bright and sharp as if she were no more than twenty, bored into him. Jaylin blinked, he knew those eyes. The color identical to Dani's.

Malik moved to his side and stared at the elderly woman along with him, his twin clearly as stunned by the resemblance. *Jaylin, do you see it?*

*How could I not?*

"Who are you?" Malik asked, an edge to his voice.

"With respect," the older man barked. "Are you sure they're good enough for her?" he said in an aside to the woman. "They look too rough for Daniella."

"Maybe a bit around the edges, Blake, dear." She patted the man's forearm. "But I've done my research. They're not the usual scoundrels mercenaries tend to be."

Not getting answers, Jaylin asked Malik's same question, though tried for a little more tact. "Considering we are standing inside a jail, you'll pardon if I dispense with the pleasantries. Who are you, and how do you know Dani?"

"My name is Elise Alltryp. Daniella is my granddaughter."

"This can't be true. She told me you were dead." Malik said this with patent skepticism, nearly as rude to her as he'd been to the guard, short of the name-calling.

"A lie, obviously, since I'm standing here. More apropos, a ruse perpetrated by my bastard of a son, which I've only recently become aware of." Her wrinkled face tightened with anger, creating more furrows and grooves. "It galls me to no end that cad is the fruit of my loins and my dear departed Joseph. He's spinning in his grave, I just know it."

"Are you here to help us get her back?" Jaylin pressed, needing to move the conversation along.

"Hotheads," the man grumbled.

"Yes," she said, "but very handsome hot heads." Her shrewd gaze scanned him from head to toe before giving Malik the same very thorough once-over. "I can see how the two of you could catch a young woman's eye, although your manners leave much to be desired. Too long flying around space is to blame, I'm certain. I'll leave that up to my granddaughter to fix."

"We don't mean to be short, ma'am, but we don't have much time. I assume you were the one who posted our bond."

"Yes. I'm also prepared to pay the impound fee on your ship so you can go after Daniella. Before I help further, I'll need assurances, however."

"Name them," he and his twin said at once.

She smiled. "Ah, I do admire enthusiasm and conviction. Which leads to my request." She straightened, or as best she could at ninety, and, with steel in her aged backbone, she stared them down one at a time, though her gaze ultimately zeroed in on Jaylin. "There have been quite a few salacious headlines. I want to know your intentions. If this is a game—"

"Far from it," he said without hesitation. "We are quite serious about Dani. Our top priority is to stop this arranged marriage to Ivar."

Her mouth twisted with distaste. "That cannot be allowed to happen. I've heard some awful rumors they are killing off brides." She shook her head, shuddering at the thought. "After you rescue Daniella from this horrible fate, then what?"

"Once she is safe with us, we don't plan to ever let her go again. It may take some convincing because we have some issues to address, but I feel certain she will understand we were meant to be together, that she is the perfect third for our triad."

"This is what you call marriage in your world?"

"It is similar, except our bond will be for life."

"As it should be. I was married to my Joseph for sixty-three years. It should be a lifetime commitment, not a game of round robin like our young folks play these days." She tilted her head thoughtfully. "Both of you intend to marry her, to complete this triad as you say?"

Jaylin stiffened, tired of the constant judgments and head shaking. Nusapphra had same sex unions, Elzor was killing off infertile brides, the Artruvians had turned asexual when their mind power increased and now procreated in a petri dish, but Trilor got the brunt of the criticism for their practices, although divorce didn't exist in their vernacular. "We are Trilorian," he explained. "It is our way."

"Don't get your back up, young man. I've lived a long time and have seen a lot. Live and let live, I always say. Your arrangement doesn't concern me if it is what my granddaughter wants."

His defensiveness eased somewhat. "It is, even if she doesn't know it yet."

Her smile reappeared, as did the twinkle in her green eyes. She considered Malik a moment. "And what about you, young man. Are you of the same thought?"

"I can barely think about anything other than finding Dani and getting her into our safekeeping. From what she's shared, there has been little joy or love in her life. Jaylin and I want to change that. As far as our triad is concerned, I can assure you, it will indeed be for life."

Hearing his twin's vow, Jaylin had a hard time containing a shout, such was his relief. But he would celebrate later once they had Dani in their arms again. A task they needed to get on with.

"Something about this doesn't make sense," Malik stated while frowning down at the woman. "If you care for Dani as you claim, why weren't you a fixture in her life? Why come forward now when she could have used your help dealing with her father's animosity any time in the preceding twenty-five years?"

A good question, one Jaylin wanted answered, too, but he didn't like the rising volume in Malik's accusatory tone. *Calm, brother. To get Daniella back, we need her cooperation, as much as the guard's.*

An almost imperceptible nod of his chin was the only acknowledgement Malik gave him while he awaited Elise Alltryp's answer.

"It saddens me to hear my son treated her so poorly. Trust me, I would have stepped in had I known. Like Dani, I was lied to and led to believe she was dead."

Malik stiffened beside him, equally as shocked. Before either of them could say more, the old woman's face fell, making her appear more wizened than her years, which he didn't think possible.

"I can see you are surprised. Imagine my reaction when I saw the recent headlines. First, I was overjoyed to learn Daniella lived, but it turned to fury at Daniel for keeping her from me all this time."

"Why would he do this?" Jaylin asked.

"I've asked myself the same thing over the past several days, and I don't like the answers I'm coming up with."

"Explain what you mean," Malik urged.

"I think he may have been responsible for his wife's death, and his business partner."

"You think he had them killed? Why?"

She shook her head, glancing at her escort. "Maybe I shouldn't have said anything. I have no proof. And it's hard for me to believe Daniel would do such a thing."

"They need to know what they're dealing with, Miss Elise," the older man told her. "Especially if your boy is capable of killing his own wife."

"Perhaps you should start at the beginning," Jaylin suggested.

She nodded, drawing in a steadying breath before she began. "Daniel and Ella were married for two years before Daniella came along. I didn't approve of the marriage. Years younger than him, I thought her only interest she had in my son was his money. It ends up I was correct."

Her voice dropped to a murmur, hands tightening on the crooked handle of her cane as she spoke of distant memories.

"Despite our differences, Ella never prevented me from seeing Daniella whenever I wanted, mostly because she was rarely home. A horrible mother, she left her to the care of a nanny most often. I wondered why because she was always such a sweet, good-natured child." Her faint smile over a fleeting memory held a wistful sadness. "I saw her once or twice a week, arranging my visits to avoid Ella, or doing so when I knew Daniel would be home. Holidays were strained, otherwise, this arrangement worked well for almost two years. One day, when I arrived for a prearranged visit, they were all out. I blamed it on a schedule mix up, but my calls to my son went unanswered. I became worried as the days went by, and I phoned Ella, something I never did, except she didn't respond either. A week became two. I went by his office, demanding answers, but was told he was on a family holiday in Europe." She looked up, not trying to hide her distress. "No one had said a word to me. I called every day until Daniel returned. When he did, over a month later, I barged into his office ready to rake him over the coals for such boorish behavior. That's when he told me Ella and Daniella had been in an accident while abroad and died instantly."

She appeared stricken, pain ravaging her face.

"Perhaps you should sit," Jaylin murmured.

Her escort moved closer and put his hand beneath her arm.

She went on as though she hadn't paused. "A glider collision he told me. I was devastated, and the blows didn't stop coming. He told me there would be no services because he'd already had them cremated. I didn't know what to do or how to grieve. And Daniel had become distant, the spark gone from his eyes. I blamed his grief. Now, I'm not so sure."

"I don't understand," Malik said.

"Neither do I," he agreed. "How do you jump from a tragic accident to murder?"

"Maybe we should discuss this later. These are my suspicions, nothing more, and you don't have much time."

Jaylin glanced at his brother. *What do you think?*

*I think it's bizarre, but so is lying to your mother about your daughter's death and keeping it a secret.*

*Bizarre is an understatement.* "Please go on, ma'am, just try to be brief."

Uncertain, she looked between them, at her man Blake, and then did something that convinced Jaylin more than her green eyes did Dani was absolutely her granddaughter. She bit her lower lip.

*Are you seeing what I'm seeing?* He sent Malik the question through their telepathic link.

*The tears in her eyes are real, and that mannerism is all Dani. I have no doubt now, despite all these wild tales and incredible lies who she belongs to.*

*I almost wish she weren't the bastard's daughter.*

His brother grunted his agreement.

Dani's grandmother didn't notice, too busy saying to herself, "How do I make this brief?"

"You were telling us your suspicions," he prompted.

"Oh, yes… Daniel wasn't right after the tragedy. He immediately went back to work like business as usual."

"This isn't unusual, for a man to deal with loss by keeping busy," Jaylin suggested, he'd done much the same thing after Mahlia.

"I thought so too, but other things didn't add up. Like his business partner's sudden departure from the company. He told me Derek needed to retire early for health reasons and that he bought out his shares of the company. He changed the name about the same time."

"And you think Ella was cheating on Daniel with Derek?" Malik asked.

"I know so because his wife told me."

"Woman," her escort groaned. "You did not go snooping around on your daughter-in-law's lover."

She harrumphed. "I'd known the boy for years. He and Daniel were college roommates. It was acceptable for me to go round for a visit and express concern for his health."

"You're like a dog with a bone," Blake observed with a slow shake of his head.

"Yes, and it paid off. His wife was a basket case when I arrived. It seems while on a business trip to Europe, Derek died tragically."

"Well, I'll be damned," Blake breathed.

"Yes, all of them off in Europe at the same time… Coincidence? I think not. Granted, as I said, these are merely my suspicions. I've never mentioned it to anyone until now. I've tried hard to convince myself I'm making more of it than it was, but Daniel has never been the same since. And there were all the lies. I'm sure he never expected me to find out he'd bought out Derek's shares from his widow. I wasn't much for business dealings and never kept up with financial news. I pay a man to do it for me."

Malik cleared his throat, like he was anxious for concrete answers. "None of this explains why he has been so distant with his daughter, and why he lied to you about her death."

"I'm coming to that. Time went by and Daniel never moved on after Ella. He dated, but had a different woman on his arm every night, never settling down. I wasn't getting any younger and wanted grandchildren. I told him so, repeatedly. I also suggested he get professional counseling for his grief. Something which went over like a lead balloon. We argued, which is all we ever seemed to do when together." With strain showing on her face, she walked to one of the molded plastic chairs and sat down. "About five years after the tragedy, during one rather contentious exchange, Daniel let something slip. He'd had a few shots of whiskey, so the whole lurid story came out. He caught Ella in the act with his partner, and during the heated exchange that followed, he told her to pack and get out, and not to think of taking Dani with her. That's when she told him the daughter he loved wasn't his."

"Alltryp isn't her father," Jaylin restated. Though shocked down to his toes by the revelation, it explained a lot.

"It's what he believes," she added.

"And you don't?"

"Look at my eyes, young man. I can't deny her, and I never will."

"But he did, by hiding Daniella away from the world,"

"Back then, the world didn't follow Daniel's every step, and didn't give his two-year-old daughter another thought. I had no cause to suspect he would lie about something like this, until my granddaughter came back to life two weeks ago."

"None of this makes any sense," Malik muttered.

"I agree. I've puzzled over it long and hard. The best I can come up with is Ella gone, no one would ever know the truth. Daniel's a proud man, and his hard-as-nails reputation means everything to him in business. It was either disown Dani, a motherless child of two, and admit his wife had duped him into raising another man's child, or quietly raise her as his own, hoping no one notices she exists and doesn't ask questions."

"Punishing an innocent child for her mother's actions is the definition of insanity," Malik exclaimed.

"I suspect Daniel of having many things, my boy, sanity isn't one of him. That she grew to be the spitting image of her mother and served as a constant reminder of how she'd used him, lied to him, and betrayed him with his best friend and business partner is terribly unfortunate."

"You two better turn out to be the men of Daniella's dreams, or you'll be answering to me," Blake said in a low grumble. "The sweet girl has had enough crap dumped on her for a lifetime, and she's barely started living it."

"I can't argue with you about the crap part," Jaylin replied, "and I can say with one hundred percent certainty, we *are* the men of Daniella's dreams."

Elise Alltryp grinned and nodded her approval. "Good, good. Knowing the sordid details, you can now sally forth, get our girl, and start making her dreams come true. And between the two of you, big strong strapping boys that you are, I expect you'll protect her from all of Daniel's plots in the future."

Jaylin glanced at Malik. They didn't need their mind link to agree on this fact. "I can speak for the both of us when I say, once we get Dani back, she won't have to worry about seeing your son, let alone becoming a pawn in any more of his malicious schemes."

"That's what I like to hear," Blake stated baldly. "And no offense, Ms. Elise, but your son is an ass."

"You're not telling me anything I don't know, dear."

"He is also a hateful, narcissistic bastard who loves only himself and his precious money," the older man stated, his face angling down to the old woman, his brow arched. "And for the life of me, I can't figure out how he can be kin to you. It must be a personality defect, or perhaps you dropped him on his head as a child."

She lightly slapped her driver's arm. "Blake, you are too droll, and so very honest. I'm glad I lured you away from Daniel's employ."

The older man, silver glinting at his temples shrugged. "I call 'em like I see 'em, Miz Alltryp. Besides, a head injury would explain it quite well." He raised his gaze and met Jaylin's head-on. "I met Miss Dani on her trip to Elzor. She's a sweet girl and doesn't have any business with the likes of Ivar who would use her as coldly as her father has done all these years."

Malik corrected him on one point. "Dani has no business with anyone except me and my brother."

Jaylin walked to her grandmother and took her hand. "Have no fear Dani will blame you in any of this. She knows the man her father is. And though she'll be hurt and angry because of his lies, her biggest regret will be lost time with you. She'll be thrilled to know you aren't gone, and her grandmother is a kind, intelligent, considerate woman. And, after meeting you, I can say on my own behalf, I am heartily glad it is you she takes after."

The old woman blinked up at him in surprise. "You are the dominant one in the pair, the one your people call the first twin?"

"Yes, ma'am."

"I'm genuinely surprised you are so intuitive. I heard you were all hard asses."

His eyes flew wide, and Malik laughed outright. "He has his moments, ma'am, believe me."

She reached up and patted his cheek in a motherly gesture. "Nothing a good woman can't fix, dear. Now, before you go, and I know you must, I mentioned assurances. I have one more. This condition you'll find on a much smaller scale than rescues from faraway planets and lifetime vows, but it is important to me. I ask before you whisk Daniella away to the other side of the universe you bring her for a visit. With my husband gone, and my son not the kind of man I'd hoped he'd be, she is the only family I have."

"Agreed." Jaylin would do anything to get out of here and get to Dani—give up a kidney, pay daily penance, stand at a whipping post for a thrashing—

which his lovely third might demand if given the option. This minor task was nothing in the scope of things.

"And I'd like for this visit to occur soon. I'm not a spring chicken to be waiting at your leisure."

Malik moved beside him. "It will be one of our top priorities after we leave Elzor with Dani safely on board."

"Now," Jaylin added, "about our ship."

"It's stocked, fueled, and ready for departure. Blake arranged it all. He knows more about it than I. I have also paid your outstanding fines which were coming due soon. You and The Renegade are a closed case where the Council is concerned."

"We will repay you," Malik promised, moving toward the door.

"Consider this a wedding gift. Now, snap to and go get my granddaughter before the unthinkable happens and my son marries her off to a walking, talking, blue Elzorian corpse." She shivered. "I'm not a racist, truly, but those people give me the creeps."

Despite the gravity of the situation, Jaylin, who agreed with her assessment of Ivar, smiled at the old woman's candor.

# Chapter Fourteen

Dani awoke to blackness, confusion, and impending panic. The last thing she remembered was being led from the only home she'd ever known, forced into a chauffeured car with two of Daniel Alltryp's hired goons watching over her, then taken to a nearby space terminal, and carried onto an awaiting shuttle. Carried, not because she couldn't walk, but because she was kicking and screaming, her compliance at an end. The final straw, seeing Prince Ivar waiting by the steps of the shuttlecraft with a smug look on his eerie blue face.

Once inside, it took two of the goons to strap her into a seat. Ivar had watched until she'd been secured then took the chair across from her. She had ignored him, staring out the window at what could very well be her last glimpse of Earth.

Not long after takeoff, she'd gotten woozy, sick to her stomach, and after that, remembered nothing, until waking here. Wherever here was. She rolled to her side, trying to get her bearings, no matter how futile her efforts with a blindfold covering her face.

"Don't move. The effects of the sleeping gas will wear off shortly."

She startled at the nasal sounding voice coming out of the darkness. Instinctively, she reacted, scooting on the cold, hard surface to get away. As she did, a wave of sickness overcame her. She gagged, but thankfully, nothing came up.

"Stupid woman, did you hear me say not to move?"

Breathing in through her nose, she croaked, "Who are you? What do you want from me?"

"From you, I want nothing. That is the point."

She heard boots striking metal as he drew near. He tugged off her blindfold, the sudden brightness making her squint. It took her a moment, blinking the entire time, until she focused on a hook nose and blue skin. He was Elzorian.

Twisting, she looked for Ivar and his men. "Where am I?"

"My ship."

"Your ship? But who are you? And where is Ivar?"

"You ask a lot of questions for a captive. It's annoying." His narrow-eyed gaze swept over her face. "You are attractive, in your pasty white, redheaded way. I imagine it wouldn't have been difficult for Ivar to take you to his bed, even though you are beneath his lineage. Now he'll never know, will he?"

"I don't understand. You don't want Ivar to beget an heir? I thought the whole planet was desperate for one of the sons to procreate."

"Not all. There is a faction that wants the rightful successor to reclaim the throne."

"Who?" Then, despite all she'd been through, enough to rattle her brain, least of all the gas used to knock her unconscious, she figured it out. "You're the heir."

"Yes, or at least my father was until he passed. As his first-born son, the crown should have passed to me, not my younger brother, Ingvar, a second son."

"Ivar's father," she breathed.

"Yes, he stole the throne claiming I wasn't of pure blood." An icy edge of contempt clung to hi words. "You see I am the product of royalty and an off-worlder. Until recently, those unions were strictly forbidden. Now, because it suits those in power, they changed the rules. Since it is legal, I want my rightful inheritance, and you stand in my way."

"I won't marry Ivar. I don't want to. Send me anywhere other than Earth, or Elzor, and I'll stay hidden. I promise."

"It's too late. You know too much."

"Only because you told me. Why did you freaking tell me?" she screamed.

"It matters not, once I sell you, you'll disappear where no one will listen to your jabbering."

"Kidnapped and sold at auction. Let me guess, as a sex slave to the highest bidder." Her eyes rolled clear to the back of her head and despite her predicament, her voice dripped with sarcasm when she said. "Gee, how original. I'm getting damned tired of this, I swear."

"Shut up. I came down here to learn one thing."

"And you expect me to tell you?"

"Yes, unless you want me to be beat it out of you."

She scowled. This wasn't a new twist, but at least he hadn't already backhanded her, kicked her in the ribs, or threatened to rape her.

"What does your father get out of your marriage to Ivar?"

"He isn't my father, and what else does Daniel Alltryp want other than money or power. Elzor can't give him the latter, so I'll give you one guess."

"Our planet has no wealth, except the research fees we earn from exploration."

"Bingo."

"Speak English, girl," he snapped, "not this gibberish I don't understand."

"Alltryp Universal is close to a new energy source they've discovered in the North region. He expects to make billions."

It started out as a low wheezing noise and grew louder. It took Dani a moment to figure out he wasn't having some sort of respiratory attack, but was in fact, laughing.

"New energy source, oh my, how absurd."

"Now I don't understand," she replied, eyeing him as if he were crazy.

"If there was something of value up there, don't you think our scientists would have found it? We've been leeching off unsuspecting exploration teams for years. Throwing out some radioactive dust particles here, burying a potential new energy source there. It's the only way we stay afloat." He laughed louder. "Oh, this is too funny. Your idiot father sold his only child into a marriage with certain death as her first anniversary gift for a bunch of gypsum and irradiated rock."

"Although I love the idea of anyone getting the better of my father, since I'm the child who was sold, I fail to find the humor."

"No, I suppose you wouldn't." He slid the blindfold back in place, squeezed her jaw, and shoved a rag in her mouth, muffling her cries of protest. His footsteps sounded again, this time growing fainter as he moved away. "You're wasting your breath. No one on this ship is going to help you.

They are loyal to the rightful King of Elzor—me. Relax while you can," he advised, his voice distant and echoing faintly in the hold. "You go up for bid in twelve hours. I'm anxious to see what the going rate is for red hair, generous curves, and a pair of extraordinary tits." She could hear his chuckle until the door slammed shut with a bang.

Dani lay there, stunned. Bound, again, with her hands behind her back, again, and her feet tied, again! Like a recurrent nightmare or a bad case of déjà vu, she was helpless to do anything about it. As she lay there, wallowing in self-pity, she started to get ticked. Especially when she considered in less than a month she'd been kidnapped three times. Evidently, it was the crime of the month, and all her abductors owned the same "how-to" manual.

She tried to get up on her knees. Without a plan, she wasn't sure why, other than she felt compelled to do something. The hard, unyielding floor hurt her stiff joints.

Didn't criminals have blankets or mattresses? Her butt hurt, at the same time she couldn't feel her numb fingers and feet, and she was convinced the gag had permanently adhered to her dry lips and tongue. Barely able to swallow, she had to concentrate hard to breathe through her nose, which the amount of dust in the air made more difficult. Clearly, this class of kidnappers had never heard of cleaning and didn't own a broom. She could feel the dirt from the floor, gritty against her skin.

A tickle started building in her nose. Trying not to think about it failed, so Dani wiggled, trying to rub her itchy nose on her shoulder. Sneezing while gagged was not a pleasant experience. She knew about it firsthand, and, in fact, she could write a book on it.

The thud of something hitting the floor behind her startled her still. Then she heard footsteps. Fear swept through her. Anyone, or worse, anything could be coming her way.

Panicked, she rolled in what she thought was the opposite direction. But sightless, pinpointing the direction of the noise wasn't easy. She learned this when her chest met something hard. An instant later, fingers curled around her upper arms.

A scream erupted from her throat, surprisingly loud with her mouth parched and muzzled.

"Quiet, and don't move."

Restrained and so stiff every movement made her body groan with pain, it wasn't a hard order to follow. And recognizing the man who issued it, made it so much easier.

"We're getting you out of here, but I need you to stay still and be quiet while I take care of a few things. Can you do that for me, *pershada*?"

She nodded her head furiously, praying Jaylin would see her response, because she wasn't able to answer him any other way.

"Good girl. Be patient for a little while more. I'll be back."

She heard him move away.

Still hurt and furious with them both for tricking her, she should have been ticked, but never had she been so glad to hear anyone in her life. In light of her situation, she couldn't work up a good case of righteous indignation, and despite the deception, she still trusted him. He'd rescued her from a similar situation, including impending rape. She'd do as he said and be patient, relying on him to save her once more. Later, when she was safe, she planned to give them both a piece of her mind in a good, old-fashioned ass chewing.

There was a distant thud, some shuffling noises, and another two solid thumps which resonated with a tinny sound, as though hitting against metal. She imagined Jaylin systematically taking out her attackers. Muffled shouts and pounding footsteps followed.

Terrified, she let out a scream when hands at her waist lifted and carried her. More shouts and a few sizzles hissed nearby, like the crackle of an electrical current. An instant after, she landed on the floor with a thud of her own. She groaned, every muscle in her body sore, now her bones ached, too.

"Sorry, baby. No time to be gentle. We're under attack." She felt a tug at her blindfold, and a flood of light blinded her. Next, something sawed through the bindings at her wrists. "Squint and slowly open your eyes. Try to recover fast, Dani. We're in a bind here."

Prying her eyelids open, she blinked, trying to focus. First, she saw Jaylin's scruffy blond bearded face, undeniably the most beautiful sight in the universe. Next, with her vision adjusted, she realized he'd dropped her on the floor behind some crates and had crouched in position beside her. Heavily armed with weapons sticking out of and bulging in every pocket, as well as hanging from a belt around his waist, he looked ready to take on anything that came at them.

The sizzling sound from earlier repeated as he returned fire with a blue-and-orange light spewing gun. A man let out a blood-curdling scream, which was followed by a loud crash, and a solid thud which shook the floor beneath them.

Instead of firing again, Jaylin's silver gaze darted her way, quickly assessing. Just as fast, they swung back and resumed scanning for threats. "The odds are twelve against one, at least. I can use you once your vision comes back."

"I can see you now." It came out mumbled behind her gag. She tugged at the cloth, except it was tied in place. Finding the knot behind her neck, she tried to untie but her fingers weren't working yet. She started tearing at it, frantic to get it off.

"Hang on." He fired a few more shots for cover then reached out and, with a wicked looking blade, carefully cut through the binding.

She spat out the wad of cloth and sucked in a ragged breath.

"Better?"

Parched and unable to speak, she nodded. But it wasn't true; far from it. The gag had left her so dry she couldn't produce enough spit to wet her tongue which had stuck to the roof of her mouth.

"Water," she croaked.

He shot several times in succession, and ducked down. Leaning over her, he used the knife to release her ankles. "You'll have to do the rest. Rub to get the blood flowing again while I hold our position." Before he went back to blasting anything that moved, he also plunked down something beside her. It looked like a canteen.

Priority one for Dani—water.

With both hands, she reached for it, dropping it twice. Thank heavens he hadn't removed the lid. The next moment, she silently cursed that he hadn't because her numb fingers wouldn't work from being restrained so long and she couldn't get the damn thing open. After several unsuccessful attempts to open the flip top with her thumbs, she pried it open with her teeth. She drank greedily, letting the coolness of the water bathe her tongue and throat, not caring in the least when some dripped down her chin and onto her top. She would have climbed inside and swam around in it if she could.

As she guzzled, shots, shouts, and screams went on all around her. Once she'd satisfied her immediate thirst, she lowered the shiny silver container and wiped her face dry with her sleeve.

Jaylin glanced at her, once again giving her a head-to-toe appraisal.

"How did you get out of jail?" she asked, a rasp still in her voice.

"A long story, for later."

"Thank you for coming for me."

"Baby…" His short, one-word reply, told her how silly he thought her comment.

She sat up, moaning as her shoulder and hip joints, in one position for so long, cried out in pain.

He fired a rapid series of shots, then crouched next to her. His free hand touched her cheek. "How badly are you injured? I'm sorry, Dani, I haven't had time to check."

"You've been rather busy." She couldn't manage a shout yet and was almost drowned out by the constant fire around them. Leaning in, she tried again. "I'm not injured, just stiff. They tied me and left me here awhile. Nothing seems to be working very well yet, but I don't think it's permanent."

The top crate on a high stack nearby took a direct hit, sending a shower of wood chips and packing straw raining down on them. He moved, covering her with his arms and tucking her into his chest. Once it stopped, he went back to firing.

Dani scooted closer. She wanted to hug him, to hang on tight, except her shoulders ached from where she'd been tied with her hands behind her back. Leaning into him would have to do. For good measure, she buried her face in his side. He put out incredible heat, and his scent gave her comfort, despite the battle going on around them.

"I'd hold you, sweetness, but I'm kind of occupied."

"I understand." Once again her words were muffled, this time by his shirt.

"Are you certain you're all right?"

She wanted to say no, instead, she tipped her head back and looked up at him as she lied. "I'm fine, but what I'd like more than anything is to get out of here."

"Me, too, Dani. I'm working on it."

As she watched, he angled his head and squinted through the sights of a long-barreled silver-and-blue weapon. The Global Police back home used something similar, called a fusion disintegrator. Jaylin aimed and shot twice. When it discharged, hisses rather than screams permeated the room. She recalled the weapon, true to its name, disintegrated an enemy. More than one hiss told her he had eliminated multiple targets.

"Damn, I'm almost out of charge," he muttered.

His comment triggered another memory about the weapon; it used a great amount of energy per shot, but was limited to around four before it needed recharging, or changing to a new power cell.

"I can shoot. Do you have something uncomplicated I can use?"

"I was hoping you'd say that. Are your fingers still numb?"

She flexed the fingers of both hands a few times, testing them, then made a fist. "They're almost back to normal."

"On my belt, in the holster." She looked and saw the grip of another weapon. She eased it out and palmed it. "Do you know it?"

"Yes. It's a photon blaster." With her thumb, she switched it on.

"Good." He sounded relieved. "Stay low and aim true, Dani. And whatever you do, don't hit the walls."

An image of them being sucked into space by a hole she made was terrifying, but she murmured, "Okay," sounding surprisingly calm. With shaky hands and legs like rubber, she scooted over to a shorter box on the other side of him, one she could see over the top of while kneeling. Never having shot at live targets before, she whispered to herself, "It's us or them. You can do this."

From her vantage point, she had a good angle on a man behind a set of metal barrels. She could see the top of his head whenever he rose to fire. Taking careful aim, she squeezed the trigger.

The discharge knocked her to her backside. Shouts erupted from the men on the other side of the large room, as a deluge of water poured down on them.

He ducked again, aiming a huge grin her way. "Wet weapons are often useless. Smart girl."

"I am?"

"You hit the water tanks."

"Oh."

He frowned. "You seem surprised."

"I was aiming for the man behind the barrels."

Jaylin stared at her a moment. Then, in a move so fast she didn't have time to blink, he took the weapon from her hand and re-holstered it.

"Why'd you do that? Did we get them all?"

"Those barrels are marked flammable. If you'd hit what you were aiming for, we'd be smoldering cinders right now, no matter the amount of water spraying from those tanks."

"I'll be more careful."

"No."

"Why? Aren't there more bad guys?"

"You can't shoot for shit, baby, that's why. If I give you the blaster, and you miss again, which odds are you will, there's a hole in the hull and we're all dead." She grimaced, knowing he was right. She'd had the exact same thought a moment ago. "I thought you said you could shoot."

"I can. I've just never actually used live ammunition before."

"What?"

"I used simulators. Some of the guards back home weren't so bad. There was a simulator on the grounds. They took pity on a bored, lonely girl and let me tag along to their training sessions."

"Fuck me, you've only shot while playing video games?"

She scowled at him. "The professionals use it for training."

"They also have field experience where they used real weapons. Creators, deliver me!"

As they argued, Jaylin resumed fire.

"How can I help? You said you needed me."

He said nothing for a moment, but managed to pick off another man, based on the screams. "You went to college, right?"

"Yeah."

"Ever go out drinking to one of your bars?"

"Of course, it's a requirement for graduation."

He glanced at her, then up toward the ceiling. "Grant me strength, she's being cute."

"What do bars have to do with the pickle we're in?"

Even as he aimed and systematically pulled the trigger, his lips twitched.

"Be serious, I'd like to get out of here today."

"Did you ever play darts while out drinking?"

"Sure."

"For real?" he asked sharply. "Not any of that fake simulator shit."

"Yes, I played real darts," she snapped. "Steel tipped points with an authentic bristle board, not the sellout electronic kind. At home, Daniel had a game room with billiards, snooker, and darts."

"Yeah, but were you any good at it?"

She rolled her eyes. "I'll kick your ass at darts and 9-ball the first chance we get. What does any of this have to do with the jam we're in?"

"Answer the question, Dani," he growled. "Are you any good at darts?"

"My friends and I won a trophy in a competition once. So, yeah, I'm pretty good."

She couldn't hit a battle cruiser with a photon cannon if she had it on radar lock and dead to rights, evidently, but she carried her team at darts that night, scoring more points than anyone on either side. It was one of her fonder memories from school. Donna, one of her few lasting friends, had helped her sneak out. Without guards walking two feet in front and behind her, scaring away anyone who might have tried to talk to her or given her a glance or a smile, she felt like a normal college kid.

"Why are we having this conversation now?" she asked him.

Crouching, he drew her closer. "Remind me to have Malik give you a lesson in following orders when we get back. You're due. After I kiss you senseless, that is." He withdrew an evil-looking red-tipped dart about four inches long. "This is a pellet dart. Embed it somewhere in your target's body and it does the rest of the work."

"How?"

"You don't want to know."

"I do, or I wouldn't have asked."

"What's gotten into you?"

"Other than being lied to by every man in my life, you mean?"

"Dani…."

"Never mind. What do the darts do?"

"Upon impact, they release tiny pellets into the victim which migrate to the bloodstream. There they expand and clog the large vessels. In under thirty seconds, your attacker's heart will stop, dead."

Grimacing, she shuddered at the image his description created. "How awful."

"It is. But if it comes down to them or us, who would you rather it be?"

"Them, of course."

He gripped her shoulders and pulled her within an inch of his face, all humor, teasing, and threats of spankings gone. "Be straight with me, Dani. There's no shame in not being able to take a man's life."

"I'm tired of being kidnapped, bound, and bruised. The gag and blindfold were the last straw. I want out of here."

"You're sure? If not, I'll find another way."

"I'm sure."

He claimed her with a fierce kiss, murmuring gruffly against her wet lips when he ended it. "Be careful, keep your head down, and do exactly as I say. Exactly, Dani. I'm counting on you being in one piece when we're through here, today."

She swallowed, wanting it, too. "Keep low, and follow orders. That I can do, I swear."

He searched her face for a second, then nodded. "Follow me. When I stop and provide cover, we have a target within range. I'll give you the location, and you'll take them out with one of these darts. We've got six, so make them count. Got it?"

"Got it."

"Let's go."

Liking her head on her neck between her shoulders, she kept low as she scurried behind Jaylin, who was much quieter and more agile, despite his size. She blamed her clumsiness on the lingering effects of being restrained for hours, or it could be the fact she had to pee. But it would have to wait. No time-outs for potty breaks allowed during mercenary rescue missions.

Besides, Jaylin's head would probably explode if she mentioned it.

Abruptly, he stopped, which meant she had to, or run into him. "To my left, behind the red-and-white striped crate, at nine o'clock."

Crouching behind him, with her hands on his shoulders, she popped up and scanned for the target. He hadn't seen them move and she had a clear shot. "Easy pickin's," she whispered in his ear.

"Go for it."

Easing around to his side, she got down on one knee. Lining up her shot, she took a deep breath and released. The man didn't react much at first, as if her dart was no more than a mosquito bite. He reached down, pulled it out and turned their way, searching for the source. She ducked, leaning into Jaylin who also crouched down.

"I don't understand," she whispered. "I hit him dead center in the thigh. Maybe it malfunctioned."

"It acts in thirty seconds, remember?"

She stared back at him while, silently counting. At fifteen, she heard a clatter.

"His gun hitting the floor," he explained. A few seconds later, they heard a choking sound and a thud. "And that was him keeling over."

Dani mentally filled in the one word he'd left off. He'd keeled over dead. She felt the blood drain from her face, and she began to shake inside.

His hand came to her cheek. "Doing okay, sweetness?"

"I don't think so." She wanted to throw up.

"Breathe, Dani."

She nodded, sucking in a big gulp of air.

"You don't have to go again. I'll do it, but I'm a lousy shot, so cross your fingers." Already, he was moving into position.

She shook her head. "No, you'd need cover, which I can't give you. l can do it."

"You're sure?"

"Yes."

"Then let's get this done and go see Malik on the Renegade."

Breathing in slow and deep once again, she strove for a calm she didn't feel. After a moment, she met his gaze and nodded. "Okay, I'm ready."

He wound a hand in her hair and pulled her to him for a hard, quick kiss. "That's my brave girl," he whispered against her lips before he released her. "Follow me, stay close, and keep your head low, like the last time."

He was on the move again, pausing to peek around a crate. With a jerk of his head toward the wall, he ran to it, bent at the waist. She followed, thankfully without tripping and falling flat on her face. Once to cover, they dropped down, their backs against the metal storage box.

"To my right, up on a scaffold. There are two of them." He passed her two more darts before he shouldered his weapon and took aim. "Now, baby."

As Jaylin provided cover, she peeked out and saw the two men. They shifted from behind some bins when his blaster shot above them. This worked to Dani's advantage because they exposed themselves, giving her clear targets. In rapid succession, she threw, hitting one in the back, the other dead center in a rather plump ass cheek. Jaylin continued shooting, while she counted. With the same precise timing, they dropped their weapons at fifteen seconds, and fell, one after the other, at thirty.

"We're almost to the doors. Once outside, Malik can transport us up."

She stared at him a beat. "Why can't he do it now?"

"Something in here is causing interference. We have to get to the hall. Then we're good to go." He stepped around her, while tugging on her sleeve to get her going. "C'mon."

Running while folded in half wasn't easy, doing it while blasters fired her way made it twice as hard. She must have flinched and blinked because she didn't see Jaylin stop until the last second. The water pooled on the floor made it slippery, and she skidded past him, beyond the half wall where he knelt. For a moment, she was without cover. A blast of weapons' fire exploded just as his hand dug into her waistband and he yanked her back.

"Sorry," she whispered. "I slipped."

He nodded, which she found odd until she glanced his way and saw he'd gone ghostly pale. "Backtrack." His usually smooth voice sounded gruff. Her strong, fearless, badass captain was rattled. "This time," he urged, "stay focused, eyes wide open, and whatever you do, stay behind me."

On the move again, they stopped once while he fired and dropped a man crouched on a thirty-foot-high stack of shipping crates, and another time when he passed her dart number four, pointing out a man moving up behind them. It seemed her aim was true for more than stationary targets because she spun, threw, and caught him square in the chest. The impact toppled him before the dart did its job.

She was out of breath the next time they stopped, from the exertion and the adrenaline rush from the danger.

"Two darts left," she whispered.

"Mmhmm," he acknowledged while checking his weapon. He tossed it away and withdrew a long black knife.

"Jaylin!" she squeaked.

"It's dead. No use to me now."

"And you're left with only a knife in a gun fight!"

"And your two darts." Once he'd handed them both to her, he twisted, and peeked his head out to plot where they went next. A spray of old-fashioned bullets whizzed by his head. He jerked back just in time. "They're getting low, too," he murmured, "or desperate."

She watched his face as he glanced around, plotting their next step. He stared thoughtfully at something, and was on the move again, this time to a crate resembling an old-time steamer trunk in the corner. He raised the lid and looked inside. "Dani, here," he ordered while he reached in and removed some of the packing, mostly straw. Then he lifted out two smaller boxes containing what looked to her like grenades.

"Can we use those?"

"Not unless you want to go for a spacewalk today."

"No thanks."

"Didn't think so. Get in."

She jerked back, before turning to stare at the trunk. "You mean inside there?"

"Yes." His unwavering gaze met hers. "Now is the time to follow orders, Daniella. And to trust me."

She hesitated a split second more, then she nodded, and climbed inside.

"Curl into a ball on your side."

She did this, too, with the help of his big hands guiding her. Next, he pulled his black blade, and, as easy as slicing through butter, punched several air holes in the top.

Once finished, he caught her wide-eyed stare. "Obsidian sabre, I never rescue beautiful captives without it."

"I can see why."

"Stay inside and be quiet. I'll be back for you."

He started stuffing in the straw he'd removed. Before he covered her completely, she whispered, "Jaylin."

His beautiful silver eyes cut to her.

"Please, be careful."

"After your dead eye with those darts, the rest are *easy pickin's*." Returning her cocky words with an equally cocky grin—badass mercenary captain that he was—he dropped the remaining straw and shut the lid.

She could only see four slivers of light coming in through the holes in the top. With a dart in each hand, ready to throw if the lid came open, she waited, straining to hear something that would indicate he was coming back. Without anything to mark the slower-than-normal passage of time, she started counting in her head.

One-one thousand, two-one thousand, three-one thousand...

At thirty-eight-one thousand, a loud crash made her jump. Not too close, yet near enough to jar her nerves jagged from the last few hours, not to mention the past two traumatizing weeks. She continued her count, panic setting in as she passed sixty, and well into an all-consuming freak-out when she hit one hundred twenty.

On top of everything else, she felt a sneeze coming on. Damn straw. She rubbed her nose, when it didn't help, she pinched it, willing herself not to sneeze and give away her location. She thought she'd conquered the impulse, but as soon as she let go and drew in her next breath, the sensation returned, except worse.

Squinching her face, closing her mouth, and blowing out while she held her nose closed only made her ears pop. She tried praying and a combination of everything else, but nothing worked. To make matters worse, footsteps approached, growing louder.

She opened her eyes wide, having read somewhere it was physically impossible to sneeze with your eyes open. More prayers followed that it was true.

The thudding footsteps stopped, replaced by the scrape of boots on the floor. She held her breath. When the crate creaked and the lid started to open, she became convinced she couldn't believe a damn thing she read. The sneeze was upon her as the top came off the box.

"Ah-choo!"

Nothing followed for a heartbeat then she heard a low rumble of laughter.

Her lashes flew wide and she took in Jaylin's gorgeous face smiling down at her. He reached in and lifted her out in a cascade of straw.

"What are you doing?" she hissed. "They'll see us."

"Targets neutralized," he said while he crushed her against him. "You were awesome, baby, unbelievably brave. I don't have words to describe it. For a second, however, when you slid through that puddle, my heart stopped and I thought you were gone." He buried his face in her neck, his lips moving against her skin as he whispered, "Thank the Creators for saving you."

Her arms wrapped around his middle, squeezing him back. "You caught me. I think you had a hand in saving me, too, honey." His arms flexed so tight she couldn't breathe. "Please," she squeaked, "say we can go now. I am so *not* cut out to be a commando."

"Yes, baby," he murmured, while pressing a soft kiss to her forehead. "We can go."

Jaylin didn't put her on her feet, instead, carrying her swiftly through a set of sliding doors leading to a short hall off the immense cargo bay. And, thank heaven he did because with the threat over, she crashed, hard, her body trembling, and both legs limp like noodles.

Once out in the hall, he flipped open a handheld communicator.

"I've got her. Transport, now."

The tingling sensation hit, and the corridor wavered as a dozen Elzorian guards burst through the doors after them. She buried her face in Jaylin's neck, holding on tight, prepared for this to be her last living moment before laser fire sliced them to ribbons.

It didn't happen. Rather than certain death, she was swept up in a swirl of bright light and the sense of disorientation that transporting caused.

# Chapter Fifteen

"Jaylin! Daniella! Thank heaven! I thought I was too late. And considering my damn bad luck, it's a miracle I wasn't."

As greetings went, it wasn't the most eloquent, and far from polite, but Malik's frazzled voice had never been more welcome or sounded so sweet. It took a moment to regain her equilibrium and longer for her eyes to focus, but in time to see him charging toward them, hair wild and sticking up all over his head as if he'd raked his fingers through it.

When Jaylin stepped out of the glass transport booth, his arms around her went slack, as others, longer and leaner, surrounded and cradled her.

"See to her. I'm getting us out of here." Jaylin strode to the lift, his long legs eating up the distance in seconds. He passed by the half door and was up the ladder, gone in a blink.

Still hazy and weak, she clung to Malik's shoulders, her fingers digging in. A sob escaped her, the reality of their narrow escape setting in.

"I've got you," he murmured, moving in the opposite direction of the hall leading to her bedroom, and the bed she longed to curl up in and sleep for a week. Carrying her as easily as his brother, he took her straight to the small medical clinic and laid her on the exam table.

"I'm shook up, Malik, not hurt."

"Humor me."

Her clothes seemed to melt away then his insistent, yet gentle fingers examined every square inch of her. After he declared her uninjured—like she'd told him—he had her open her mouth and swiped a testing swab along the inside of her cheek. After sliding it into an electronic sleeve, he pushed a button on the end, and waited no more than three seconds before he looked at the display.

"You're dehydrated," he announced. "We'll take care of that right away."

Turning to the wall-mounted touch screen, he typed a moment. The room darkened, warm air began to blow, and a blue light mounted in the ceiling came on. Her skin tingled as though tiny fibers trailed over her everywhere at once. It felt odd, though not unpleasant. After a few moments, Malik removed what looked to Dani like a large wet towel from the bottom section of the metal cupboard. Though soaked, when he laid it over her, covering her from shoulders to mid-thigh, its warmth soothed her, so she didn't complain.

"What does the blue light do?"

"It eliminates infectious organisms in the room, including those on your skin."

"Wow. Earth doctors still use topical antiseptics. You've got some impressive new technology."

"This isn't new. It was developed and put into use on Trilor before I was born."

"So long ago?" she teased, thinking to lighten the mood although he couldn't have been too much older. He didn't take offense, leaning over her with a gentle smile, his eyes more golden than brown—so handsome.

"So, what's your plan of treatment for dehydration, doc?"

Arching his brow, his lips twitched in a hint of a smile. "First, an infusion of electrolytes then it's off to bed for you."

"I have no problem with that. When do we start?"

"We're almost through." He angled his chin to the towel draped over her.

Nearly dry, it had been dripping wet only moments ago. "Where did the liquid go?"

"It absorbed through your skin. You don't use the R.I.D. in your world, I gather."

"Uh..." she intoned, trying to decipher the acronym.

"Rapid instillation device," he explained, talking quietly while he leaned a hip against the table's edge, fingers stroking her mussed hair from her face, clearly waiting for his R.I.D. to work its magic.

"We don't have anything like this. It's amazing."

"What do you use?"

"I.V.'s I guess, which require needles, tubes, and bags of fluids."

He looked horrified. "Thank the Creators you have me to care for your health now."

She looked up at him, his still-rumpled dark hair blue-tinged from the overhead light. His features, not as serious now, took on a softer appearance. She didn't know whether to reach up and drag his face down for a kiss, or smack him for lying to her. After this latest ordeal, she had to decide what to do. She felt safe with him, and with Jaylin, but after their deception, could she trust them again?

Still holding his entrancing golden gaze, she saw it change, becoming dark and troubled, as if he knew what she was thinking. They both could read her too easily.

"What's wrong?"

She sat up, needing to be alone, to think. With her latest trauma behind her, and the relief of Jaylin's rescue and seeing them again fading, she had to decide what to do. They'd lied to her and hurt her, badly.

"Lay back, Dani, we're not finished." His hands came to her shoulders, holding her still. "What is it? Are you in pain?"

"Yes," she snapped angrily, though it sounded more like a sob, and she didn't want to cry. She tried to pull away, but he was too strong. "You lied to me."

"Dani—"

"It was a cruel trick. I'd begun to have feelings for you, as a cyborg, and couldn't understand them."

"I'm sorry, we both are. I haven't had feelings for a woman since our wife died."

"You were married?"

"Yes, Mahlia died of an unexpected illness five years ago."

No longer masking his feelings, she read the pain of his loss, after all this time. "I'm so sorry."

He nodded, his brows knitted together. "I won't lie, I was devastated, and swore I'd never love another woman. Then you came along and stirred up all sorts of emotions I didn't want to feel. I was confused, Dani. Jaylin knew I was fighting your pull. Playing along like I was a cyborg was his way of taunting me, pushing my buttons, trying to wake me up—and it worked. I'm falling in love with you. We both are."

"Why should I believe anything you say?" she whispered. She wanted to, yet couldn't let herself.

"We need to talk, all three of us," he said. "Once you've rested—"

"Good idea." She swung her legs over the side. "If we're done here. I'll go do that now."

"Wait," he ordered. "Let me shut down the equipment and I'll escort you."

"I don't think that's necessary," she told him coolly.

"I say it is. You had to be carried in here minutes ago. I won't risk you falling. Now, do as I say and lie back down."

By his tone, she knew he was serious, and bossy, like Jaylin when it suited him. He removed the now-dry towel and adjusted the lights. When the blue had faded and the regular lighting came back on, it illuminated the form of the man in the doorway. His casual stance, arms crossed over his chest and leaning with one broad shoulder against the door told her he hadn't just arrived. And here she sat, naked again. She mimicked his position and folded her arms covering her breasts, suddenly uneasy in their presence.

His silvery gaze flicked to Malik. "Everything checks out?"

"Yes. Other than the bastards not feeding her or giving her water, and the bruises from the restraints." His comment brought their attention back to her, both looking at her wrists. Following where they stared, she saw how her closed arm position pressed her full breasts together, plumping them up and creating a deep line of cleavage. She loosened them, but a nipple peeped out over one forearm.

"I'd like a robe, please," she whispered.

"No need," Malik said. "After I clean you up, you're going to bed."

"I can do it myself, so that won't be necessary, either."

"Again, Dani, I say it is." His tone was softer, though no less firm. To Jaylin, he asked, "Are we on our way?"

"Yes, I laid in a course back to Earth."

She almost choked on her gasp of surprise. "You're taking me back?"

Not waiting for a response, she leapt off the table the next instant. When Malik attempted to steady her, she slapped his hands away and stormed to the door.

"Get out of my way," she demanded, her palms flat against Jaylin's chest, pushing when he didn't comply. Except he didn't budge an inch from the force of all her strength. "Move!" she hissed, angry tears filling her eyes.

"Dani…" His hands covered hers.

"Don't touch me," she cried, trying to snatch them back, but he held tight.

Arms encircled her waist from behind. "Sweetheart, don't—"

"Stop telling me what to do," she shrieked. Wrenching free of Jaylin's hold, she spun on Malik, her fists connecting soundly with his chest. "Cyborg, my ass. I can't believe I fell for your bullshit." Her words came out broken by angry sobs.

Steel bands enveloped her, pinning her arms to her sides as Jaylin buried his face in the bend of her neck. "That is my doing, *pershada*."

She jerked uselessly against his hold. "I didn't hear him explaining away his lies in the days and nights we spent together."

Malik's big hands bracketed her face, tipping it up to his. "You're right. I could have dispelled your misperception."

"Call it what it is. You lied, both of you did." She tried to pull away again, but it was a waste of energy. Stark naked, she was trapped between their tall, muscular bodies. "I can't believe you're taking me back to Earth, to him." Angry and hurt, she said in a ragged voice. "I won't go. Take me to Nusapphra."

"Sweetheart—"

"Now!"

"No, you're our third, dammit," Malik growled, his temper flaring. "And you're not going anywhere without us."

This outburst was so unlike him, it sobered her enough for Jaylin's whisper to penetrate. "I'm sorry, baby, but haven't we made it clear you're a part of us now? And it's for a lifetime, so you're going to have to find a way to forgive us."

"Then why are we going to Earth? I don't want to see my father, I mean, Daniel, ever again."

"You don't have to, Dani. Never again." Malik's voice had grown husky with something other than anger.

"If that's true, then why take me back?" She directed her question at Jaylin, as she twisted to peer up at him.

"We have important unfinished business to attend to." At her disgruntled look, he added, "It has nothing to do with your father, sweetness. I promise."

Taking in the unguarded look on his face, and his unwavering silver-eyed stare, she believed him. The tension seeped out of her tired muscles. She swayed against them, knees weak, as fatigue set in. Suddenly, bed sounded like an excellent idea.

As tired as she was, she didn't miss the concerned look Jaylin shot over her head, one blond brow raised in question. She turned back just as Malik answered. "Crashing physically after all she's been through is expected. Emotionally, she's seems surprisingly stable."

"Damn straight. I don't like being lied to, or manipulated."

"And we won't do so again. That is our vow." Firm in his conviction, he didn't blink as he met Jaylin's gaze. "Right, brother?"

"Absolutely. Honesty in a triad is essential." The brush of his lips against her hair sent a tingle throughout her body. Except she wasn't over her snit yet, and something Malik said needed explanation.

"Wait. You said I seemed stable. Was this in doubt? Did you think me otherwise?"

Jaylin caught her chin in his hand at the same time Malik's swept up and down her back soothingly. "We both regret the deception, Dani, but that wasn't what he was referring to."

"I don't understand."

"What happened on the Elzorian ship would shake a seasoned soldier. Something you are not."

She glanced away. "I'd planned never to think of it."

"How's it working so far?"

"Well, considering you two have ticked me off royally, pretty good."

"And when your anger has cooled?"

"I'd prefer not to talk about it."

He bent close until his gorgeous eyes were only inches away. "I don't think that's wise, sweetness. Malik and I have been in the military, we've both been in battle, we know what you can expect to think and feel when the dust settles and you have time to reflect."

She remembered the clatter of their guns hitting the floor and the loud thud of their fallen bodies, brought about by the dart thrown by her hand. A heaviness hit the center of her chest as she averted her gaze.

"Whenever you're ready to talk," he offered. "We're here for you."

"That's anytime, Dani," Malik murmured close to her ear. "Day, and especially at night, when memories tend to resurface."

"Stop being so sweet and concerned when I'm mad at you."

Fingers nudged up her chin, but no one said more until her lashes swept open. "We're serious," Jaylin uttered, unwavering in his regard.

"I know," she whispered.

A long pause followed, until she broke the silence.

"Can we make a pact during future heart-to-hearts, I get to wear clothes?"

The tautness in Malik's arms eased, and the skin around Jaylin's eyes crinkled.

"Or, I could wear clothes and you two could be naked."

He eased back, a grin touching his lips. "She's being cute," he observed, running his thumb the length of her jaw.

"When is she not cute?" Malik replied, pressing a kiss against the side of her head. "But I take cute as a positive sign forgiveness is forthcoming."

"You're not out of the woods yet," she grumbled.

"Then we'll have to work harder," her light twin replied, touching his mouth lightly to hers. Like her, they knew she would fold under their combined efforts. The question was how long did she make them squirm?

"I think a hot shower is in order," her dark twin suggested. "It will ease your sore muscles and help you relax. Followed by a massage."

"Sounds nice. Is this also part of your healing treatment?"

"If it puts you in a forgiving mood, absolutely."

"We'll use the shower in my quarters. I'll go gather what we need." Jaylin captured her lips again, this time quick and fast. Leaving her in the circle of Malik's arms, he moved toward the hall.

"He said we," she said after a moment.

"Yes, I heard him." He gathered her still stark-naked body closer.

"Are you both planning to join me?" She didn't say so, but she hoped his answer was yes.

"Yes. You'll find Trilorian twins are very attentive when it comes to their woman."

"It better be a large stall to fit all three of us."

"Remember the captain's big bed? The shower is equally impressive." He lifted her into his arms and followed in Jaylin's direction.

"Is carrying me to and fro being attentive? Both of you tend to do that at every opportunity."

"Do you mind?"

"No, although it's rather disturbing when you are fully clothed and I'm naked. Don't you have an exam gown, or a blanket, something for me to put on?"

"It makes no sense to examine someone with clothes on, so no, I don't keep clothing in here," he replied. "And if I did, you'd only have to remove it again to get in the shower. As for a blanket, also unnecessary. The ship maintains a constant seventy-two degrees by your planet's measurement. You can walk around naked or sleep without covers, if need be."

"You'd like that, wouldn't you? Having me run around bare."

"We wouldn't complain, no." Amusement resonated in his voice.

"I notice you're saying we, a lot. Do you two do everything together?"

"Not always, we are twins, but separate beings. However, when it comes to important things, like caring for our woman, we tend to do things together."

She hadn't noticed he entered Jaylin's room and arrived at the bathroom door until he set her on her feet. Then, he took her hand and led her inside.

"What if I don't want to take a group shower?"

"You will once you're under the water with us," Malik assured her, squeezing her fingers.

Jaylin was busy adjusting the water temperature, his golden skin bare, the muscles across his broad back bunching and rippling as he moved. Although she tried not to look, her gaze dropped to his butt, tight, lean, and sculpted atop thick corded thighs.

When Malik handed her off to him, he led her into the steamy, more than roomy-enough-for-three shower and steered her under the multi-head sprayers. At the perfect temperature, she let her head fall back so the water soaked her hair and ran down her body. Making it better, several nozzles sent out a warm mist from the sides. Closing her eyes, she relaxed while his fingers went to work, massaging shampoo into her hair.

The soft click of the door latch told her without looking Malik had joined them. She peeked, unable to resist, and took in the sight of water sluicing down his smooth, muscular chest as he picked up a sponge. Again, she tried to keep from it, but she followed the rivulets coursing down his body. Fully erect, his length extended toward her, as if reaching for her hand in invitation.

Damn. How was she supposed to make either of them squirm when they were using such underhanded tactics?

He squirted green gel on the sponge and began to wash her front, the light herbal fragrance of the soap filling the air. Breathing it in had a soothing effect, as did the sudsy hands gliding over her skin. Not since she was a small child had someone helped her bathe, and until now, she didn't know what she'd been missing to have a man do it. Doubly wonderful when there were two. The scents, the warm spray, and twenty massaging fingers made for a dreamlike, sensual experience.

"Lean your head back," Jaylin murmured. Starting at her forehead and working backward, he used a handheld sprayer to rinse it free of suds. "Conditioner?"

"Yes, please, or I'll have tangles."

"We can't have that," he replied, and by his serious tone, she knew he wasn't teasing. He would know about working snags through long hair, since his thick mass was nearly the length of her own. Collecting a generous amount of a light, cream-colored substance from a wall dispenser, he began to work it through the wet strands.

She sighed, his fingers incredibly relaxing. Lost in sensation, she swayed slightly on her feet, until Malik began to wash her breasts. Avoiding intimate parts until now, a jolt of arousal swept through her. His touch changed her relaxed sigh into a gasp of delight. It also earned her a mouthful of water. Spitting and coughing, she grabbed his forearm, holding on. This pressed his hand more firmly against her breast.

"I didn't mean to startle you, *trilana*. But the tanks aren't unlimited, which is another reason we'll share our showers when we can."

She blinked away droplets of water, tipping her head back to meet Malik's eyes well above her own. They'd become dark gold, the brown less prominent with his growing desire. She couldn't look away as he palmed one breast from underneath, and washed it with the sudsy sponge. Without rinsing, he did the same to the other before he passed the sponge to Jaylin, who had finished her hair.

He twisted the wet skein with one hand and held it on top of her head while he washed her back. Malik, in the meantime, massaged her soap-slick breasts, paying close attention to the nipples which had peaked to hardness from all the attention.

Dani's free hand grabbed his other arm, holding on while she arched her back, seeking more of his touch.

He arched a dark brow at her while grinning. "Didn't I say you'd want this once you got in?"

"No one likes a smarty pants, Malik."

He chuckled and, with the sprayer, rinsed her breasts, sending rivers of soap over her belly, her smooth mound, and down her legs.

"My turn," Jaylin murmured. He took up the sprayer and rinsed her back, the spray stronger now, like hundreds of tiny massaging fingers. It felt good, but nowhere close to how Jaylin and Malik's twenty felt when they moved lower.

"Spread your legs for us, Dani."

She glanced down to find Malik gazing up at her, waiting for her to do as he asked. Jaylin's hands on her hips, gliding down her outer thighs, told her he was taking the same position behind. She inched her feet apart.

"Wider, please," he requested.

Not as patient, Jaylin slid his palms to the inside of her thighs and showed her precisely what they wanted. "Just like this," he murmured.

They each took a leg and worked upward, kneading her muscles as they went. It felt beyond good. She became self-conscious when they ran out of leg and the backs of their fingers grazed her pussy. Shifting, she closed up tight, but this only trapped them between her legs.

"You can't still be shy after all we've done, sweetness." Jaylin's lips grazed her lower back.

"I, uh, I've never…in the shower."

"We know, Dani. This is another first we have the pleasure of introducing you to," Malik said, his gold-brown eyes melting into hers. "Put your hands on my shoulders and hold on."

"Why?"

He didn't get time to answer before Jaylin, who slid his arm around her waist, raised her left leg and draped it down the length of Malik's back.

Open for them now, soapy fingers over her bottom. A palm cupped one cheek while a thumb dipped into the cleft and parted the halves. Fingertips slid into the furrow, teasing over her rear opening.

They didn't neglect her front either. Large soapy hands bathed her inner thighs, moving upward to glide through the folds made slick without the benefit of soap. If not for a supporting arm at her waist, she would have been on the floor, her legs shook so badly.

When two fingers entered her drenched center, another slid inside the tightness of her bottom, both at one time, it was too much. Her head fell back and she cried out, her words unintelligible, other than, "Oh, my freaking God!"

They didn't let up, fingers and thumbs moving in and out, sometimes twisting at the same unhurried pace. Pressure built low in her belly when Malik leaned in and sipped her clit between his lips.

Drawing out her sensual torture, Jaylin continued for several breathless moments, then added a second finger in back.

Both men working in tandem were her undoing.

Like a rocket, she shot to the summit and flew apart. A burst of white light exploded before her eyes, while her body convulsed in orgasm, each time with them better than the last.

Head spinning, the thud of her heart pounded in her ears. She was helpless and limp like a rag doll when Malik slid her leg from his shoulder. His hands on her hips steadied her as he turned her around, her back to his chest. He lifted her by the waist, while Jaylin parted her thighs, moved in between them, and thrust up inside her still-rippling channel.

"Heaven," he murmured, and wrapped her legs around his hips.

As she clung to his wet shoulders, the fingers of one hand twisting in the length of his hair, his hands curved beneath her ass. Molding a cheek in each palm, he supported her weight while fingers parted her from behind. Circling and dipping into her rear entrance, they spread soapy slickness wherever they touched. Then, the tip of Malik's cock was there, pressing firmly.

Filled with Jaylin's thick cock, taking another from behind would challenge her beyond the two fingers of moments ago, she tensed in apprehension.

Malik uttered an impassioned groan. "So tight... Relax, Dani."

She whimpered, her arms gripping Jaylin's neck while she arched her back, instinctively pulling away. Taking one of these big, powerful men was intimidating, both driving into her at once seemed impossible. But Malik wasn't going anywhere, even when her tense inner muscles clamped down hard on the portion of his cock already embedded.

"Easy," he hissed, his hands on her waist, holding her still. "Unclench your muscles and relax."

"I can't. You're too big."

"No, baby, we're just right," Jaylin insisted between kisses. "You're our third, which means you were made to take us this way. Breathe in and out slowly, and concentrate on letting your muscles go slack. When you do, Malik will glide right on in."

She shook her head. "It's impossible."

One of his hands left her bottom, coming up to cup her jaw, angling her face up to his. "Not only is it very possible, it's happening. I'm embedded deep, and Malik is halfway there. Once you relax and allow us both inside, we'll make what you felt earlier pale in comparison. Now, be our good girl and do as I say. In a few moments, when you're screaming our names while coming for the second time, you'll know I'm right."

Arrogant, bossy, and dominant, Jaylin's commanding voice and the steel in his silvery eyes gave her no choice except to comply, that and the fact she was sandwiched between two men.

"Would you stop if I asked?" she whispered.

"Of course, we'd never force you to do something you truly don't want. We understand this is new. You're feeling vulnerable, but you aren't hurting. I can tell by the heat engulfing me, and how your wetness is drenching my cock. You want this, Dani." He pressed closer, the graphic imagery of his words said in a soft whisper sent a wave of arousal rushing through her. "You've dreamed of it."

"Relax and give into it," Malik said against her ear. "Let us make your fantasy come true."

Dragging in another deep breath, she took stock. Jaylin's touch was gentle, his lips soft, the easy caress of his tongue playing over her own, and the fingers at her breast circling one taut nipple. Add to this Malik's open mouth moving along her neck and shoulder. She was helpless against their dual assault on her senses. And, when she asked herself if she really wanted them to stop, she knew Jaylin was right—darn him. She didn't. Lastly, after the mind-blowing climax they had given her, she wanted to please them both in equal measure.

She could do this, had dreamed of this.

Concentrating on unclenching her inner muscles and letting them slacken, lasted about two seconds before the multitude of other sensations inundating her at once couldn't be ignored. Like the glide of their tongues on her wet skin, the way Jaylin's chest hair abraded her nipples, and when Malik slid her wet hair off her back so he could lick along her spine.

He growled with pleasure when, as Jaylin predicted, she relaxed and he glided right in, up to the hilt.

"That's it," he uttered, his hot breath against her neck, sending shivers along her skin. "We're both inside you now, and it's incredible."

Motionless beneath the warmth of the shower, their hearts pounding, limbs entwined, bodies melded as closely as three people could be. It came to her in that moment their pulses and breathing were also in sync. Lost in the moment, she closed her eyes, barely able to wrap her head around the intimacy she felt with them both.

"I didn't know…" Dani breathed.

"I did, although stubbornly denied I could find it again," Malik replied.

"I knew from the start, and from now on expect the two of you to listen to me, without questions."

Her head came up, biting back a smile at Jaylin's extraordinary arrogance. She couldn't resist calling him on it. "I'm not sure this is the proper moment to gloat, Captain."

"I keep telling you, sweetheart, you're going to have to get used to it." Her giggle made Malik hiss again, the involuntary movement squeezing him tight.

"Sorry," she whispered.

Jaylin, who took no offense at their teasing, murmured against her lips, "If you two will stop goofing off, we can get on to the screaming, and paling-by-comparison part."

To prove his point, he moved, easing out while Malik stayed home. All humor faded when Dani felt him glide along every nerve ending inside her. She thought nothing could ever feel as glorious, until he sank back inside, stretching and filling her once more. This time, while Jaylin drove home, Malik slid out, lighting up sensitized nerves along the way.

Her head fell back, her moans of pleasure rising in the steamy stall, when the action was repeated a moment later, in reverse. Jaylin's mouth opened on her throat, as Malik nibbled on an earlobe, both keeping up their alternating in-and-out motion.

As the minutes passed and they kept at it, they merged their rhythms so they both moved into her at once. The fullness, the stretch, while they took ownership of every scintilla of available space, drove Dani to the brink. She hovered there, overwhelmed by sensation, and cried out, "Too much."

"It's never too much," Malik declared low in her ear. "You need to accept it. It's a lot, two men claiming you, but don't fight it. It's how we were meant to be."

"I'll come apart."

"We want you to," Jaylin insisted. "Surrender to us, and we'll catch you."

Still, she resisted.

"Hold her legs," he said to his twin.

As second, Malik didn't hesitate to comply with his first's command. When he did, the hand on her bottom let go, and slid between them. Jaylin located her clit with his thumb.

Her moan turned into a whimper, and her eyes fluttered shut.

"No, *trilana*, look at me."

Compelled to obey, she met the intensity of his gaze.

"Don't deny who you are. Surrender," he repeated.

"I can't."

"Yes, you can. Yield to us. You will not withhold what is ours to claim."

She intended to shake her head, except Malik's fist in her hair held her still. He wouldn't allow her denial either.

"Submit to us, Dani," he demanded in a soft stream of breath against her ear. "It's destined to be."

It took a split second, but clarity came to her. She wanted this, all of it, and, most of all, she wanted them. When she surrendered like they demanded, a feeling of freedom swept through her. She unclasped her hands from behind Jaylin's neck, and moved one arm backward to snake up behind Malik's head. Her fingers entangled in their hair, clinging to them both, as she answered at last. "I don't want to withhold anything from you. Not ever again."

Four strong masculine arms tightened around her. As one, they slid out and surged deep, only to repeat the motion, driving unceasingly into her body. Malik growled in her ear, nipping then using his tongue to ease away the sting of the bite. Jaylin's lips sealed over hers, his tongue demanding, flicking against hers at the same pace his thumb worked her clit. Swept up by their passion and the intensity of their combined dominance, she trembled, unable to catch her breath.

"Feel the connection, Daniella. When we spend inside you and complete the claiming, it will be this way for the three of us from this point on, forever bonded in a sacred triad."

"Yes," both she and Malik answered together.

"Come with me, both of you, and seal our triad bond."

With a jolt, she felt the connection he spoke of, like an electric current flowing between them. It sparked and sizzled, bonding them as one. Robbed of breath, she savored the tightness of their arms around her, the groans of pleasure intermingling with her own. Her two men thrust once more and stayed firmly planted, exploding together, filling her with the hot splash of their seed.

She thought she heard them groan, *Our trilana*. It sounded more like ragged whispers in her head, although couldn't be sure in her sexual haze. When no one said anything for a long time as they all tried to recover, she assumed she was mistaken.

Energy spent and too drowsy to join in, Dani listened to their soft banter back and forth.

*I'll be damned if you weren't right, brother.*

*You had doubts, Malik?*
*I did, after, but never again. She is perfect.*
*As I told you from day one.*

Her head came up, sensing something wasn't quite right. She looked first to her sated silver-eyed twin, next twisting to search eyes she knew would be liquid gold from spent passion.

*Something's wrong,* she heard Malik say, his concern showing in his darkening expression and the lowering of his voice. The funny thing was, his mouth remained tipped down in a frown — unmoving.

Jaylin took her chin in his hand and angled her face to his, eyes searching. *She's flushed, but this is expected after what we shared.*

*No. It's something else.* Aloud Malik asked, "Is something hurting, sweetheart?"

"No, nothing like that." She felt their tension ease. "Why can I sometimes hear you talking in my head, yet your lips don't move? Not by so much as a twitch."

They gazed at her briefly then at each other. For a moment, she thought she'd made a mistake, or hallucinated it, until Jaylin's words sounded in her head.

*It's the connection.*

Like before, his mouth didn't move.

"You're telepathic?" Stunned, her head whirled with a million questions at once. She settled on one for now. "But we connected before. Why can I hear your minds speaking this time and not then?"

Gazing down at her, Jaylin's voice came into her head as clearly as if he were speaking aloud. *This is about more than sex, Dani. The other times, you didn't trust us, not completely. You weren't ready, and, frankly, neither was I. Now, with us all in acceptance and the claiming complete, we have formed an unbreakable bond.*

"I felt electrified."

*As did I.* His grin flashed briefly, accompanying his soundless response. *It's a phenomenon of the first time. As the bond becomes stronger with time and each subsequent joining, you'll feel it grow stronger, and we'll share a greater intimacy.*

"More intimate than this? I don't think it's possible."

Jaylin and Malik glanced at one another and grinned.

"What?" she asked.

*Jaylin didn't mean physical intimacy, Dani,* Malik explained, *more of mind and spirit.*

She flushed, better understanding their amusement. "I'm not sure what you mean."

*With a stronger bond, you should be able to mind-speak to us.*

*Really? That's awesome.*

Jaylin frowned, but when his gaze darted over her shoulder to his brother, it eased into a slow, sexy grin. *You like the idea?*

*Yes!* She looked between them, both relaxed and smiling, as they should be considering what they'd just done. *So, this speaking in each other's heads, it's what you've been doing all this time?*

*Yes, and when a set of twins forms a triad, the gift is extended to their mate.*

*That is so cool.*

*As the water will be if we don't get out soon.*

Enjoying the interaction and intimacy too much for it to end, she protested, *But I don't want to, not yet.*

*We'll do this again, often.*

Her grin grew wide at Jaylin's assurance. *How often?*

He chuckled. *What did I say, Mal?*

*Yeah, yeah, you were right, as usual. How long are you going to rub it in?*

*About two weeks, which is how long both of you held out.*

Malik's arms flexed from behind, giving her a firm squeeze. He also whispered in her ear, "See? Damn annoying."

"Nothing wrong with my ears, brother."

She giggled, enjoying their teasing banter.

*In this case, I'm damn glad he was annoying, and persistent, or we may have never gotten our reward.*

She rolled her head on his shoulder until she could see his face. *What do you mean?*

*After Mahlia passed, we lost faith.* His dark brows gathered. The memories would always be with them both. Time might allow the rawness to fade, but Dani knew, because their first wife meant something to them, it would never fully go away.

*I understand, Malik. You loved her. Maybe if you talk about her more, it will get easier. Please, feel free. I won't mind.*

He nuzzled his chin against her wet hair, breathing deep, before going on. *Thank you, Dani, that's sweet. Maybe someday. My point is we gave up hope for any kind of satisfying future.* Jaylin battled back where I, as he said, got stuck. *There is an old Trilorian proverb which says those who are lost may wander, but if they are determined and fight their way back to the light, they will be rewarded. I didn't understand it until recently, when you entered our lives.*

Jaylin buried his face in the bend of her neck, nuzzling and inhaling as Malik had. *You are our reward.*

*And I have you to thank, brother, for having enough determination for the both of us.*

Moved to tears by Malik's sentiment, Dani swallowed hard and bit them back. *You're going to make me cry.*

*None of that, baby. We're reconciled and bonded as a triad. This is a happy day.*

*Agreed*, Malik said. *And we have more cause to celebrate since our third is so special she's already able to mind-speak.*

*I am? But I thought you said it took time?*

*Usually it does.*

Excited, she twisted to beam up at him. *Will you teach me?*

*Sure, lesson one, keep doing what you've been doing so easily for the past few minutes.*

"What?" she asked aloud.

Chuckling, Jaylin laid a finger against her lips. *Try again.*

*Try what again?*

She started. His finger had kept her mouth from moving, and the words sounded in her head. *Holy smokes! I did it.*

*You sure did.* Malik chuckled.

Jaylin grinned. *You're a natural.*

Her arms flexed around him, while her head tipped back and she kissed Malik's cheek. *So cool!* she repeated against his wet skin.

*Which reminds me...* He reached over and waved a hand over the sensor, ending their shower.

*Malik! I didn't mean cool temperature, but cool impressive.*

*We'll have to explore your special talent while conserving our water, Dani.*

*Talent. I like that. What else can we do?*

*Dry off and have you again, in a bed?* he suggested, while easing from her body.

*Works for me, brother.* Jaylin's hands on her bottom lifted her, so she slid up his chest. He pulled out, too, leaving her feeling empty without them.

At the shower door, he passed her off to his twin who stood waiting with a thick thirsty towel.

Jaylin grabbed one for himself, using it to dry her back.

Malik took the front, rubbing her skin to warm her and spending an inordinate amount of time on her breasts. The peaks were hard and achy before he moved down her belly and farther below. When he crouched to dry her legs, he placed a kiss on her mound, rosy and tingling from all the rubbing. There he lingered, with little licks and strokes at his leisure.

*I get her pussy this time. Face to face, I want to watch her pretty green eyes lose focus, and feel those sweet whimpers against my lips when she comes.* Like a kid calling dibs on his favorite toy, he projected this idea in her head. She would have rolled her eyes if she hadn't been so relaxed from the attention.

*Deal.* Jaylin also stooped, his face level with her bottom, while his tongue busily lapped droplets of water from her cheeks. *I've been dreaming of claiming her ass since I first saw it bare, round, and beautiful on the pirates' ship.*

*Hello! You remember I can hear you now, don't you?*

*Certainly,* they answered together.

*Don't I get a say?*

*No.* Yet again, their response, succinct and high-handedly arrogant, was simultaneous.

*What if I'm not in the mood?*

Jaylin's mouth opened along the fullest part of her bottom cheek, and his teeth nipped lightly. *We'll get you in there, that's what.*

Malik's response contained a bit more tact. *There are two of us, sweetheart. You don't ever have to worry about not being in the mood.*

*But you've worn me out; another round might kill me.*

*Impossible,* Malik declared as he rose, pausing to swirl his tongue around each hard-tipped nipple. *Great sex has never been fatal.*

*Tell that to all the old men who've keeled over when their ticker gave out.*

*Dani, Jaylin and I are in our prime. You're a healthy twenty-five-year-old woman. And you're a human female. I know you've got the ability to climax repeatedly, if your partners know what they're doing. You can trust neither of us will ever disappoint.*

He tossed the towel into the open receptacle which fed to the auto-wash—an awesome machine—which would have it fluffed, folded, and back on the shelf, ready for the next time one of them needed it.

*To prove it,* he continued, *let's use Jaylin's big bed. After the cramped shower, I'm ready to spread you out and get adventurous.* He strode to the door, tossing over his shoulder, *Come on, you two. I've got five years of celibacy to make up for.*

She twisted to find Jaylin staring after his brother in surprise. *I thought you were the dominant one.*

Head turned with a single brow arched in challenge, his hands slid around to her bare backside and squeezed. *Is that really in question?*

*No.* She shook her head as she thought it, making doubly sure the fact he was in charge wasn't in doubt.

*I'm glad we're clear.*

"Vitamins," she murmured. "We need to lay in a supply."

Warm and rich, his laughter wrapped around her as he scooped her up and made his way to the huge bed in the other room. When he reached the edge, he stopped and tossed her in the air. Landing with a bounce and what she felt certain was more than one lewd jiggle, she settled beside a reclined Malik, watching as Jaylin followed her in. He rolled her onto her side facing away from him, and curled up behind her. Then, like they hadn't all come in spectacular fashion moments ago, they started up again.

Breathless from their kisses and the hands moving over her, she couldn't help wondering if this hunger would be something they shared forever, too.

Malik's voice echoed in her head while he sucked on a taut nipple. Jaylin rolled her to him enough to take the other. *Trilorian males are known for their stamina. You, however, may need the R.I.D. occasionally to keep up with us.*

*Fuck me.*

*We heard you, Dani,* Jaylin said in mind-speak as he gave her butt a smack. *And are happy to oblige.*

She shot him a glare over her shoulder. *Does this thing have an off switch?*

He gave her a wink, while his second answered. *For a naughty girl who asks in order to hide things from her men, no, it doesn't.*

*Seriously, you'll hear everything?*

*He's teasing, Dani. I agree, though, you'll have to swear to only use the power for good, if you want to find out.*

She grinned. *I have ways of making you talk.*

She moved her hands, one in front and back, seeking out Jaylin's thickness, and Malik's spectacular length. Intent on teasing them back to readiness, she was the one surprised upon finding them hard. Encircling one in each hand and squeezing them tight, she pumped both slowly, marveling over how they were up for another round so soon.

*I think I'm in trouble with you two, aren't I?*

*Not yet, but if you don't wrap your lips around one of us soon, you will be.*

*Jaylin!*

*She's too chatty, brother,* Malik complained, though he was obviously amused, and very aroused. *Can't you control our woman?*

*I'm taking her ass, you're in charge of her mouth this time.*

With surprising agility for such large men, they moved onto their knees. Jaylin flipped her face down and, with his hands on her hips, lifted her so his brother to slide beneath. Malik's hands spread her legs as she was lowered to straddle him, his cock gliding easily into her primed, very wet pussy. His arms came around her, one gliding up her back while the other went high, his fingers spearing into her hair and holding her still for his devouring kiss.

Behind her, Jaylin spread her cheeks, his tongue circling the tight hole he intended to take. He moved away a moment later. She bit her lip, anticipating the press of his broad shaft as it stretched her wider than she had been before.

Instead, she jumped when something cold and slippery hit her skin.

"Easy, sweetness, just a dab of slickness to ease the way." His long fingers delved and gently twisted, warming it as he worked it inside her, the task made easier by Malik's hands on her ass cheeks holding her spread wide. "You're ready for me, baby," he announced, a raspy urgency in his voice, "and I can't wait a moment longer to be inside you."

She couldn't either, needing to the sense of oneness she'd felt with their earlier joining.

Though larger, when he pressed into her, she didn't get the feeling of apprehension she expected, maybe because he had so thoroughly prepared the way, or perhaps, because of the anticipation of the fullness, the incredible stretch, and the overwhelming presence of having her two men inside her again. Her lips left Malik's, parting on a low, throaty moan of pleasure.

Like in the shower, they moved within her as one, driving her to new heights, fingers teasing, tongues tasting, cocks relentless in their pumping. While Jaylin's girth tested her limits, Malik's length plumbed her to incredible depths until she felt each thrust low in her belly. As promised, they pushed her over the edge — three times before she lost count — and outpaced her with their stamina while she collapsed, spent from the mindless pleasure they gave her.

# Chapter Sixteen

Dani came awake slowly the next morning, muscles she didn't know she had aching from overuse. She thought Malik had been kidding about using the R.I.D. to help her keep up, but now wasn't so sure. She'd lost count of the orgasms they'd given her.

Two in the shower, several more while in bed, and another after a brief nap, then a brief reprieve had been called due to hunger. With her keeping Malik company while he cooked, Jaylin had gone to the bridge to check their course and whatever else needed to be checked on while in auto-navigation mode. Neither let her far from sight, however, and were sweetly affectionate with touches and tender kisses, considering the puffy sensitivity of her lips from so much activity.

After they ate, she'd ended up dessert for her men, who had spread her out and taken her right there on the galley table. Jaylin had to carry her to his big bed when she didn't have the energy to walk following two more stunning climaxes, which made a grand total of seven…or was it eight? She shifted in the bed, groaning softly.

"Sore?"

Tipping her head, she found Jaylin staring down at her, twin lines creasing the space between his sandy brows.

"A little, I feel drained more than anything."

"You'll build up your endurance in time."

"Any more and I'll be dead."

Stirring next to her, Malik joined the conversation. "I told you that was impossible, at least with me around. I forbid it."

She tilted her head down to see him grinning up at her from where he lay at an angle to her, his head pillowed on her thighs. Her face flushed noticing his face was only inches away from her sex.

Jaylin's thumb swept over her cheek. "How can you blush after what we did to you yesterday?"

His observation made the condition worse as heat spread to her ears and down her neck.

"I think it's adorable." Malik moved forward and pressed his mouth to the top of her mound. The brief caress didn't seem enough for him, and he moved lower, flicking his tongue out to dip into her slit and tease her clit with a quick back and forth. Behind her, Jaylin shifted higher on the pillows and pulled her back against his chest. With her upper half open to his hands, he began playing with her breasts and teasing her nipples.

Instantly aroused, she geared up for more, despite being sore. It didn't take long with his fingers circling her pebbled nipples before she arched into his hands and moved restlessly against them both.

Bold as brass, she told them, "You two are like addictive drugs I can't seem to get enough of."

"I feel the same way, baby, but we won't be taking you again this morning." Jaylin's declaration was as deflating as a needle pricking a full balloon.

"Why not?" she asked, more than a little disappointed.

"Because it's too soon." Malik nuzzled his stubbled chin into the vee of her thighs. "We used you well. Not being used to two men, we pushed you farther than we should have." His fingers extended and stroked lightly over her mound once more, before giving it a little pat. "You are pure temptation, your body something I'm becoming addicted to, too. You need time to recover, though. There's a whirlpool tub in my room. You'll have a soak and be pampered today. Tomorrow will be soon enough for more."

"I'm fine."

"So you say, but those are my orders, Dani."

"And mine," Jaylin agreed. "Even if we say no penetration today, it doesn't mean you can't come for us in other ways."

"This is true," Malik stated as he propped his forearms on her thighs. "Fingers and tongues can be very therapeutic, I've found."

His thumbs spread her apart and he dipped his head, touching his tongue to her clit. As if challenged to top him, Jaylin took both nipples between his fingers and rolled them. Soon they had her writhing on the bed, so much that when Malik spread her legs for better access, her hips arched, almost knocking him from his face-first perch. They chuckled at her response but weren't ready to stop.

Since she was unable to lie still, Jaylin assisted her by stretching out his long legs and moving her in between them. Next, he wrapped his ankles on the insides of her calves, holding her pinned and wide open for his brother to give her pleasure.

With Jaylin pulling and pinching her nipples harder, she arched her back, whimpering, while ready to come from his touch alone.

"She needs more." He angled her face up for a kiss at the same time he shifted both their legs wider.

This gave Malik unobstructed pussy access, which he didn't hesitate to explore, as he licked, sucked, swirled, and tongue fucked her.

The stimulation beyond what she could bear, Dani shattered, her body bucking hard then quivering limply with orgasm number eight—or, was it nine?—in less than twenty-four hours.

Jaylin ended his ongoing kiss, his mouth moving up her cheek and coming to rest at her temple. Breathing hard, she exclaimed, "I need a white flag.

Malik's head popped up, a dark brow quirked in question, his lips glistening with the evidence of her climax.

"On Earth, it's a signal of surrender."

"You did that for us yesterday, several times, without a flag." He chuckled when her eyes rolled up to the ceiling.

Jaylin did, too, her breasts shimmying from the rumbling vibration in his chest, which still supported her upper half. He sat up, shifting her into her brother's arms. "Malik will put you in the tub while I check on our progress. We'll have breakfast together after your bath."

"At the galley table?" Images of being taken thoroughly at the exact spot the night before made her squeak, "No thanks, I'm good."

He leaned over her. "I know what you're thinking, baby. You'll join us, eat to keep up your strength, but nothing else. We'll honor your white flag until tomorrow." Lowering his mouth for another kiss, this time whisper soft, he then stood and began to dress.

Reassured, she lounged against Malik and watched. "How long before we arrive?"

"Three more days."

"Are we taking the long way to Earth?"

"No, and considering what today is, we have no reason to delay."

She blinked up at him, not understanding until Malik murmured in her ear, "Happy birthday, Dani."

Twisting, she took in his slow grin. "I'd forgotten." As what this long-awaited day meant to her sank in, she murmured in wonder. "I'm free of him, at last."

The bed shifted, the cause, Jaylin's knee on the mattress as he leaned over her once again. "You were free of him the instant we claimed you as our third."

"Let's not go back," she urged. "Forget this business; leave it unfinished."

"Can't do it." Malik pressed a kiss against her shoulder, then shifted her up the bed, stretching out alongside her with his head propped on his fist. "We made a promise to someone special from your past which we intend to keep."

She frowned, unable to imagine who it could be. "Who?"

"Your grandmother."

Dani sat up so fast Jaylin had to dodge to keep from being head-butted, and Malik was knocked to his back. He didn't complain, instead, he moved into Jaylin's vacated spot on the pile of pillows stacked against the headboard. Her eyes darted between them seeking answers. "It isn't possible, she's dead."

"That's what your father wanted you to believe, sweetheart."

"He's not my father!" Her chest ached as she went from angry denial to sadness in the course of a second. "If Daniel Alltryp isn't my father, then Elise Alltryp can't be my grandmother."

Sitting on the edge of the bed, Jaylin reached for her hand, squeezing it tight. "It's not true what he told you."

"How do you know this for sure?"

Malik reached up, tilting her face down to his. "Because your gorgeous green eyes are like hers, Dani. There is no denying the resemblance."

"But my mother told him I wasn't his child, and she didn't know who my father was. Why would she lie about something like that and play such a cruel trick on me?"

"We may never know, baby." Jaylin smoothed his thumb across her knuckles. "However, I'd stake the Renegade's title on the woman we met being your grandmother. It's not only the striking likeness of her eyes, but her character. She's kind, giving like you, and was truly shocked your father kept you from her all these years. She wants to meet you and, though I know she would have helped us regardless, made bringing you to meet her part of the deal for posting our bond and returning our ship."

"None of this makes sense," she whispered. "If my father hadn't thought I belonged to another, my life may have been very different." She looked down at her hand clasped in Jaylin's big one, and Malik's arm around her waist. They were strangers to her grandmother, yet took one look and became convinced of who she was. "If I look like her, why couldn't my father see it?"

"Your grandmother thinks he was blinded by anger, crushed by the betrayal of two people close to him, ones he thought he could trust. He took it out on you, who grew into a living reminder of her."

"There is something else, Dani," Malik began.

"Perhaps that should wait," Jaylin cut in.

"She deserves to know," his twin replied.

"I'm not so sure."

She leaned forward, her hand cupping his determined jaw. "Please, Jaylin. I know you want to protect me, but don't keep me in the dark any further. I've had twenty-five years of it."

"You're right. I'm trying to keep you from being hurt more than you've already been. This will be difficult to hear, and we don't know it's a fact."

Her hand gripped his harder, drawing from his strength as she prepared for yet another blow. "What is it?"

"Your grandmother thinks your father may be behind your mother's death."

"And, perhaps his ex-partner, the man she betrayed him with," Malik added.

"Oh my God!" she breathed in horror.

"As I said, there is no proof," Jaylin reminded her.

"His own mother thinks it's true." She closed her eyes while trying to grasp what she was hearing. "But why not get rid of me, too? Why keep the bastard daughter?"

Jaylin's fingers flexed around hers, tugging her close, until her head rested on his shoulder.

Malik moved, too, sitting up and curling his long body around her back as if he could shield her from this hurt. Close to her ear, he tried to explain the unexplainable. "Your grandmother thinks, on a subconscious level, he suspected the truth."

"I seriously doubt that's the case because it would mean he had a small shred of humanity within him," she said raggedly, thrown for a loop by these revelations.

"She could be telling herself this to explain away her own child being so evil. But the fact is, for some reason he kept you. Once the decision was made, he had no choice except to keep up the pretense and maintain his reputation. I don't suppose disowning a motherless child is good for business."

"So, once again, it comes down to his greed," she whispered. "I hate having his blood running through my veins."

Jaylin's fingers combed her hair, and his lips moved against the top of her head when he spoke. "Your grandmother said much the same. Think, Dani, if you have his blood, you also have Elise Alltryp's. We didn't meet with her long, although from what we saw, I think you'll be proud to call her family."

She sat up. "And she's why we're going back to Earth? To visit?"

"We gave our word," Malik answered. "And she made us promise to do it first thing. She had us quaking in our boots she was so demanding."

"I'm sure you could outrun her with your long legs."

"Probably, but her cane gives her reach."

An image of a cane-wielding old woman making Jaylin and Malik Sin-Naysir quiver with fear made her giggle. "I can't wait to meet her." Bubbling with excitement at the prospect, she shoved Jaylin playfully and demanded to know, "Captain, can't this bucket of bolts go any faster?"

He stiffened, a sudden scowl tilting his lips downward. "Are you insulting the Renegade? A ship that has served you well three times? I'll have you know she's in tip-top shape, and we've upgraded all her systems."

Surprised by his vehement reaction, she wasn't sure what to say. "I, um… I'm sorry, it was a joke. I didn't mean it."

"Here's another lesson to learn about your captain, Dani," Malik murmured in her ear. "Don't dare mess with his bridge or insult the other woman in his life, the Renegade."

Crawling to where he now sat at the side of the bed, jerking on his boots, she came up on her knees and enveloped him for a change. Thinking he couldn't possibly be this upset about a joke, she pressed her face into the side of his neck and moved one hand down his chest, teasing a finger along the open collar of his shirt. "Can you forgive me, Captain Jaylin? Never would I insult this fine, well preserved—"

"Is that another crack?"

"No, no, I, uh, meant well maintained. I can tell you've put your blood and sweat into making her a first-class space cruiser."

Malik choked back a laugh, while Jaylin tipped his head and stared at the ceiling, as though counting to ten or praying for patience.

While in the position to do so, she tried buttering him up, well, more like seducing him by tracing her tongue around the outside of his ear. She whispered, "I'd do anything to prove how sorry I am."

She found herself flat on the bed before she knew how she got there and a steely eyed blond alien more handsome than sin staring down at her.

"You'd do anything, huh?"

Realizing her mistake, she tried to think what they *hadn't* done to her. She had three orifices, and all had been thoroughly used, so she felt safe nodding and saying, "Yes, sir, Captain."

"Malik, I think a spanking for insulting our ship is in order. Teach her the Renegade provides her shelter, protection, and, in the future, will allow her men to keep clothes on her back and food on her table."

And Malik, who she could see grinning from the corner of her eye, was no help because he agreed to this plan and gave a hearty, "Aye, aye, sir!"

"Hey, I was only teasing," she exclaimed.

He stared down at her. After a moment, his lip twitched, the laugh lines next to his eyes standing out.

"You are, too," she guessed. "Aren't you?"

Malik laughter burst free then Jaylin's mouth curved into a wicked grin. "Of course, I'm teasing, but let this be a lesson to you."

"Another one?" she huffed.

He bent and kissed the pout from her lips. "Yes, never try to outdo a master at his own game. You'll lose."

"I'm not teasing." Malik gave Jaylin a shove and moved him out of the way.

Dani found herself rolled to the center of the bed, with yet another big man on top of her, this one with glimmering gold eyes. Unlike her, he'd known this was a game from the start and his smile had never wavered.

"You're not?" she asked breathlessly, bewitched by his good looks and the smile that came readily now.

"Hell no." Shifting them again in the big bed, Dani found their places reversed, with her on top, looking down at him. This gave him free access to her bottom, which he claimed with both hands. "I've been eager to turn this glorious round ass rosy red again."

"Malik!"

"I'll be gentle." Her dark twin winked, which had Jaylin chuckling this time.

"You two are in cahoots against me!"

The bed shifted and lips not belonging to Malik—he was still busy grinning up at her—found her ear.

"Never, baby. As a triad, we're in cahoots *with* you." He threaded his hand in her hair, tugged with enough pressure to tip her face up to his, and kissed her until she couldn't think, let alone protest further. The next instant, he bounded off the bed.

"Carry on, you two," Jaylin called while he strode to the door. "I'm for the bridge. Someone has to fly this bucket of bolts."

Malik buried his face in her neck, his body vibrating with his laughter as he rolled them again. When they came to a stop, with him draped over top of her, his legs in between hers, she gazed up at him and whispered, "I'm in it deep with you two, aren't I?"

"Yes, *trilana*, but we're going to make you love every minute of it."

He kissed her breathless after that, paddled her bottom playfully—playful his word, the two dozen swats still stung, though deliciously so—and carried her to the whirlpool tub in his bathroom, climbing in with her for a relaxing soak before breakfast.

# Chapter Seventeen

The glider pulled up in front of a huge two-story house with six white columns gracing the façade, and a wide, welcoming front porch with appealing rockers. She could imagine her grandmother sitting there in the evening, watching the ducks and swans floating down the river at the edge of the lush front lawn.

As Malik helped her out of the vehicle, Jaylin exited the other side and rounded the back to join them. Her gaze was locked on the black lacquered front door. When it opened, a petite, white-haired old woman stepped out. She had tears in her eyes though her mouth tipped up in a huge grin.

"Daniella?" she asked.

"Grandmother Alltryp?"

Having moved to the top of the half flight of wide steps, she put her hands on her narrow hips and frowned down at the three of them. "I'll have no formality, do you hear? It's Nana Elise or Nana. I won't answer to anything else."

"Nana," Dani whispered, moving forward.

Jaylin was at her side, but not to stop her. He bolted up the steps two at a time and caught her nana's arm, assisting her as she started down the stairs to meet her.

"Your cane, ma'am," a man called from behind her.

"I don't have time for such nonsense when I haven't seen my granddaughter in twenty-three years."

"Do you have time for a fractured hip?"

Dani recognized the kind man who had driven her on Elzor what seemed like an eternity ago. "Blake?"

"Miss Dani, glad to see you again, especially hale and hearty. You've had a rough time of it since we last met."

"That's the understatement of the millennium." Malik had come up alongside her, his hand resting low on her back.

"Blake works for me now, dear," she explained when she stepped down from the last step. "Thank you, Jaylin." She smiled up at him, while patting his forearm. "You are a big strong boy, aren't you?"

His eyes widened, and Dani couldn't help laughing at his startled expression. It changed quickly to a sob as the old woman turned green eyes upon her, identical to the ones she saw staring back at her from her mirror each morning. "Oh, Nana, it is you."

"No crying, or I'll start blubbering, too." It was much too late for that, however, and they went into each other's arms sobbing.

"Here we go," Blake grumbled. "Once the waterworks start, there's no shutting 'em off."

Pulling away, Dani wiped away her tears to no avail because more replaced them. Blake, who had walked down to join them, produced tissues.

Sniffling, Nana gazed up at Malik, patting him, too. "You aren't as stout as your brother, but you're very tall. Bend down, dear," she tapped her finger to her cheek, "I'd need a ladder to come up to you."

As thrown as Jaylin by her candidness, he still didn't hesitate to lean down and kiss her nana's wrinkled cheek.

"Now then," she said, beaming. "I've looked forward to your visit and do hope you can stay for a few days, at least. Tonight, I have a quiet supper planned, so we can chat. And, my man of affairs will arrive with the papers in time for coffee and dessert."

"What papers?"

"You're of age now, dear. He'll be transferring your trust fund over to you, and there's the matter of my will."

"Your will?"

"Yes, I'm disowning Daniel. You will be the heir to my estate, which includes a controlling interest in Alltryp Universal."

"Father doesn't own it outright?"

"No, it is an old family business. I just let him vote my shares."

"He'll be furious."

"Pshaw, who cares? He doesn't frighten me. He kept you away from me and treated you miserably from what I hear." She gripped Dani's hands. "I'm so sorry for what he put you through. I knew he was angry at Ella but still can't believe he'd ever be so cruel to an innocent young girl. It's like I don't know him."

"I'm not sure I want him to know I'm really his daughter. Let him think as he does and maybe he'll leave us all be."

"Inside, he knows, even if he won't admit it. No one can look at you and deny you're an Alltryp. Although, it's entirely up to you, dear. I won't say a word. If one day you decide to confront him, I'm sure your young men will keep you safe while it happens."

"You can trust that we will," Malik said with conviction.

"They are very protective," Dani explained.

"Which is as it should be." Smiling, she put her curly white head next to hers. "I have faith they will help to repair the damage Daniel has done."

Their steadfast presence behind her gave her the confidence to reply. "The patch has already begun, Nana."

"I'm so glad for that, Dani dear."

"Can I ask…?" she began, but thought better of it. "Sorry, I'm asking so many questions, and we haven't even made it inside."

"Here or there doesn't matter, does it? Ask away," her grandmother encouraged with a gentle pat to her cheek.

"Why did you maintain the trust after you thought I had died?"

"Now that's something I've asked myself often over the years. I considered starting a foundation in your name with the money, yet couldn't bring myself to do it because—and this may sound silly—it was my only connection to you. Now I'm glad that my selfishness kept me from it."

"I don't think you're either silly or selfish." Dani bit her lip. A million credits was a large sum. She couldn't imagine how much controlling interest would amount to. No matter her nana's fearlessness, she didn't feel the same. She worried about her father's greed. He also had power and influence which could haunt her and, by extension, Jaylin and

Malik. He'd shown time and again how vindictive he could be when crossed.

"There is something else." Wisdom and insight gleamed in eyes so like her own. Traits she hoped she didn't have to wait decades to gain.

"The trust is very generous, and I'm thankful for it, but I don't need anything else. I'm worried about the will. Won't father know if you change it?"

"Not until I'm dead. And I don't plan on cocking up my toes for some time."

"I pray not. I've just found you."

"Oh, my dear. My regret is our reunion has come so late and as your new life is beginning. One which will take you so far away."

"Come with us," she blurted out, not knowing if it was possible, or if Jaylin and Malik would agree.

"And travel in space?" She shook her head vigorously, sending her glossy white curls bouncing. "This old bird intends to keep her feet planted on good old terra firma." She waved her hand toward the driveway. "I won't even get into one of those newfangled air gliders."

"But, Nana, they've been around for almost a century."

"As have I, Dani. I prefer my Cadillac, and, as long as the government maintains the road system, it's how I'll travel. Build a highway to Trilor, and I'm there."

Dani gave her a watery smile. "I'll miss you."

"You can come back, sweetheart."

She twisted to look at her men.

"Of course, you can," Jaylin agreed, confirming what Malik had said. "Our business takes us this way often."

*I thought we'd go to your home on Trilor.*

*We will, briefly. To be official, we must register our triad formally with the state — in person. Afterward, we can go anywhere.*

Really?

*When children come along, we'll want to settle down,* Malik advised, *but we have plenty of time to decide where later.*

An image of twin boys, one blond, the other dark, popped in her head. Or a daughter with her, and her nana's, green eyes. She liked either idea.

*You mentioned wanting to travel.* Jaylin cut into her thoughts of family. *What better way than with us?*

"On the Renegade?"

He laughed. "Yes, on our old bucket of bolts."

"I'm missing something I think."

At the bewildered expression on her grandmother's face, Dani realized they'd been moving in and out of their link.

"I'm sorry. How rude of us."

"What, dear? I'm confused. Please tell me I'm not going suddenly senile."

"No." She smiled. "I'm so new at this triad mind-speak thing, I sometimes don't realize when I'm doing it."

"Mind-speak?"

"Yes, Jaylin and Malik are telepathic. All Trilorian twins are. And when they take a third, she gets the ability, too."

"How fascinating. Can you teach me?"

Malik fielded her question. "I'm sorry. For you to learn, we'd have to find you a set of twins, Mrs. Alltryp."

"It's Nana." She whispered in an aside to Dani,

"He's the dark one, and the second, right?"

"Yes, he's the younger brother, and his name is Malik," she answered, delighted with the interaction.

"Ah, now I remember. It will take me a little while. They are both so handsome it's rather distracting. As for twins for me, Malik, I'll have to pass. I'm too old for courting and all that nonsense, but come inside and you can tell me more about it." She took Blake's proffered arm to climb the steps.

Dani smiled after her, bursting with happiness. Needing an outlet, she jumped to hug Malik's neck, welcoming how he bent, assisting her in doing so, and how his arms clasped her tight to return the affection.

She did the same with Jaylin, squeezing him as hard, and growing warm inside when he kissed the top of her head.

"I'm so glad you've found her, Dani," he said.

"I love her already."

"It's settled, then?" Malik asked. "We'll have regular visits with Nana?"

"Yes, please." She grinned, beaming.

As they flanked her, each taking a hand to follow the older couple into the house, her grandmother's voice drifted down to them.

"I can't wait to tell the women at the club my granddaughter has snagged not one, but two handsome men."

"Won't they be shocked?" Dani called up to her.

Elise Alltryp, having gained the top step, gazed down on them, her green eyes twinkling with mischief. "This is my book club, dear. Our staple is steamy romance, including a ménage on occasion. They'll be titillated more than anything."

Dani gasped, releasing their hands to cover her mouth. With a preference for contact, each man moved in close, Malik's arm curling around her shoulders, while Jaylin slid his around her hips. Both chuckled as they urged her up the stairs.

"My nana reads steamy ménage," she uttered in shocked disbelief.

"I'm old Daniella," her voice called from the doorway. "Not dead."

As she flushed hotly, her men, unable to contain their amusement at the feisty old woman, tossed back their heads and laughed.

\*\*\*

While looking out the guest bedroom window later, instead of appreciating the moonlight glistening on the water, or the shadows of the weeping willows gracefully swaying in the breeze, or the coolness of the night air through the open window which made her nana's lacy curtains flutter, she couldn't stop worrying what her father was plotting next.

It had been a bittersweet, tear-filled reunion with her grandmother, but her stories and wit had also provided plenty of laughter. She'd been glad Jaylin and Malik were there to share it with her. Things had taken on a definite businesslike tone when Nana's attorney—what she called her man of affairs—had arrived during dessert. Discussions of trusts, wills, codicils, and a head-spinning amount of financial and legal terms made her nervous, and turned her thoughts to what her father's reaction would be. The fact he was out millions of credits in his deal with the Elzorians made her stomach know with fear; Daniel Alltryp wasn't a gracious loser by any stretch of the imagination.

"Do you think my father will retaliate?" she asked in the quiet of the room.

"He can't be pleased," Jaylin acknowledged, "except what can he do? You're legally an adult now. He'll have to find another way to pad his bank account. Besides, he should be the one worried about retaliation."

She stopped, picturing Jaylin on the Elzorian ship—deadly and determined. And Malik had blown a pirate ship to bits without remorse. The two of them against her father would be a formidable force, but she didn't want war. "Perhaps we should go."

"After our visit, Dani," he asserted firmly. "We aren't in the habit of running from trouble, and aren't going to start now because of your father."

"When he finds out about the will—and I'm certain he will no matter what Nana thinks—he'll freak out." She began pacing, moving back and forth at the foot of the bed while two sets of worried eyes followed her. "I don't mean to seem ungrateful, but I don't want it. I want to travel with you."

"Your grandmother is spry for ninety," Malik commented. "And under Blake's watchful eye, she's likely to live to one hundred, or more."

"He watches her like a hawk," Dani acknowledged without slowing. "It's very sweet."

"He's like the son she should have had," Jaylin put in. "Were you listening to your options, Dani. The attorney said if you don't want it, when the time comes, you can sell your shares, or hire a CEO to run the company for you and sit back and rake in the profits."

"I haven't a clue how to run a huge company, and why do I need to rake in anything more than the million I have. My real worry is father will contest the will. He could drag it through the court system, and the media, making it ugly. I don't want to think about those headlines."

"We'll help you figure it out. Right now, you need to rest. It's been a long day." Malik patted the space left for her in the middle of the wide mattress.

She gave it a skeptical glance. Though a king-size bed, the breadth of their shoulders would leave little room for her. She'd be wedged in between them, like the filling in a Trilorian sandwich. The idea held merit, except with her nerves on edge, she couldn't think about lying still, let alone going to sleep.

"Come to bed, Dani. It's late." He added a hint of steel to his order when she didn't immediately climb in.

She looked at the antique clock on the wall of her grandmother's guest room. "It's only nine o'clock."

"He means we're getting a late start making love to you, baby." Leave it to Jaylin to be frank. At least he put it sweetly and hadn't used the f-word. "Now strip off the robe and get over here."

This made her stop. Mind-blowing sex would distract her and help her sleep. So why the hesitation? Deciding it an excellent plan, she shrugged off the cotton robe and let it fall at her feet. Beneath it, she wore a simple cotton sheath, borrowed from her nana. She almost laughed at the grimace of disgust on her light twin's face.

"The hideous granny gown goes, too, and if you're wearing panties under that shroud, Malik's pleasure will be delayed because I'll spank you myself."

Amused golden-brown eyes met hers, the ends crinkled due to his broad smile. He winked and sent a thought to her head. *Told you so.*

*Told her what?* Jaylin asked, joining in through their link.

*Your view on women's undergarments.*

*A damn waste of time. As is this conversation.* So quick she didn't have time to move, he leaned forward with a long arm extended and grabbed her wrist. He yanked her forward so she landed on top of him. The next second the gown was whisked over her head and tossed to the floor. Jaylin's hum of approval at finding only bare skin underneath reverberated in the room.

*We'll have to be quiet*, Dani warned. *Nana's room is down the hall. In fact, maybe we should wait until we're back on board the ship.*

*Not a chance*, came his unequivocal response.

*We'll muffle any of your noises.* Malik rolled toward them and spread kisses along her shoulder.

"Only *my* noises?"

"Mostly your screams when you come," he whispered. "You're a moaner, and tend to get loud."

*I like her moans.* While Jaylin projected his opinion, he grinned.

Heat flooded her face until her cheeks felt scalded. *Good grief, I had no idea. We definitely can't do anything tonight."

*Wrong, we're doing plenty, and probably more than once.* He dragged her up his chest until her breasts dangled over him, then he sucked on a nipple, drawing hard.

"Jaylin!" His name came out in a prolonged moan.

Malik chuckled. *See what I mean?*

*Please, stop.*

The blond head at her breast did so, but only to angle up and pin her with an incredulous look. "Dani, the woman's ninety, reads trashy novels, and is a mother. Do you think she's forgotten people, especially newly bonded young people, have sex?"

To her, the s-e-x word rebounded off the walls when he said it aloud. She put her hand over his mouth.

*If you embarrass me when I've just reunited with her, I swear Jaylin Sin-Naysir, I won't have sex with you ever again.*

He stared at her, deadpan. A heartbeat passed before he burst into laughter, Malik joining in.

*What? You don't think I can hold out?*

*We put a one-day halt on sex after our first full claiming and you were begging for more by that night.*

*I didn't beg, Malik.*

*No, I believe your precise words to me were, 'I was celibate for twenty-five years, which beats your puny five. I have more time to make up for than you, and I have no intention of waiting.' But wait you did.*

She glared at him. *How did you remember that word for word? Are you sure you're not a cyborg?*

He growled, and sitting up, pulled her from his brother's arms. At the last moment, he twisted her so she landed facedown across his lap. Then with loud cracks resounding like ancient gunshots in the room, his hand fell hard twice on each cheek.

"Malik," she hissed, not feeling the swats as much as her embarrassment. "The sound of a spanking is worse than sex noises."

He didn't stop, more spanks and cracks following.

"Ouch! Stop!" she squealed at a decibel level grandmother would have to be deaf not to hear.

"I think you hit a nerve, Dani," Jaylin observed, sounding amused and not the least bit concerned. "If you want him to stop, I think an apology is in order."

"For what? Calling him a coldhearted machine? I rest my case."

A flurry of rapid-fire swats, at least a dozen, probably more, rained down on her backside. At this point, she rethought her remark. It was a low blow, knowing Malik had disliked her thinking him a cyborg.

"I'm sorry, honey," she cried, meaning it. "I know you're not a machine, Malik. You're very much a man. My man!"

The cacophony of spanks and her pleas ceased. It occurred to her the latter, in the heat of things, was louder than his hand colliding with her rear. She collapsed over his lap, wilted with relief, until he flipped her again, this time perching her stinging behind on his hard thigh.

"I am a man, Dani. One who isn't afraid to take you over his knee for a bare-bottom spanking when needed. Though never, ever, will I do more. I love you too much. And don't let big brother fool you, he is of the same bent."

"You love me?"

He grunted, halfway between a growl and a laugh. "Is that all you got from my lecture?"

"No, I understand you'll spank me if I'm bad, but I'm rarely bad, except recently when you or Jaylin tick me off. More important to me is the other part. You said you love me, is that the truth?" Her voice shook when she asked it again, hoping beyond hope despite the joys they found in their physical joining their hearts were engaged as well.

"Dani, sweetness…" No longer amused, Jaylin moved closer, his thumb wiping away the tears wetting her cheeks. She hadn't noticed till now she'd been crying. "How could you doubt our love after what we've shared?"

She looked away. "I'm sorry. You haven't said the words, so I wasn't sure."

"But we connected and sealed our triad," Malik replied, sounding confused. "If love didn't exist, our bond wouldn't have formed."

Her head came up, searching for the answer in first silver, and then golden eyes. "Truly?" she asked.

"Yes."

She pushed at his shoulder, turning to do the same to Jaylin. "One of you might have mentioned it."

"I'm sure we did," he replied as he caught her hand.

"You didn't; I would have remembered."

"I thought we did, too," Malik agreed, while frowning.

"We talked about sex, had incredible sex, and experienced a connection—the sizzling electrical thing—and a host of other sensations and feelings, but love never entered the picture." Joyful, disbelieving, and angry all at once, she blew out a breath to steady herself in order to finish. "The reason I would remember is because no one has ever told me they loved me before."

"Never?" Malik asked, a catch in his usually steady voice. "Oh, sweetheart, love was definitely in the picture."

Overwhelmed by the flood of emotions, she crumpled against his chest. She didn't stay there long, pulled from Malik's arms by insistent hands a moment later. Looking up into Jaylin's eyes, she saw love reflected there, and a flash of quicksilver anger a moment before he pulled her astride his lap and crushed her to him. "I could kill Daniel Alltryp for doing what he did, and for making you doubt your worth. You are loved, *trilana*. We'll shout it from the mountaintops if that's what it takes for you to believe it."

A sob worked its way up from inside her chest at his impassioned words.

Malik moved against her, making it so she had a man at both her front and her back. Strong arms encircled her, holding her so tight she knew they'd never let her go. Liquid heat dampened her thighs as a thick cock pressed hard against her bottom, while another nudged insistently between her thighs.

Wanting to be closer and wishing she had the power to meld with them both, she lifted an arm and wrapped it around Jaylin's shoulders, fingers twisting in his long hair to drag his face down to hers. She kissed him, whispering, "I love you, Jaylin."

After a moment, she broke free of one set of lips and twisted her head to another. Her free arm snaked up, hand threading through short wavy hair. "I love you, too, Malik."

While his tongue dove inside, Jaylin's mouth found the pulse at her throat.

"You'll hear the words every day, sweetness, so you don't ever again have to wonder or guess."

As they embraced, they alternated kisses and caresses, and increased the restless movement of their hips as their need soared. This went on for several long, wonderful moments, before Dani broke for air.

"We probably should stop before we can't."

"We declared our love, you said it for the first time too, and you want to stop?" Malik asked, sounding more shocked than before.

"You were the one who said I was a moaner."

His gaze shot over her shoulder. "Brother, we need to get back to the Renegade soon. Once we're on board, we can fuck her how we want, show her loudly who she belongs to, and how much she is loved without worrying about who might overhear."

She blinked up at her dark mate in surprise, but asked Jaylin in an incredulous whisper, "Did he just say the f-word?"

"I do believe he did, *pershada*. Either you or I have corrupted him."

*You both have*, Malik answered, coming across a bit frustrated. *Now, can we get back to making love to our third? Further, can we limit comments to our mind link. I'd rather not test the theory that the sound of a threesome won't give her ménage-savvy grandmother a heart attack. We can take turns keeping her quiet with our tongues and other things.*

*Are you taking charge?* Jaylin asked him.

*Damn straight.*

*Then I appoint you acting captain because your plan sounds like an excellent strategy to me.*

*I thought you might approve.*

They both looked at Dani, brows raised, as if daring her to protest further.

*Don't look at me! I'm not arguing.*

Malik rolled his eyes—replicating her frequent bad habit—while Jaylin grunted in disbelief.

*What?* she demanded of them both.

*Baby, you'd argue with the Creators as they invited you in through heaven's gates.*

She giggled, finding that hilarious. *But you love me, so it must be part of my charm.*

*She's being cute again, Mal.*

*Can we get on with tongues and other things now, please? I rather like the idea.*

Jaylin chuckled. *Now she's being cute and downright naughty. I don't think you spanked her hard enough, brother.*

*I beg to differ. My bottom is still warm.*

*All the better*, Malik said. *We can dispense with the preliminaries and get right to the matter at hand.* When she looked up at his pun, he winked. He also curved a hand around a taut cheek, and squeezed. *You should do the honors this time, Jay.*

*With pleasure.*

*Not fair. What did I do?*

*She wants a list of her offenses, Mal.*

*Hmm, sassiness should top the list.*

Her lower lip curved down in a pout. *That's not illegal.*

*And being cute, which always makes me hard, but its damn inconvenient now with a punishment impending.*

*Sorry, brother. I must disagree with you there. Getting us hard should always earn a reward. Being naughty and cute at the same time, now that should get double the spanks,* Jaylin suggested.

Suspicious, she narrowed her eyes. "You're teasing again, right?

"We are always serious when it comes to spanking," Malik whispered in her ear. *Jaylin, in particular.*

*But he said he didn't punish.*

*No, I said I leave it to Malik most times. I didn't mention it because he enjoys it so much.*

*I have to admit to the love of a good woman and a good spanking, so I have no trouble being the disciplinary twin.*

*Gee, thanks for the support.*

Jaylin's fingertips ran lightly over her bottom, drawing small circles on her skin. *My specialty is a different kind of spanking altogether.*

*What does that mean?*

*He gave you a hint, Dani.*

*When? Wait. I must have missed it. Are you two using super twin code again?*

Malik laughed. *There is no such thing.*

*Oh, well… then please explain what the heck you're talking about? My butt is on the line.*

*There's the sass again*, Jaylin pointed out.

*Think back, Dani. He said with pleasure*, Malik reminded her.

"I still don't get it."

"Ah, but you will," Jaylin murmured. His hand slid down to the lowermost curve of her cheek and palmed it. After giving it a good squeeze, he released her, except it was back in a blink, landing with a crisp swat. It stung, though not much, and he rubbed it away with an unhurried, sensual caress.

Her breath locked in her throat, body alive with sensation as she stared into his burning gaze.

*You like that?*

She inhaled shakily, parting her lips to answer, but another spank and slow caress made her forget what she had planned to say.

He grinned. *I'm thinking that's a yes. What if we up the ante and make this a group project?*

Malik didn't need further invitation. His hand, on her other cheek, swatted firmly, although nowhere near as hard as before. It warmed her skin, heating it further when he followed the spank with some very nice rubbing.

Jaylin gave her another firm swat, and yet another, before he turned her to face Malik who accepted her into his arms. He arranged her legs to straddle his hips before he lay back against the pillows, bringing her down on top of him. His lips took hers, his tongue caressing both thorough and deep, while others, open and warm, trailed down her spine and over her bottom.

Malik continued his drugging kisses, but his hand moved between them. His thumb found her clit while two of his fingers slid inside.

"Dear heavens," she whispered.

*Shh, baby, think it, don't say it.* Jaylin smacked twice more, then laved and licked her hot skin, soothing away any remaining sting.

After swatting the other side two times more with his free hand, instead of rubbing, this time Malik's fingers curled beneath her bottom and slid her up his chest until he could catch a nipple between his teeth.

Holy mother of…

She couldn't finish her thought because Jaylin, while still licking and moving his lips over her bottom, glided his fingers through her wetness, transferring her juices to the tight hole in back. After he'd made it slick, he settled the pad of his thumb over the tight pucker and pushed inside.

It sent her over the edge, her body shaking with the force of her release. But it wasn't enough for her two diabolical dominants who prolonged it by swatting her behind and simultaneously pumping into both her front and rear holes — oh, the joy of four hands on her instead of two.

Malik moved to her other breast, and sucked the untouched nipple hard. Another orgasm hit on the crest of the other, or maybe it was one long sustained release. She didn't know, nor did she care at this point, breathless from trying to keep from screaming with pleasure and waking the entire house.

As she began to come down, Jaylin rose to his knees and pulled her hips back, positioning her ass high in the air. Malik's erection sprang up between them. It seemed only natural to encircle him with her hand. Squeezing and stroking wasn't enough. He wanted more and pushed up in the bed.

His fingers slid into her hair. *Take me into your mouth, Dani.*

She didn't need to be told, anticipating what he wanted and eager to do so. She engulfed him, which thankfully muffled her cries, as Jaylin plunged into her pussy from behind.

In minutes, while sucking greedily and being pumped into hard, she felt another orgasm building. With all her might, she fought it, wanting the two of them to catch up and go over the edge with her.

Jaylin knew, however, and brought his hand down hard on her ass, not in the sensual swat of the moment before, but for real. The smarting smack sent her reeling, and she lost control just as Malik cried out his release, and he followed an instant later.

Licking and sucking more slowly, she didn't stop altogether until his body relaxed. That's when she collapsed on top of him, limp and shaky. Although he had come, too, Jaylin continued to glide in and out, the unhurried thrusts, incredible.

His fingertips ran lightly over her upturned bottom while Malik used one hand to comb through her hair, moving the other in a slow caress down the length of her spine.

After several more minutes of gentle touches and relaxed pumping, Jaylin stopped, bent forward, forward, nuzzling his face into her hair. He kissed her tenderly on her shoulder, before he eased out.

Hands beneath her arms dragged her up and rolled her to her side. Face-to-face now, Malik licked along her lower lip, before plunging inside, while another long body stretched out behind her and molded against her back.

A second set of lips spread a line of kisses over the bend of her neck, and up the side. Brushing her hair back with his chin, he bared her ear and sucked on the lobe, something which always made her toes curl. As he did this, Jaylin mentally projected his question into the blissful moment. *Now do you get it, pershada?*

"Mmm..." Her hum of approval came out like a purr.

He chuckled. *I take it you don't have any more questions.*

*Only one.*

*What's that, sweetheart?* Malik's words resonated in her head.

*When can we do it again?*

Curving into a smile, Jaylin's lips tickled her ear. Soon, his hearty chuckle mingled with her feminine giggles, which ultimately coalesced with Malik's low and equally amused laughter.

\*\*\*

The sound drifted down the hall to the old woman in her bed. It pulled her from the gripping tale of adventure she was reading and made her smile, happy for her beloved granddaughter and the two men who so obviously loved her. Deciding it was late, and past time to call it a night, she set her book on the nightstand and switched off her light. In a shaft of moonlight, the cover gleamed emerald green, on it a beautiful redhead embraced her doting men, one blond, the other dark-haired. Both young and breathtakingly handsome, they looked at her as if she was the reward they waited what seemed like a lifetime to receive.

# Epilogue

"Are you sure you want to do this?"

Looking up into Malik's concerned face, his golden eyes glittering with warmth, all aimed at her, Dani couldn't believe he was the same serious brooding man she'd met three months ago.

She lifted her hand to his cheek before standing on her toes and straining to place a kiss on his lips. He still had to bend his head so she could reach. "Having you here with me helps, and, although it won't be pleasant, I need to put this behind me once and for all."

Large hands bracketed her hips as Jaylin leaned in close, his chest solid against her back. He repeated for at least the third time, "We're both here for you, Dani. If it gets too much, say the word and we'll have you out of here in a flash."

She angled her head, nuzzling her face into the side of his throat. "My heroes," she sighed. "Although I think I'll be fine. What can he do from behind a high voltage security shield?"

"Words can hurt, baby. Especially his, you know it better than anyone."

"If he does anything to upset you, *trilana*, we're shutting this down." This warning came from Malik, but he stared at his twin when he said it.

"Agreed." Jaylin nodded.

An alarmed sounded, and her father appeared in the doorway, a guard by his side. He wore a loose-fitting, standard-issue boxy top and bagging pants, both cut to accommodate the electronic shock shackles at his wrists and ankles. Another encircled his neck, resembling a dog collar. If he got out of control, a zap would allow the guard to step in and haul him out.

He was pale, haggard, and had lost weight. She hadn't seen him in several months, but he looked like he'd aged at least ten years.

"If I knew it was you, Daniella, and your two guard dogs, I wouldn't have agreed to the visit. Take me back," he demanded of the guard.

"Keep a civil tongue, Alltryp," the uniformed man warned, to which her father scowled. He also cooperated when led to a three-foot-wide circle on the floor.

Once Daniel stood in the center, the guard stepped back and activated a handheld device. A low hum and a flash preceded the appearance of a wavering transparent force field shooting up from the floor and caging her father. Jaylin had explained this device on their shuttle ride up to the orbital prison. If he moved beyond the perimeter, he'd get hit with enough voltage to render him unconscious.

"This won't take a minute," she began softly. "I have something I wanted to say. Afterward, you won't need to worry about any more unannounced visits from me."

"What an unexpected gift," he sneered. "Get on with it."

She raised the sealed envelope, relaxing her grip when she realized she'd crumpled it. "This is from Nana Elise."

"She isn't your grandmother, you twit. I thought I explained."

"Shut up, Alltryp," Jaylin growled. "She will say what she came to say, and you will listen without any more lip. Do you understand?"

"And how are you going to make me comply, *captain*? Touch the force field and you'll be twitching on the floor."

"Officer Simmons?"

The guard nodded and twisted a dial on his device. Daniel opened his mouth, yet no sound came out. His eyes widened and his hands came up to tug uselessly at the collar around his neck. Locked in place, it wasn't going anywhere. As he panicked, Dani grimaced and looked away. Malik's hand found hers. His fingers opened her clenched fist, interlaced with her own, and held tight. As he did this, Jaylin's hand moved up her back, slipped beneath her hair, and wrapped around her nape.

*If this is too much, sweetheart, tell me, and we're gone.* His fingers flexed on hers, while Jaylin's squeezed firmly, both giving her the strength to reply.

*I'm okay, but can you get him to stop?*

Malik cleared his throat. The guard looked at him, a brow raised. Jaylin gave a small shake of his head to which the man shrugged and adjusted the dial, this time to off. Daniel's hands fell away from the collar as he gasped for air.

"This device is a prototype. In addition to the modes that incapacitate during an escape attempt or noncompliance, the collar can act as a silencer. The electrical impulses interfere with the vocal cords so the inmate has no choice except shut up." He caught Dani's horrified expression and added, "It looks and sounds worse than it is. All that choking was exaggerated. I can assure you, it's painless."

"It's abuse is what it is! I'll file a complaint," her father exclaimed once able to speak again.

"Go ahead. I'll get you a copy of the inmate control policy. This jewel has been added to the list of trail equipment. I have to fill out forms in triplicate every time it's used. I hate paperwork and avoid it at all costs, though, in your case, I might enjoy it. Now quit your bitchin' and let the little lady speak."

"Thank you, Officer Simmons," she said, appreciating his explanation, but hoping to move this along.

"No problem. You tell Blake I said hello next time you see him."

"Of course, he speaks well of you. He asked me to tell you he'd be calling soon to set up a game of cards."

"Should we send for tea and cakes for this reunion?" Alltryp sneered.

"Why are you always so nasty?" Dani snapped.

The twitch of his eyebrows said she'd surprised him. Rarely had she stood up to him. Instead being the obedient daughter, her life controlled to the nth degree by this intimidating man. But he didn't look so scary now, especially in his bright-orange prison issue uniform, replacing a business suit.

It wasn't lost on her, she'd gone from one authoritarian figure to two. The difference? Jaylin and Malik loved her, wanting only to keep her safe and make her happy. Her father had wanted to use her for his own gain, to have a living breathing outlet for his anger. What she wouldn't give to have had Jaylin and Malik at her back while growing up.

Ready to end this drama, she opened the envelope.

"You told me the reason you hated me is because I look like my mother. It's irrational to blame someone for something they have no control over. Even more so to blame someone for something someone else did. Rather like kicking the cat for your own screw up, isn't it, Daddy?"

"Don't call me that," he barked.

"Why? You said you loved my mother once, and you dreamed of having a little girl to love who looked just like her. Well, the joke isn't only on me anymore." She pulled out the lab report, unfolded it, then turned it so he could see. "I *am* your daughter. Here is the proof. You'll have plenty of time to sit in your cell and think back on the last twenty-five years and how you treated your own flesh and blood."

"What kind of trick is this?"

"No trick. Simple science. Can you read this number, Daddy?" She shook the paper. "It says 100 percent without a doubt I am your daughter and that of your once beloved Ella. Your wish came true. Something you could have found out for yourself if you hadn't been so entrenched in your loathing of my mother and using me as a target for your misplaced retribution." She released the report and watched her father's gaze follow as it floated to the floor. It landed print side up, the result glaring in bold red print. "You wasted years on bitterness and hate. You could have had my love, given readily, but you chose to be miserable and alone. Now all I feel for you is pity, although I shouldn't." She met his eyes for the last time. "After today, I don't want to see or hear from you ever again. These two men are my family now, and I love them. As for you, from this point on, I have no father. For me, you cease to exist."

Jaylin moved in closer, his hand leaving her neck to curl around her shoulder, and tuck her into his side. "You told me you loved your wife in the beginning, Alltryp, so you must have had a heart once. If it's still in there, buried somewhere underneath all that malice, use it to look at your daughter, and see the loving, giving, wonderful young woman she has become, somehow — incredibly, so — despite having you as an example. But her beauty, both inside and out, is lost to you. If you ever get out of this hellhole, do not contact her. You're officially out of her life. If you try, so help me, I don't care if you're a decrepit, feeble old man of ninety, I'll make you hurt."

"No," Malik countered, his tone low and ominous in the stillness of the room. He moved past her, and sidestepped into a protective position guarding her front while staring hard into Daniel Alltryp's eyes. "Bother her again and you won't have to worry about my brother's wrath because I'll kill you myself."

Resting a hand on his back, Dani felt the tension vibrating through his body. *I'm done here, Malik*, she told him through their link. *Let's go.*

When he turned, her hand remained raised and ended up splayed on his chest. He grasped her fingers and squeezed. *Yes, sweetheart. You've done what you came to do, and we've said all there is to say. Let's get you back to the Renegade.*

***

Though Jaylin brimmed with pride at Dani's bravery and determination in facing her asshole father, at the same time, his heart ached that she had to do such a difficult task. He wanted to scoop her up, hold her tight in his arms, kiss away her anguish, and protect her from any more cruelty ever touching her again. She would welcome his actions except for the last, saying it was impossible, pain and loss were part of life. But he and Malik had vowed to do everything in their power to minimize it. They'd all had more than their fair share of both.

Jaylin agreed it was time to end this, and went to the door, rapping hard twice in a signal to a second guard outside they were done. He waited as first Dani then Malik passed through and were in the hall before he glanced dispassionately back at Alltryp.

He sat stunned, his eyes fixed on the lab report on the floor.

"Stupid fool." The older man's head came up, tears in his eyes. His regret came too damn late as far as Jaylin was concerned. "You spent a lifetime amassing wealth, trying to fill a void of some kind, except you had everything you needed in the palm of your hand. For lack of a kind word, a smile, and a hint of a father's love, you pissed it away. The irony is she's more priceless than anything you manipulated to get. I get feeling betrayed, but killing your wife and your partner didn't ease the pain, nor did tormenting an innocent young girl because she happened to look like the woman you once loved. Thirty-five years at least, wasn't that your sentence? If I'm not mistaken, when you next see daylight, you'll be as old as your mother is now. Enjoy your cold, lonely cell. You earned every minute of it."

Having twisted the knife even more for Dani's sake, he had the last word, and left her murderous father—who ended up as the only bastard in this scenario—without another thought.

The End

## The Renegades' Reward

# Maddie Taylor

**Other titles currently available from Maddie Taylor**

### The Barbarian's Captive

(Primarian Mates, Book 1 of 4)

Light years from home, plant biologist Lt. Eva La Croix and her all-female exploration team land on a planet they believe is a perfect substitute for the dying Earth. They are set upon by huge alien hunters, and Eva is captured by the barbarian leader. Tossed over his shoulder, she is carried back to camp and claimed as his own.

Despite her fear, she is captivated by the gorgeous, dominant male with his long, gleaming black hair, smooth bronze skin, and glimmering golden eyes. Expecting her full compliance, he strips her and prepares her for an intimate and very thorough inspection. Horrified, Eva protests, but quickly learns defiance will be met with swift consequences, including a bare-bottom spanking until he proves to her who is in command.

Deemed compatible, she and her teammates are whisked away to the barbarians' world where they are mated to these powerful men. While pampered and protected, the women are expected to submit to their male's authority and bear their young. Will Eva learn to adapt to their unusual beliefs and old-fashioned ways? Can she sacrifice her independence and surrender to this dynamic, highly sexual alien male who has conquered her body, and perhaps her heart? Or when escape is imminent, will she flee with the others, never to see him again, and feel the rampant desire that now surges through her blood for her compelling barbarian mate?

**His By Command**

(Primarian Mates, Book 2)

Leading an all-female crew on a deep space expedition weighs heavily on Maggie Vohlmer's young shoulders. Their mission, find a habitable planet to replace the dying Earth. While a landing party comprised of her best and brightest scientists is exploring a promising new world, they are attacked. Maggie is left with an untenable decision, pursue a powerful enemy who has taken eight of her own, or leave them to their fate while protecting those still under her command.

Unexpectedly, their ship is seized by the same enemy, aliens who are gorgeous, human-like men, except for their incredible height, long, glossy dark hair, and extraordinary gold, teal, and violet eyes. Maggie and her crew are further shocked when they are whisked away to the aliens' world where the males make the rules and their women are expected to submit.

As leader of the Primarian Space Fleet, Commander Roth is dedicated to protecting his people and planet from otherworldly threats. With so much at stake, he doesn't have the time for a mate.

But fate has other plans for him, sending him the perfect match in the form of the curvy, blonde captain. Except Maggie refuses to surrender willingly, and Roth refuses to bend. Both struggle to deny the passionate chemistry that flares hotly between them.

As the Odyssey's captain, Maggie will not give up the fight for their freedom, not while her mission to save the people of Earth is unfulfilled. Can these two dedicated and determined leaders find a way to coexist? And will Maggie, who tries her mate's patience at every turn, find a way to rescue both of their worlds, while learning to acquiesce to the dominance of her unexpected mate?

**His Rebellious Mate**

**(Primarian Mates book 3 of 4)**

Staunchly loyal Eryn Lockwood heads up security on the USIF Odyssey, an all-female research ship charged with finding a new world to call home. Her team is guarding a group of scientists exploring an uninhabited planet when they are set upon by a band of powerful alien warriors. Entranced by Eryn's long auburn hair, fair skin, and green eyes, the fiercest of the attackers gives chase, and claims her for his own. As his would-be mate, his old-fashioned ways infuriate her, especially when he takes her over his knee for some firm-handed discipline.

Though a fiery passion ignites between them, Eryn remains steadfast in her need to escape. To fulfill her mission and save her people, she commits an unpardonable act, something she'll never forget...and he can never forgive. Returning to Earth, she attempts to pick up the pieces of her life, but thoughts of her gorgeous, golden-eyed alien consume her.

Master Warrior Ramikin, the biggest, baddest, and most skilled fighter on Primaria, has never been bested—until now! And by the beautiful Earth woman destined to be his! Furious, he lets her go, resolved to eradicate her from his thoughts. But Eryn's face haunts his dreams, and he lives every day, yearning for what can never be.

An alliance between their worlds thrusts them back together, although not everyone is in favor of mingling their two species. When anti-integration zealots assault Eryn, it is Ram who races to her rescue, but he arrives seconds too late. With her life hanging by a thread, the deep, mate-bond between them becomes clear. Is there hope for the independent, rebellious soldier and the proud warrior she betrayed? Will they be able to put aside the past and come together to fight those who would tear them apart? And, as they accept their fate, can Eryn and Ram recapture the passion they once shared?

**Marshal's Law**

(Jackson Brothers, Book 1 of 3)

When Janelle Prescott is thrown from her car as it careens off a slippery road, she expects to wake up in a hospital. Instead, to her utter disbelief, she wakes up in a jail cell which looks like something from an old western movie set. It is there, hurt and alone, with no idea what happened or how she will get back home, that Janelle first meets Aaron Jackson. As she regains her wits, however, Janelle realizes that something is terribly amiss, and her worst fears are confirmed when she learns that Aaron is the marshal of Cheyenne County, Wyoming…and the year is 1878.

When an injured, apparently addle-headed woman falls into his lap, Aaron takes it upon himself to keep her safe and nurse her back to health. Truth be told, he is instantly attracted to her despite her sharp tongue and her bizarre story — a story which he is quickly forced by the evidence to accept as genuine. After Aaron takes her under his wing and into his family's home, the two clash frequently, but Aaron is more than ready to lay down the law…even if that means a good, hard, bare-bottom spanking for this feisty brat from another era.

Having little choice, Janelle must learn how to live as a woman in the Old West, including submitting to the firm-handed marshal who, in spite of everything, seems to have laid claim to her heart.

## Captain My Captain

(Club Decadence Series, Book 1 of 7)

Special Forces Captain Tony Rossi is back from Afghanistan and ready to settle into civilian life. He has his business affairs in order and is now ready to get on with the personal business of Megan Sinclair. Kept apart for 15 years by distance and circumstance, those barriers no longer exist and Tony is ready to claim his woman. Will she be willing to accept his belief in a traditional relationship where the man is the head of the household? What about his part-ownership in the local bondage club? He is determined to win her, no matter the obstacles that get in his way.

Megan, for her part, has loved him since high school but believes he just thinks of her as a cute kid sister. When she realizes that Tony is interested, it's a double-edged sword. As an independent businesswoman, can she conform to Tony's old-fashioned beliefs and demands and be spanked? Can she bring all her secret fantasies to life and submit?

Finally, when they are both available to work on a relationship, life interferes. Megan accidentally becomes embroiled in the conspiracies of a local drug dealer with ties to a Mexican drug cartel. Tony must keep her safe at all costs, something that now she is not at all sure she wants. When fantasy meets reality, bottoms get sore, and suddenly that's not quite so much fun. Or is it?

Also by Maddie Taylor

**Published by Breathless Romance**

### Primarian Mates Series

The Barbarian's Captive
His by Command
His Rebellious Mate

**Published by Blushing Books**

Everything Christmas
(Part of The Naughty List Boxed Set)

The Gift

Hero to Obey
(USA Today Bestselling Multi-Autor Anthology)

Hero Undercover
(Multi-author Anthology)

The Juniper Bride
(Part of the Sons of Johnny Hastings Boxed Set)

Surrender My Love

### Club Decadence Series

Faithfully (Prequel)
Captain My Captain
You Said Forever
Little Light of Mine
Unbind My Heart
Second Time Lucky
What About Love

### Decadence LA Series

Master My Love

### Decadence Nights Series

Hooked
French Kiss

### The Red Petticoat Saloon Series

Claiming Coral

### Published by Stormy Night Publications

Mistletoe Magic
(Part of A Very Naughty Christmas Boxed Set)

Gideon's Redemption

Innocence Enslaved
(with Melody Parks)

Lanie's Lessons

The Trail Master's Bride

## The Jackson Brothers Series

Marshal's Law
Jackson's Justice
Wild Wisteria

## Pleasure Bay Series

Dimitri's Desire
(with Melody Parks)

Mastering Mariah
(with Morganna Williams)

## Sweet Trilogy

Sweet Salvation
Sweet Surrender
Sweet Submission

## Other Independent Publishers

# His Naughty Christmas Angel
(Part of Put Your Ho Ho's On Anthology)

## About the Author

USA Today and #1 international bestselling author, Maddie is a lifelong reader who became a romance junkie as a teen with her first romance novel, The Wolf and the Dove by Kathleen Woodiwiss. From then on, she was hooked, and gobbled up everything she could get her hands on, whether contemporary, historical, paranormal or sci-fi. If romance was to be found between a strong alpha male, and a sassy, adventurous and ofttimes defiant yet loving woman, Maddie was all over it. As an author, she stays true to those themes writing steamy erotic romance, with a side of kink, and adding elements of intrigue, danger and suspense to her plots.

Maddie started writing as a hobby. Her stories stayed private while she raised a family and worked full time as a registered nurse. It wasn't until 2012 that she decided to take the plunge and submit her first book for publication: Captain My Captain. She went on to publish eleven novels the first year.

As always, Maddie thanks her readers for supporting and embracing her books. Please post a review so she knows what you're thinking. Constructive, earnest reviews are always welcome and Maddie takes all of your recommendations to heart.

***NEWSLETTER***

Keep up with Maddie by subscribing to her monthly newsletter @ http://ow.ly/erNZ30dQRKW Get updates on upcoming books, book promotions, low and free book information, free content, and giveaways.

Made in United States
Cleveland, OH
29 March 2025

15601721R00187